About Bobbie Darbyshire

Author of five novels, Bobbie Darbyshire won the 2008 fiction prize at the National Academy of Writing and the New Delta Review Creative Nonfiction Prize 2010. She has worked as a barmaid, mushroom picker, film extra, maths coach, cabinet minister's private secretary, care assistant, adult literacy teacher, and in social research and policy. Bobbie hosts a writing group and lives in London.

You can find Bobbie on Facebook and Twitter @bobbiedar, or visit her Amazon author page.

Also by Bobbie Darbyshire:

Truth Games
OZ
The Posthumous Adventures of Harry Whittaker
The Third Bus

CW01498766

Love, Revenge & Buttered Scones

Bobbie Darbyshire

Best wishes
Bobbie Darbyshire

Cinnamon Press
:: small miracles from distinctive voices ::

Published by Cinnamon Press,
Office 49019, PO Box 15113, Birmingham, B2 2NJ
www.cinnamonpress.com
The right of Bobbie Darbyshire to be identified as author of this
work has been asserted by her in accordance with the Copyright,
Designs and Patent Act, 1988. © 2010, Bobbie Darbyshire.
First published in Great Britain by Sandstone Press, 2010
Print Edition ISBN 978-1-78864-159-3
British Library Cataloguing in Publication Data. A CIP record for
this book can be obtained from the British Library.
Designed and typeset in Adobe Caslon Pro by Cinnamon Press.
Cover design by Adam Craig © Adam Craig.

Cinnamon Press is represented by Inpress.

In memory of Roger Hurrey,
who cheered this book on

Love, Revenge & Buttered Scones

Excerpt from the Inverness Library Events Bulletin

Book Group Update - January 2000

The December meeting was well
attended, and our discussion of
George Orwell's Homage to Catalonia
was enriched by Angus Urquhart's
eyewitness recollections of the
Spanish civil war. We were also glad
to welcome Sara Ross of Princes
Street Publishing as our guest for
the evening.

In an exciting change to the forward
programme, Miss Ross has persuaded
Princes Street's bestselling author,
Marjorie Macpherson, to lead a
writing workshop at our February
meeting. So for January we're reading
her latest book Heart of the Glen
(copies available at the library).

The Book Group meets in the Reference
Room on the third Friday of each
month. 7 till 10. All comers welcome.

Dearest Marjorie, No one speaks to my soul as you do. I mean you no harm. Why will you not answer me?

Henry Jennings' last letter to me, I have it by heart. Has he forgiven me, I wonder? Has he found a way through?

I wish I could stop thinking about him. I want to be writing again, immersed in some make-believe world where he can't follow. Lord knows I've tried, but each project dies on the page, because he may read it, and what will he make of it?

So I've seen I can't dodge this. I must first write about Henry, as honestly as I can, and hope that then he'll stop haunting me and let me move on.

I'll start with that last letter he sent me, try to recall in what frame of mind I received it, how I came to act as I did. It dropped on my doormat between Christmas 1999 and the New Year, forwarded by my publisher, arriving the same day as a request to run a workshop for a reading group in Inverness. The combination was disconcerting. I don't know which unsettled me more.

The Inverness thing verged on an instruction. *It's high time you went public*, emailed Sara from marketing. *It can only add to your sales now. Let's start with some low-key events and build.*

I took calming breaths. I find it hard, saying no. I gathered myself and picked up the phone.

'Come on now,' Sara scolded. 'You're going to have to face this sooner or later. Just a toe in the water, we won't broadcast it. I'll be surprised if it gets picked up. And trust me, I'll square everything with the librarian. She's warm-hearted, you'll like her. I know she'll take perfect care of you.'

I don't know why, but as Sara banged on I was beginning to waver. Was it Henry who was changing my mind? Or the kind Scottish librarian? Or my fondness for Inverness, one of the gentler places on this benighted planet? Whatever it was, my nerves were subsiding. The craving to meet my readers was outweighing the fear. I was saying yes.

'That's marvellous,' cried Sara. I had to hold the receiver away from my ear. 'You'll be fine, I promise. They're a lovely bunch. You won't regret it for a minute.'

What had I done? I put down the phone expecting panic to hit, but it didn't. Instead I found the small, irrevocable act of courage was giving me a lift. An infusion of luck and capability. It had me looking at Henry's letter, too, with a different eye.

Reading your books is like meeting my better self in a dream...

Dear Henry. He was a decent man, I had no doubt of it, as genuine as any of us manages to be. He was lonely, that was all. Had need, as each of us does from time to time, of an imaginary love. I'd been a coward not to reply to him.

But please, Marjorie, don't be alarmed. I completely understand that you are separate from me. You have only to say and I will stop sending these letters. Until you do I cannot help but hope.

He wrote from the heart, he deserved careful answer. I'd sat down to do it once or twice, but whether I resorted to truth or fiction I found my words would inevitably cause him anguish—it is no small matter to puncture a dream. So I'd kept putting it off. It was bad of me—I make it a rule to answer fan mail by return, if only with brief thanks, so why not Henry?

The truth is, I liked him. Liked getting his letters. Didn't want them to stop. His comments on my books were pleasing—he saw the things I'd put in that no one else spotted, connections and echoes that I flatter myself lift them a touch higher, make them more than mere pot-boilers for the romantic fiction market.

I don't have you on a pedestal. I'm sure you are as fallibly human as the next person. But I know that a woman who can write as you do is a woman I must love.

Nice one, Henry. And I liked the photograph he'd sent me. His eyes. His ingenuous smile.

Okay, I'll come clean, he appealed to me. I'd even sunk to making a few enquiries, rung round for business references to check if his letters were a wind-up.

They weren't. He was just what he said and what his photograph displayed. Forty-one years old. Shortish, roundish, shy. Engagingly old-fashioned, somehow marooned outside the flood of modern life. Ex bank manager, now sole embodiment of HIJ Associates Financial Advice, working from his home in Guildford. Only one discrepancy. He claimed to be a widower, but one of my sources indiscreetly let slip that Mrs Ingrid Jennings, the missing I from HIJ, had deserted with a stockbroker seven years since. A forgivable spin on a lonely heart's life, I decided.

I have 'Heart of the Glen' at last. I haven't opened it, just weighed it in my hands. I've learned not to rush or spoil...

There was a rhythm to his prose that suggested he would never desist. My discomfort was growing as I kept failing to answer him. And then, that morning, at last I thought I saw how to do it. Meeting my readers. Meeting Henry.

So little divides kindness from cruelty. I meant well, that's my excuse, but it hardly serves. So thank goodness—though I take no credit for it—thank goodness it turned out more or less for the best in the end.

At least, I believe and hope it did. For Henry, and for the others too.

Henry Jennings, Peter Jennings and Elena Martínez. Those were their names.

I wasn't with them that dark February morning at the turn of the millennium, rattling over the privatised points between the fields of mad cows towards Inverness. I'd gone up earlier, decided to make a week of it, research the next book, do a bit of misty reminiscing and moseying around.

No, Henry, Peter and Elena, in various states of excitement, each was travelling alone that day. Each stared alone through a rain-streaked window, anxious for the journey to be done and the future confronted. And at intervals each sought solace for a nervous stomach in the buffet car.

In Henry's case, the dash from his seat was so furtive that it drew the attention of all who witnessed it. He'd jumped out of his skin at Kings Cross at the sight of his brother, with tatty backpack, slouching ahead of him towards the front carriages. Landed, sweating with panic, in his first-class compartment at the rear. What on earth was Peter doing on this train? Such an unkind blow, it seemed deliberate, yet he could think of no reason. Fighting paranoia, he decided that only strong drink would do the job properly and managed to fetch it without bumping into the lout.

Peter's trip to the buffet was also reluctant, in his case because of penury. The fare was a rip-off, he was down to a fiver and some loose change, and he had no idea where he would spend the night. Reward? He must be off his head—this had to be some nasty bastard's idea of a joke. Ha ha, fucking hilarious, mocking an unrecognised genius. Just wait till he caught up with whoever it was.

Elena waited in line for food behind Peter in a state of fretful impatience, her one thought to track down her quarry in Inverness. Was *el malo* still alive? He must be, he had to be, she willed it to be so.

Henry Jennings, Peter Jennings and Elena Martínez. Swaying towards the buffet car and back to their seats. Negotiating the doors that slid shut in their faces. Stepping around children and over dogs. Seeing and trying not to see the sleepily entwined couples whose body language said, 'We just travel between beds.'

Henry tried not to see the couples because he wanted Marjorie in his arms so badly he could barely draw breath. He was weary of sharing his life with ghosts. He prayed that this journey would deliver a real woman to him at last.

Peter tried not to see them because the chance would be a fine thing. All the women he knew had grown tired of ooh-aahing his poems and lending him money. Plus women were trouble. Was this paper-chase some ratbag's idea of revenge?

And Elena tried not to see them because the miles and days were piling up between her and the bed she belonged in, which might not be kept warm for her return.

Unpacking their little paper carrier-bags alone. Henry, a clutch of brandy miniatures plus a large packet of prawn-cocktail-flavoured crisps. Peter, a can of bitter and two KitKats to last him eight hours. Elena, orange juice and a chicken-salad sandwich on wholemeal. The rage was consuming her. She must stay strong for what was to come.

Henry, Peter and Elena. Each agitated. Each alone. Each seeking release in Inverness.

Chapter One

Henry

There was a dark pink envelope in among the manila, addressed in an italic hand that Henry didn't recognise.

He wasn't fooled for a moment—it was junk mail no doubt. Likely another of those introduction agencies. A few hundred quid for six phone numbers, a champagne dinner for ill-assorted strangers. Jumped-up computer dating. He'd given up on all that, but he was still on their mailing lists, salt in the wound.

Sure enough, there was nothing inside but a printed flier. A flimsy bit of rubbish, not up to the style and weight of the envelope, folded blank side out. Open it up, just a cheap-printed ad for some damn thing—

He stared.

Marjorie Macpherson! It was a flier advertising Marjorie Macpherson!

He had to sit down. He had to take this in. He pushed the breakfast crockery aside and sank onto the kitchen chair, smoothing the paper flat on the table.

SHAPING THE STORY   How are novels invented? Have you ever wished that you could invent one? Spend three hours with Marjorie Macpherson and discover her secrets. Join her 7-10pm, Friday 18 February, in the Reference Room of the Inverness Library. All welcome.

There was a computer graphic of a quill pen, and a fragment of local street-map with the library shown in red. That was all.

Except the envelope.

He picked it up. Looked inside. Sniffed it. Examined the points and flourishes of his name and address, the blurred imprint of the postmark.

London. Not Inverness. London.

Did Marjorie send this? Had she answered him at last? Could it be?

Second class. No message.

Of course. He remembered. He'd bought 'Heart of the Glen' on the Finchley Road the day he called on that client. He'd used his MasterCard. Targeted marketing, that was all this was.

He could ring the shop. He remembered the garish shopping centre. Which of the glossy book-chains had it been?

Although actually, no, he didn't want to ring. They would only confirm it was a promotion, and he wanted to believe, or pretend to believe just for a while, that it wasn't. That Marjorie's hand had touched this envelope, her tongue had moistened the flap, her fingers had guided the pen, shaping his name, shaping the story, calling him to Inverness.

Damn it, what did it matter who'd sent it? Friday the eighteenth of February, the Reference Room of the Inverness Library. He would be there, of course he would. At last he would be where she was.

What was today, the fifth? He counted days on his fingers. Thirteen to wait. It was so long, how could he sleep or eat or work meanwhile? For then he would see her, the actual Marjorie Macpherson, not his dream of her. He would see her face and hear her voice. And she would see him.

He was trembling, he realised, and leaving damp prints on the dark pink envelope. His brain was trying to dislodge the thought that was flashing in projected letters, like credits on a cinema screen. He got up and paced the kitchen, refusing to read the message in his head.

YOU'LL SEE HER. AND THEN IT WILL BE OVER.

He struggled to hold on to hope.

IT'S USELESS. SHE'LL SAY NO.

How could he tell what she would do? He hadn't a scrap of information, not even a picture of her face. The dust-jackets of her books were inscrutable, her publishers said she didn't 'do publicity shots', they weren't 'at liberty to divulge personal details'.

Yet he knew so much. Her warmth, her humour. Her solitude. She wasn't married, he felt sure. Or not happily. It was there in her writing, she was as alone as he was. And her age, he could sense that too. Not too impossibly old or too foolishly young for him, her take on life was so similar. A few years his senior perhaps, was that why she was shy?

YOU'RE MAD. SHE'LL SAY NO.

How slim the chance was. Three hours in a room full of strangers. A queue of lingering fans seeking autographs and advice. How could he win her? What could he find to say?

And then he realised.

'I'm Henry Jennings.' That was all he needed to say. She would know him—she had his photograph and his letters. Marjorie wasn't shy, she wasn't cold, she was romantic. She was testing his love, his courage. He stared at the flier, willing this to be true. She would smile and agree to a drink or a meal. Her presence would make him bold. He would become the man he could be, the man who lacked only Marjorie Macpherson to make him himself.

All welcome. He frowned. That was odd. More than odd, completely ridiculous. Her books were so popular, the event would be oversubscribed. Unless...

Yes! He banged fist on table, making the eggcup jump. For wasn't this proof that the flier was a personal invitation? He would accept. He would go. He would match her romantic gesture.

YOU'RE MAD. SHE DIDN'T SEND IT. SHE'LL SAY NO. IT'LL BE OVER.

He hammered the table. 'I'm *not*. She *did*. She *won't*. It bloody well *won't*.'

It was no use. 'What do *you* think?' he wailed. 'You're a woman. What would you do in her shoes?'

The ghost of his mother, Maggie Jennings, two years dead, beamed at him from her chair by the window. 'Well, dear,' she said. 'We can't be sure of course, but it looks very much like an invitation. And if it is, then it would be unkind, wouldn't it, to entice you all that way just to turn you down? But why don't you give them a ring?'

Yes. The phone lay on the table. He picked it up and tapped in 192.

'Hello... Scotland, please. Inverness... The public library...'

He took a note of the number, then a deep breath before dialling again, endeavouring to feel businesslike.

A friendly young woman picked up. 'Inverness Library. May I help you?'

'Good morning, yes. I was wondering. The workshop

on the eighteenth?'

'Yes?' Reassuringly matter-of-fact.

'The places, are they limited? Would I need to book?'

'No.' She sounded perplexed. 'It's only a workshop for our book group.'

'Oh dear. I see.' The blood was rushing in his head. So it was true. Marjorie had sent this.

'Were you wanting to join the group?'

'No. Well yes. What I mean is, I'm a particular fan of Miss Macpherson's, so I wonder, might I come along, just for the evening?'

'Of course. I'm sure they won't mind.'

'Thank you, thank you so much.' The excitement was tumbling out of him. He mumbled goodbye, put down the phone, and grinned through a mist of joy at his mother's ghost.

'It's true,' he told her. 'It's really happening, Mother. Marjorie sent this. She's read my letters. She wants to meet me.'

Chapter Two

Elena

'But, Elena—'

'No, Mikhail!' Furiously shouting. 'We will not discuss this more. You are wrong! I am right! Usually it is the other way, but this time, no!'

It was difficult to speak her frustration in English—she lacked the vocabulary—but with seven languages between them English was the only one they shared. For a moment she saw Mikhail's eyes blaze, as though he would shout in his turn. But then the fire went out of him. He dropped into a chair and turned his face to the window. The silence grew long as he stared into the gloomy Brussels afternoon.

'I am right, Mikhail,' she repeated. 'Only I can know this.'

Still he said nothing, watching the rain without expression.

Her fury exploded. 'Enough! You refuse to understand, then I am leaving.'

With no time for thought, she was snatching up her coat and bag, yanking the door wide then slamming it behind her, hearing the slam speak her anger more powerfully than words could do.

She marched towards the lift. He did not follow, his door remained closed. She punched the lift button.

Spain. He insisted they should end their jobs here and

take new ones in Spain. So many times she had said no, yet still he repeated she must do this stupid thing. She hated even to think of Spain.

She leant her head against the bars of the lift as it went down. The stench of cleaning fluid grew stronger as she neared the bottom. She could not hold her breath long enough to escape it. The hall floor shone wet from today's mopping and a faint haze of blue smoke hung around the concierge's open door. Elena ran out and down the steps, muttering, 'No, not now,' but it was useless. Always these smells carried her to her aunt's deathbed three months ago. She turned to walk home, head down against the freezing rain, hugging her shoulders, remembering Spain.

'Tell me, Aunt Marisa. Do not leave me without telling.'

A complaining wind rattles the shutters. The air is thick with incense and disinfectant. The struggle is over. Marisa's face is smooth and her eyes grow dim. Her fingers pull at the lace bedcover. Elena takes hold of her hand and pleads. 'Stay, Aunt. Speak. All my life I have carried this shame.'

Marisa barely shakes her head.

'I beg you, give me the reason.'

No sign. No movement. The fingers she holds are frail, knuckles loose beneath the skin like sticks. And the dying woman's features, pale as watered milk, seem unfamiliar sunk in a white pillow above a white nightgown.

As far back as Elena can remember, her mother and aunt wore black. Shoes, skirts, shawls, scarves. Juanita and Marisa Martínez, old before their time, unsmiling, silent, thin, dressed all in black and covering their hair. Speaking softly as though fearful of being too loud. Kissing her with sorrow in their eyes.

Elena bends her head, battling to calm herself, fighting the malevolence of the shuttered, creaking house. How terrible to die alone like this. Since she arrived yesterday, no one has come except the priest, and he with lips compressed, offering only the forgiveness of God, cold as the winter sun.

'What was it, Marisa? What was the terrible thing we did?'

Her aunt's eyes are closed, her breathing is ragged. She is falling beyond the reach of sound.

There is no escape. The shame will follow as far as Elena can run and waits always for her here, where she becomes a child again, shunned by the adults who mocked her as children.

Nothing has altered. As she stepped from the taxi into the square, the hush fell, a gob of spittle landed in her path. And now, behind the shutters along the narrow stone streets, she senses how the villagers mutter and shuffle like vultures. Marisa Martínez is dying. *Qué alivio!* not before time.

From childhood, Elena learned to hide her face. With eyes downcast, to keep close to her mother and aunt as they ventured to market or church, or into the mountain vineyard where they worked apart from the other women.

'But, Marisa, it was never so bad for you and Mama as it was for me. You did not have to go to school.'

The memory sends a chill through her veins. The teacher brusque, the children cruel. Each day for years, shrinking in shadows, fearing their tricks and taunts.

'Your mother is the devil's whore, Elena. *Vale!* Where is your father?'

Her father? The devil? She ran home wailing with fear.

'Alfredo was a good man,' her mother comforted her. 'But they punished him for showing care to Marisa and me. The shame was ours not his, ours before he knew us, we could not ask him to share it. And I was thirty-seven, too old to be his bride. He excused himself, he returned to *Sevilla*, we did not see him again. I did not tell him you would be born. Maybe he heard from others, maybe not. But you must not blame him, little one. Each must think of himself. *Es el mundo.*'

'Yes...' Elena remembers how Marisa sighed, paused in her incessant lace-making with longing in her eyes. '... yes, but you are a child of love, Elena. At least for one summer Juanita knew love. They vowed that neither of us should have husbands, when their own—'

'Hush,' said her mother. 'Do not let envy wag your tongue.'

'*Pero por qué, Mamá*? Why should you not have husbands?'

But no, her mother shook her head. And her aunt sniffed and resumed her work, knotting and twining the slender white threads.

Marisa's fingers fidget now in Elena's palm, picking and pulling, making lace from the air. Elena strokes them, repeating, 'Tell me, Aunt. What wrong did we do?'

She was eight years old when she learned her father's name. Twelve when her mother took fever and died, swearing her aunt to silence. Fifteen when she walked for hours, down into the valley, to board a bus to Seville and knock at her father's door.

'*Nada, papa*,' she whispered as she approached. 'I want nothing. Only to see your face and to know the reason my family is cursed.'

Too late. The previous winter Alfredo had died also and his house was sold.

No answer in Seville. Her mother dead. The village impenetrably hostile. And now, Marisa, the last who might tell her, taking the secret to the grave.

'Have pity,' Elena cries aloud. 'All my life, will no one answer me?'

She clutches the cold fingers to her cheek. The eyelids tremble. The blue lips part and move.

'Aunt?' She bends her ear to catch the sound.

'There.'

'What? Where?'

The fingers stir. She lets them go. 'There.' The hand drops, then moves again, as if to make a fist, as if to point.

'Where, Aunt. Where?' She bends her head to catch the dying whisper.

'In the drawer.'

Henry

The train reservation was safe in his wallet. Now a letter of confirmation arrived from The Royal Highland Hotel, making his heart pump faster.

Five days to go.

The flier still lay in its envelope on the kitchen table. He slid it out with feigned inattention, seeking the thrill of surprise once more.

Marjorie Macpherson...
Have you ever wished...
Discover her secrets...
Join her...

Suddenly his insides were dissolving with terror. In his mind he was at the door of the Reference Room of the Inverness Library, trying to go in. For the hundredth time he struggled to imagine it. He would arrive last not first, he'd decided, on the dot of seven. Resigned to his absence, she would be surveying the expectant faces, but as he came in her eyes would meet his. She wouldn't speak. She would smile barely a flicker. Their gaze would hold as he strode forward to take his place at the back of the tight circle of chairs.

What would he see? What would *she* see? Panic still threatened, like a cat waiting to pounce.

'I must decide what to wear,' he said loudly. He would distract himself with that.

He liked his best suit. At Mother's funeral, Peter had sniped that the snug-fitting waistcoat gave him a Mafioso air. But no, it wouldn't do—pinstripes were too formal. He substituted moleskins, checked shirt, tweed jacket, the Sunday-pub gear he'd worn in the photograph that was lying on Marjorie's writing-desk. Or beside her bed.

The thought of the photograph had his heart racing. He kept a copy among the circulars stuffed in the toast-rack. He pulled it out and scrutinised it anxiously, relieved to see how likeable he appeared, relaxed in a summer garden, smiling to camera. Himself, yet not himself.

He was breathing more easily. This was the man she would see, the man he would be. And she... she would be Marjorie.

He held tightly to the photograph.

He'd felt handsome that glorious Sunday last June, briefly confident in the role of romantic hero. He'd caught sight of himself unawares in the hall mirror as he came in from the pub, buoyed by a couple of brandies. He'd seen it could be so. He'd marched down his front path and up his neighbour's before the mood could pass.

'Hope you don't mind, Trevor, but I need my photo taking.'

'Vanity of vanities, all is vanity,' Trevor had intoned, propelling his Super-Lite chair over the ramps into his back garden. Too vain himself, thank goodness, to think of asking for reasons. 'Which background would Sir prefer? Roses, foxgloves or whitewashed brick?'

Was Marjorie perhaps wheelchair-bound like Trevor, Henry had sometimes wondered. It wouldn't put him off.

Foxgloves, he'd chosen, and the mock-orange coming into bloom. And deaf to Trevor's heckling, with courage gathered from the pub and the hall mirror, and the scent of new blossom in his nostrils, he'd smiled into the lens as though straight into his beloved's eyes.

The ghost of his mother coughed gently from her chair by the window. When he lifted his eyes from the photograph, she too was smiling. All would be well. He picked up the secateurs. He was due at Trevor's. He set off along the hall.

Where he saw in the mirror a nondescript, middle-aged man with fear in his eyes. He called to the kitchen, 'Please, Mother. You mustn't be kind. What do you really think?'

She came to the doorway. 'You've a strong chin, Henry,' she said. 'Plenty of hair. Good teeth.'

He struggled to see himself favourably. Taller than he was wide. Solvent and solid. Nice, damn it. Dependable, decent, a man of integrity. He was in with a chance, surely?

It was high time he told someone. It would help make it real.

'I'm in Scotland next weekend,' he said lightly as he drew the bolts on Trevor's French window.

'You'll be back to take me for my fitting, I hope.'

Trevor's new leg. Henry nodded. 'Monday. Yes. No problem.' After all Marjorie lived in London. He carried the stepladder into the garden. 'Inverness is where I'm off to. I've not been there before.' He set the ladder up on the uneven flowerbed and tested his weight on the bottom step. 'It isn't a client I'm seeing.' He climbed gingerly upwards, unlocking the secateur blades. 'Actually, it's...'

How should he describe her?

'It's a lass.'

'Oh yes?' said Trevor. 'Be savage, for God's sake, Henry. Be merciless.'

'What?' The ladder wobbled. He peered through the thicket of wisteria twigs.

Trevor frowned up from his chair. 'Prune to two buds it says here. It all has to come off.'

Elena

The days were passing so slowly, did Mikhail not feel them the same way? Yet he remained silent. She could think of nothing but Spain and Mikhail, Mikhail and Spain, wanting one, loathing the other.

How much she was missing him. His strong arms, his kisses, his soft Russian voice. But more than these things, without him she was beginning to dislike herself again, to feel she was a bad and undeserving person.

She unwrapped and reread the horrors found in

Marisa's linen drawer, praying for release from her burden, but it did not come. It was not her fault, yet forever she must carry the shame, as Jesus carried the sins of the world.

Mikhail had made her feel forgiven. Gradually she had told him everything, her worst, most ugly self, and still his eyes shone with love. In her whole life, no one had been this way before, accepting her fears and resentments, allowing her to speak her bitterness with honesty.

'This is who you are, Elena. Your suffering is part of you. Always I will understand.'

She should have known it could not continue. Ever since she had told him her mother's secrets, he had been seeking remedies.

'For now you can mend yourself, Elena. When you ran, the pain followed you. With the truth you can go home. Together in Spain with me you will find the cure.'

Wrong. Wrong. Why would he not understand? Nothing had changed. Spain had made her who she was and there could be no cure.

Spain, and *el malo*. 'Urquhart'—that was the evil one's name. How to pronounce it? Oor-coo-art? This name was all she knew, and the year, 1937, and the place, her village high in the Sierra Nevada behind the Republican lines. It was not enough information. How many times had she typed words into Mikhail's laptop, begging the Internet for a clue? So many Urquharts in the world, but none of them *el malo*. He was dead, almost certainly. If not in 1937, then later. Had he lived, he would be more than eighty years old.

Mikhail and Spain. Spain and Mikhail. It was no use. She could not sleep or choose. At work her colleagues asked, was she all right? She shook her head, not knowing how to answer. How could they understand when Mikhail did not?

She could wait no longer. She rang his office, but he was not there today, they said. She tried his room, his mobile, she left messages, she waited. Still he did not respond.

Her anxiety grew. Where was he? Was he still angry? She set aside her pride and ran back through the winter shadows. Braved the stench of incense and disinfectant and rode the lift again.

Her knock brought no answer. Tears blurred her eyes. She had Mikhail's key in her hand. She turned it and stepped inside.

The bed was unmade, today's newspaper on the table, an aroma of coffee in the air. He had been here, he had heard her messages, but he declined to answer them. His silence filled the room. To stay, to go, it was the same. She was broken and could not be mended.

The laptop screen flickered, renewing itself. It sparkled through her tears. A game of Minesweeper, lost with only a single bomb to find, the little yellow face, its mouth turned down, inviting her to click and play again. She took hold of the mouse and instead clicked on Google. She typed 'Urquhart' into the search box one more time.

Undiscovered Scotland: Urquhart Castle... picturesque ruins, north shore of Loch Ness... owned by Historic Scotland and open to the public

The Clan Urquhart Website... Urquhart motto: "Meane Weil, Speak Weil and Doe Weil"

Angus Urquhart... eyewitness recollections of the Spanish civil war...

What? Elena gasped. She double-clicked the site. Read hungrily.

El malo! It was he!

Book Group... third Friday of each month... 7 till 10.

Today, what was today? She counted Fridays on her fingers as the printer gave her the page. Tomorrow, yes. But time was short. She must visit her apartment, pack, tell her boss, check there was a seat on Eurostar. She headed for the door.

Then paused. Looked back at Mikhail's rumpled bed. Returned to the table. Scribbled a note for him.

I am here and gone, Thursday the 17th. Are we still angry with each other? I leave messages on your mobile. I must speak with you but cannot now delay. I find Urquhart alive! I go to Scotland. I will ring from there. Please Mikhail, answer the phone. Elena.

Leaning to put the note on the pillow, she stalled. The mattress beneath her hand was warm. She stood a moment staring at the bed. It told her nothing. She turned again and left.

Henry

The alarm went off on cue. His bag lay packed beside the bed. He tried not to think, he tried not to be afraid. He was into his moleskins and striding out bravely towards the station, taking deep breaths of the frosty air, head high among the Guildford commuters. Inverness was far away. He calmed himself with thoughts of its being an imaginary city, as approachable as the end of the rainbow.

Waterloo swept him off the train in an immense, sucking tide of workers. He had to struggle like a spider in a bathtub to break free of the flow into the Underground and join the queue for taxis.

'Kings Cross Station.' He had spoken the words. He was gliding over the river and up Kingsway, the traffic flowing fast and sure, stealing his breath.

He was out of the taxi now, checking the platform on the departure-board, swimming against another tide of commuters. He was making his way towards a train that quivered with potential like a rocket at Cape Canaveral.

The grey-suited crowds were left behind. Here were others, dressed like himself in greens and browns, backs to the teeming centre, faces to the outermost reaches. His heart was lifting on a rush of certainty. Fear and doubt were dropping away. His ticket was in his hand, his carriage was in sight. In a few minutes he would be flying, clear and straight to the heart of the glen, where his love awaited him.

Then. What? No! His brother!

In crumpled grubby black as usual. Shambling ahead with that unmistakable half-saunter-half-fidget, glancing back along the platform as he reached for a door, sending Henry bolting into his carriage, where he sat shaking and panting and confused.

How the hell was Peter here? Was this a set-up? No one knew about Marjorie. Did they?

His euphoria took a nosedive. The romantic hero tumbled from the stepladder. In a flash of clear vision, he saw himself through his brother's eyes, laughably past it, acting crazily, dotty about some stranger who would tell him to get lost, tell him, in Peter's unkind phrase, to 'get a life'.

Goddamit, he needed a drink.

Chapter Three

Peter

At the far end of the train, Peter Jennings did furious battle with himself. What was he thinking, shelling out next month's rent on a February trek to brass-monkey land? A rip-off wild-goose chase, sure as wild-goose eggs, and he the mug. But what? What con? What brand of joker? Bloody mind games. Straight through the crap, no messing, he'd give them hell, making some kind of fool of him.

Growl under his breath, then slump. Big deal, no less the sucker. Blowing the scam, then pissing off bedraggled through the no doubt freezing rain to some crummy B&B. He could see it now: massive granite, mangy cardboard cells, guarded money-up-front by a grim teetotal widow, mummified in twenty-seven layers of her own laborious knitting, her multitudinous cats in baskets mulched in layers of knitted squares and ancient fur-balls, jumping with fleas. Skint and sober into bed, with prospect of no breakfast, breathing in the unaffordable stench of the other fuckers' kippers, before another eight hours courtesy of Signal Failures Inc, scratching the bumps red-raw.

Shit.

Yet still excitement batted inside the cynicism like a fly in a balloon. The bastards had him high and hooked, one whiff and he was craving more. Potent as the cries of encore on the pub performance trail.

And yes. Why not? Keep moving. Inverness, wherever: somewhere to go. A change from waiting for Fortune to step into the corner caff, where the diet of black coffee and shortbread began to seem more repetitious than inspirational. Or into the office stacked with malign heaps of envelopes demanding to be stuffed with survey forms, plus tea to be made for the suits with privet hedges, flush with loot like big brother Henry, insulting him with their smiles.

Or for it to fall through his letterbox, like the occasional come-on: *Thank you for sending poems. Interested in reading more.* To be followed, please just once, by *YES YES YES* and large advance, not *unfortunately unable, no call for genius here, mate, and wishing you luck elsewhere.*

But now, who knew but Fortune had fallen fair, as always in the end she did, if you were her child, which definitely he was, or would be, it was only a matter of time. And okay, nothing might come of this, but a child of Fortune must fly with the wild geese, must keep the stream of consciousness flowing smooth and lucid, open to the monster of a poem that would one day rise from the depths uncoiling itself into words that no one could possibly ignore.

Yes! Chew finger-end and glare through dust-streaked window. Spray-paint signatures giving way to brave stretch of greenery, atop which Ally Pally sailing by. Yes, yesterday morning, though not through letterbox, too big for the pathetic flap in the Wind-in-the-Willows door of his mouldering, rented houseboat in fucking Suburbiton. And morning was an overstatement, middle of the night more like. Anyway long before any self-respecting poet was awake, let alone out of bed, for who gave a tuppenny toss about Personnel's mispunctuated little essays on the abuse of flexitime? Yes, Thursday, far too early, through festering dreams had come the knock knock knocking, like a frantic audition for the Scottish play, or the KGB come to grab him for the gulag archipelago, which was one sure route to make the world sit up and take note, lucky bugger, knock knock knock and a 'Sign here, mate' and the departing back of merry, whistling Postman Pat.

And there it was. It was in his rucksack now. Take it out. Examine it suspiciously. Draw savage breath. Jiffybag with typed address. Contents: a dog-eared bundle of A4, covered—in spidery script of faded blue ink—with two hundred numbered quatrains of Scottish Gaelic, signed *Angus Urquhart 1999*. Plus library compliments slip with cryptic message.

Peter, This is precious. Please return it, soon and in person. The reward will surprise you. Ask at the library. FU.

And FU too!

No dosh. No wherefore. No 'Mr Jennings'. Just, 'Do as I say.'

Cheek of the devil, like hell he would. And what in hell's name was he doing, chasing off to some godforsaken Scottish library to play some game of pass-the-parcel?

Too late. Next stop The Frozen North, and fuck it he'd had nothing to eat today and he was famished.

Elena

'Ay!'
   'Sorry.'
   'De nada.'

In the buffet car, Elena briefly registered the young man's scowl and strong blue eyes as he turned and pushed past her. The scowl warmed her. It was good to find anger beyond her own head. She stepped forward through the hot cotton-wool smell of microwaved burgers and fired some words at *el camarero*.

'That sandwich, please. And juice. *Naranja*. Orange. Thank you.' She banged her money down.

Her English was poor—she had learned it from a bored teacher. Her fury against *el malo* had swollen to encompass the language he spoke. It shamed her mouth to utter it.

Trust me, Carlos. Urquhart. Two English words. Two names. Making one filthy lie. On a yellowing, unfranked picture-postcard of the Loch Ness monster.

Blind with fury, she collided with yet more passengers and wrenched at the sliding doors. Silently she repeated the vow that was keeping her strong. I will find him, Aunt. I will find him, Mother, I promise. He will not escape.

What revenge would she have? She hardly knew. Let him only be alive—Oor-coo-art, *el malo, el bastardo*—then she would know. She would denounce him, yes, but more. She would shame him somehow, as cruelly and indelibly as he had shamed her family. It would not be enough. Nothing could be enough.

The train swayed as she neared her seat. She stumbled over someone's leg. Two faces turned sleepily towards her, then resumed their kissing. And suddenly she was back in Brussels, her hand on Mikhail's crumpled sheet. Warm, and slightly damp as though with sweat. Why was it so, in the afternoon? Was he unwell?

A child had stolen her place by the train window. The

child's mother refused to meet her eye. Elena controlled her temper—this was not *el malo*. She threw herself into another seat, beside a boy whose shaven head nodded to the 'scratch scratch' of his headphones. She ripped the packaging from her food and began bolting the sandwich, gulping the juice, barely tasting either.

There were plates in Mikhail's sink, she remembered, and a newspaper on the table. She could see the paper clearly, its headline in favour of the euro.

The bread and chicken congealed in her mouth. The headline was in French. The paper was in French.

Mikhail did not speak French.

The bed was warm and damp.

No.

She swallowed the hard lump of food, fished for her mobile, pressed redial.

'Thank you for calling. Mikhail Kilvanev is not presently available. Please leave a message.'

She hit the off button.

No. No. No.

Peter

Angus Urquhart 1999?

Back in his seat, one KitKat down and one to go, scan opening lines again.

Tha cuimhne agam gun do sgrìobh mi pìos bàrdachd
I remember I wrote a poem
nuair a bha mi sia bliadhna a dh'aois.
when I was six years old.
Tha e agam fhathast.
I have it still.

Precious, said the note from FU. Could it be? Blue treasure trail on narrow feint.

LOST BARD RETURNS FROM GRAVE?

Angus Urquhart 1999. Yesterday, crack of dawn, no one he'd cared to know. He'd only glanced at the thing to lull himself back to sleep. Then, come again, whose work was this? Leap up, stub toe, bang head on beam, grab Gaelic dictionary.

One stanza... two... then three. Surely not, yet unmistakable. The chipped, plain statements blossoming into subtext.

B'àbhaist dhomh a bhith a' sgrìobhadh tric nuar a bha mi òg.

I used to write often when I was young.

Sann, sann anns a' Ghàidhlig as bha mi a' sgrìobhadh mar bu trice.

Yes, it was in Gaelic I most often wrote.

Angus Urquhart had to be Calum Calum! Yell and whoop, boat rocking, brain exploding.

DERELICT GENIUS FINALLY FLIPS!

Be calm. Stay sane. Compare and cross-compare. It couldn't be, but strike him dead it was, it had to be. Original, unpublished and—*1999?*—blimey, a recent poem by the Gaelic bard himself! And still it went on being true.

Tha am bàrd ainmeil a-staigh comhla rium an-diugh.

The famous poet is here with me today.

Henry

He unscrewed the top of the first little Martell bottle and swigged it dry. He had to steady his nerves. He had to concentrate.

The brandy burned under his ribs. The carriage swayed as the train sped between frozen fields. He had to sort out what was what. He was acting crazily—yes all right, no doubt about it—haring off to Inverness in pursuit of a total stranger. But that was his business. Why was Peter here?

He had the compartment to himself, thank goodness, so he could pick his mother's brains. He conjured her easily on the seat opposite and begged her, 'Why?'

'Let's hope it's just coincidence, dear,' she said. 'If not, if Peter means to laugh at you or spoil your chances, then it's unforgivably bad of him. It's high time he grew up.'

Her sympathy solved nothing. Henry was hit by an acute awareness that he was inventing it. His mother vanished into the upholstery, and the carriage was as abruptly empty as an opened airlock.

He gasped for breath. The pressure built in his chest, and his pulse began to race. He felt drunk with fear. 'No. Please. Mother.'

She was struggling to re-materialise. 'It's all right, dear. I'm still here.'

Only she wasn't, not really, and he was doubting Marjorie too. Only Peter was real, harbouring grudges at the other end of this train.

Henry's swag. Henry's loot. His brother's words still stung. He opened the second little bottle and knocked it back. Five years and it got no easier. It was too bad. Grossly unfair. The whole blasted lot left to him like Midas's gold.

'You've got to stop upsetting yourself.' His mother's ghost came and went on the seat opposite. 'I've told you, your father was old-fashioned. He simply meant to appoint you head of the family.'

Dearest Mother. She hadn't minded Father's rotten will one bit. She'd continued in her home that suddenly he owned. Drawn cheerfully on the bank account he'd rushed to open for her. It was Peter who was the problem. Bloody Peter.

'Come on. Please. It's yours, of course it is. Don't be pigheaded. Don't wait for me to kick the bucket too. Take the money and have done.'

But no, his malevolent little brother, earning peanuts, living in squalor, for five relentless years had refused to touch one penny, preferring to scowl and snipe.

His mother'd had no patience. 'There was no love lost between you and Pa,' she scolded Peter. 'Henry has offered you half and you've refused it. Let that be an end to the matter.'

Had it really been his mother speaking? Taking his part against Peter? Yes, dear Mother. At the end of her life, years after he'd ceased to hope for it, she'd begun to smile at him in the old way. Just as her ghost, fully restored, was smiling at him now.

He grinned back in relief. It was a bad habit he knew, communing with thin air. It verged on the unbalanced, like his yen for Marjorie, but he'd never managed to do without it, not even during his short, mistaken marriage to Ingrid. All his life he'd had ghosts for company. And was it so unbalanced actually? Probably lots of people did it. People like him, lonely in childhood, who'd grown to depend on imaginary friends.

The second miniature Martell was empty. He frowned at the third and decided to open it, what the hell.

Damn it, he wasn't by nature a lonely child. He'd have been fine if they'd served up some other children for him to play with. But all he'd had was his mother's concentrated love. *She* was lonely, that much was obvious. Chock-full of imagination, romanticising her Scottish childhood. He exchanged another smile with her ghost, remembering the fantasy world they'd created together. Glens and mountains, battles against the Sassenachs. What great times they'd had, rescuing each other from danger and working themselves into storms of tears over each other's tragic fates. He wouldn't have missed that for the world.

His smile faded. The great times didn't last. Aged eleven, he was sent away to the bullies and bad food of boarding school. And then, when he came back, his mother's eyes seemed absent.

'I've galloped all night with a saddlebag full of oatcakes,' he told her.

'Please, dear, not now. Haven't you something you can be doing?'

He remembered, word for word, her first denial.

'I'm sorry, Henry,' her ghost whispered.

'Yes, yes, Mother,' he muttered. 'It's all right now.'

Back then though, it wasn't. He'd tried everything he could think of to earn her smile, but each half-term, each holiday, she'd continued the same, as implacably remote as his father. He'd almost preferred to be at school. Loneliness had been dumped on him like a cold shower.

Then finally, that awful summer vacation when he was twelve, there was whingeing baby Peter. And there, with Peter in her arms, he'd recognised his mother at last. Doting, concentrated, occasionally in storms of tears. But not for him.

He blinked and drained the last few drops of brandy. He was forty-one, for goodness' sake, yet still these memories hurt. Year after year he'd watched her lavish affection on his brother. From Peter's cradle to her own grave, because there was never any talk of boarding school for Peter.

Henry sighed. He'd become inured to it. What else was there to do?

Peter

Yank dictionary from rucksack, apply himself to stanza fifty-two. Yes, no mistake, it went on being true. This voice last heard in nineteen thirty-eight. An unclaimed voice, owner missing, presumed dead somewhere in Europe's evil convulsions.

Calum Calum.

Subject of his own dazzling but incomplete PhD thesis. Incomplete from idleness, drawled prosaic prof, from lack of last words was the truth. Year after year refusing to yield, sucking itself, scum and bubbles, into the sand like the tide from a child's moat.

Why? Because voice not done with speaking, that was why. Owner not dead! The famous poet was here with him today. Here in his grasp last words. And maybe not the last, not even these? For tides turned, and moats filled, and maybe even now, Angus Urquhart, alias Calum Calum, muse and mentor, the very same, was alive and spilling words like Noah's flood.

Yes! Give in to certainty. Though who FU, and why? How had this come to him? Did Calum know him? Had old man Calum read the poems of Peter Jennings? Heard him perform them? Smiled blessings from the Edinburgh Festival shadows, while he stormed it night after brilliant night with *Notes from Under Water* and talked up his Gaelic roots?

Why not? For genius was for genius to discover, and he was Fortune's child indeed. For wasn't it poor Ma with her romantic notions of her Scottish ancestry who'd crooned the songs of Calum into his cradle? And hadn't he toddled from it with his destiny issuing from his mouth, pronouncing the unpronounceable as efficiently as Hey Diddle Diddle?

Yes, until Pa came looming, bellowing, 'Peter! Bloody well shut up, or learn to speak the Queen's English, not that damned Scots drivel that sounds like German crossed with bloody Japanese. And Maggie, there'll be hell to pay, I mean it.' And Maggie'd never sung those songs again.

But hard luck, Pa, you loomed too late.

Quick. Straighten face. Tosser opposite, tea-cosy hat and organic braces, beaming like Jodrell Bank. Leaning forward with some drivel about the niceness of the day on the tip of his clichéd tongue.

Piss off, mate. Arch brow, purse lips, stare hard and... yes, success, the loop-socked loon was blushing prettily and turning his frozen smirk to the window.

Hurtling between meadows now. Green grass, fat sheep, brown mud, thin horse, grey hedgerows, sleepy cows, still some remaining *fields and farms* despite old-maid Larkin's *going going*. Plus frost there too in shadow, hollow, furrow, and maybe—if he knew what shape it was—an elm waiting to be discovered. As so was Calum

Calum. As so was he. Peter Jennings! His unheard voice soon to be acclaimed by long-lost Gaelic bard. His Byronic image, skimming this landscape, soon to be cloned endlessly behind plate glass on heaped displays of elegant, black volumes.

And the awed reviews. NEW GENIUS FOR THE NEW MILLENNIUM!

Until when, the bastards had him by the balls. He'd starve before they told him yes. Give them their way and the only venue he'd share with Calum was the Dead Poets' Society, damn them and rot them all in hell.

Henry

'I'm sorry, Mother. It really is all right.'

For yes, it really was. Miraculously, in the last three years of her life, she'd made the journey back to him. It was he who'd helped when Father died, that was what it boiled down to. Arranging the funeral and so on. And afterwards, sorting out, redecorating, showing her how to adjust the central heating. Just listening to her. Listening was never Peter's forte, whereas Henry would happily have listened to her all day.

She didn't say much about much—her main topics were the garden and the books she was reading. He'd read them too, to keep her company, which was when he discovered he liked them. Historical novels, period romances, sagas of family life, that kind of thing. Books that Peter sneered at.

'Take no notice, dear. He doesn't know what he's missing.'

His mother's ghost beamed across the empty

compartment. If he wanted, he could reach and take her hand.

He grinned at his bad habits. The brandy was coursing through his veins. There was nothing so dreadfully wrong with fantasy—it could be relied on like drink to see him through. And after all, it wasn't only his mother he fantasised about—there were the sexy women too. Other blokes did that, didn't they? Except that mostly he didn't take his fantasies to bed with him. He didn't like to sully them. He thought of them more as guardian angels, watching him muddle through the days, giving his existence some kind of point.

That was how it started with Marjorie. It was his mother who first gave him one of Marjorie's books, the year his father died. 'Try this, Henry dear. It's so sad and Scottish.' It was in one of his mother's tartan-upholstered wingbacks that he innocently turned the first page. It was in her spare room, in the small hours of the same night, that he reached the last page, weeping tears he hadn't known he was still capable of: for his mother, for her namesake heroine Maggie McConn, for his lost childhood and his failed marriage, for the whole impossibility of being alive.

He was almost weeping now, reliving how it felt to fall in love. Transcending his tears that night had come the power of the stranger whose words had unlocked them, a new ghost taking shape among the bedroom shadows. This one would be different, he knew it from the start. Her voice was real—he didn't have to invent, only to listen.

He wrenched the packet of crisps apart in triumph, showering the carriage with yellow-pink flakes. Apart from her voice, Marjorie Macpherson had been a fantasy, like his other fantasies, a way of stopping the empty future from crashing in. But now—he grinned about him at the foolish litter of crisps—now she was real beyond doubt. This evening at seven o'clock, she would be waiting for him. This time tomorrow, they would have met, spoken, begun the business of becoming acquainted, leaving the fantasies behind.

And yes, of course, his mother was quite right. Peter knew nothing of Marjorie. Peter was on this train by accident, or else it was bloody well time he grew up.

Elena

Maldita sea! She could not sit still another moment. She sprang up and paced the carriage, as though by movement she could escape the thought of the warm, damp sheet in Brussels. She saw them as clearly as if she were standing in the room. Some French-speaking woman entwined with Mikhail on the bed, laughing and easy, then turning to mock her, dismissing her with a wave. 'You were so angry with him, so difficult. Did you expect him to love you?'

No, of course. How could it be different? She had learned her childhood lesson all too well: how to be locked outside, how never to find the way in. Alone in the space between the compartments, she stared through smeared glass at the shadowy English landscape flying past and let the tears gather in her eyes. Everywhere she ran, she was outside. Spain had rejected her, and she had rejected Spain, choosing self-exile as soon as she was grown, burying the hurt.

But now, Marisa's dying gift, the explanation was in her hands. The poison that had blighted her life. Her mother's torment, suffered so young and felt so deeply, scratched onto tiny pages and buried for years at the back of the linen drawer.

The evil was done, impossible to undo or mend. The time was past, and all the people. Except herself, born of a dishonoured family, robbed of light and joy, unable to love or be loved. And he, murderer, thief of honour, Oor-coo-art, might he yet live and breathe!

Chapter Four

Henry

It was five-fifteen. He hung back as Peter took his time slouching through Inverness Station and across the square that fronted it to ask directions of a cab driver, and at last, thank heaven, sauntered off into the dark.

Henry's paranoia had grown during the day as his brother failed to alight at York, Newcastle, Edinburgh, Perth, or even—last-ditch hope—Aviemore. Edinburgh had been sheer hell. *We apologise for the late arrival of this train. The connecting service to Inverness is being held for you at platform 16. Please join it immediately.* He'd shadowed Peter, hoping to see him leave the station. Instead, for hair-raising minutes, typical Peter had gone and got himself lost, pussyfooting up and down the staircases of Waverley in search of platform 16. Henry'd had to bury his head in the FT as the fool doubled back past him. Time was pressing, they would miss the train. He'd had a job controlling the urge to shout, 'It's there, you blithering idiot, right in front of you!'

When finally Peter found his way, there was the stress of having to hide from him in only two carriages. Henry waited until his brother was on, then scurried to safety like a mouse under a skirting-board. He was dripping with anxiety. He would have to change his shirt before he went to the library.

Off they'd chugged, over the Forth Bridge and the Pass

of Killiecrankie, up into the Highlands. All at once Edinburgh seemed southerly and civilized—there were still three-and-a-half hours of remote northern miles to cover. Henry's heart had lifted at the vision of the clean Scottish air whipping itself into low-hanging clouds over moor and crag, like tethered duvets in the gloaming. Here in the station square, he took a deep breath of the same air, dark and cold. The sound of bagpipes nearby was making his skin tingle. He experienced a moment of naïve bliss.

The Royal Highland Hotel spilled light from an inner corner of the square. Ten paces and his feet were sinking in deep-pile tartan carpet.

'Good evening, sir.' A neat young man was smiling warmly, handing him a key with a heavy fob and taking his order for a roast-beef sandwich in his room. He was climbing the sumptuous art nouveau staircase and strolling along a corridor hung with amateur oil paintings of stags and mountains. His problems were lessening with every step.

Why hello, Peter. What a small world, eh? I'm up here seeing a client. How about you?

Well, good evening, Marjorie. I'm Henry Jennings.

He slid key into lock and opened the door on a quiet, comfortable room. Everything would go well. There was nothing to fear. Scotland was working her reliable magic.

Elena

The station clock showed five-twenty. With speed and courtesy, the man in the reservations office had telephoned a guesthouse and given her a map. She wheeled her suitcase fast past the taxis, for she had jumped from the train like a liberated cat and the map showed that Ness Bank was no distance.

Turning left outside the station, she crossed over and entered a paved shopping area. Beneath a lamp a solitary piper was playing to a small crowd, and she lingered a few minutes to listen. His face was sad, he looked at no one, the wail of his instrument seemed to pain him. She started down the almost empty high street. Here was the usual European mix of old and new, the bright lights of Marks & Spencer and McDonalds side by side with antiquated shopfronts in gnarled stone. Yet the place felt singular, different from English cities. Granite grey and solid. Sincere and dependable. Was this how its citizens would seem also, she wondered. Was this how her grandfather had been fooled?

Trust me, Carlos. I will bring the guns.

'Oor-coo-art.' Elena spoke the name aloud, determined to keep the flame of her anger bright. Though it burned still, it had exhausted her. She had raged so much—she needed sleep.

She needed warmth also—the air was sharp with cold. But no, where was her coat? Still on the train? She turned to run back, then remembered. The hotel room in London—she had hung it in the cupboard. How stupid to leave it there! Rushing to catch the train, the taxi waiting, thinking only of *el malo*.

No importa. Already she had found this River Ness, where the city seemed to end. Through the darkness across the road-bridge, she saw houses, not shops and, to her right, beyond the twinkling curves of a pedestrian suspension bridge, a mass of hills. How small it seemed, this 'capital of the Scottish Highlands', presiding over territories, glimpsed from the train, as vast and wild as her native Sierra.

She turned left. Fatigue was hitting like a drug. Her feet moved as in a dream, carrying her along the riverbank. She liked this Ness river—it had a soothing voice. Wide and shallow, fast-flowing over pebbles, the current made a continuous chatter of water on stones. The surface glittered with little backward-pointing waves.

She passed some rapids. White water, a natural weir, a louder, more insistent sound. There was no wind. The frosty air weighed on her shoulders like a quilt. Though she was cold, she wanted to lie down, here under these leafless trees on this gentle grass slope, and let the water sing her to sleep. Pushing herself on, she heard the cry of a roosting gull, taken up by another and then another. *Sleep. Sleep.*

At last, the guesthouse. She stumbled up the path and rang the bell, scarcely awake. The door opened. She nodded dumbly at the proprietor, signed her name in his book, took the key from his hand, found her room, closed the door behind her, let go the handle of the suitcase and fell onto the bed.

Peter

Five thirty-five.

'FU? That will be Fiona, but I'm afeart she's away just now. Could you be coming again at seven? She'll be here for you then. The library's late opening tonight.'

A shrivelled, wee besom-rider dishing out her singsong Highland helpfulness, and little to suggest foul play in this Doric-outside-playschool-inside library, dumped between windblown bus-station and multi-storey carpark. And yes, why not go back at seven, for wasn't his stomach clamouring to be plied with victuals more substantial than a KitKat?

Cash crisis looming, HOMELESS GENIUS SEEKS BED, but food, food! stomach insisting. Recce bus-station, push open waiting-room door, where yes, a bench of sorts. Later, head down on rucksack, dry and high, it would have to do.

Must take a leak. Ladies to the left of bus-station, Gents to the right. Ladies cleaner every time and graffiti more lyrical, though nothing here but 'Sandy loves me'. My arse, come on, girls, try harder.

Out again and ducking across Academy Street looking for some cheap caff. Zilch in this lane, only launderette spewing drifts of biologically-active steam. Double back and head past station, trying not to imagine nosh, while 'feed me! feed me!' stomach yelling and saliva spurting from tongue. Dear *fuck*, the need to eat! And oh boy, just in time, the Deep Pan Pizza Company rearing in horrid orange glow, reeking of hot bread.

Inside crammed, humid with sweat, décor yellow and maroon, plastic ferns and shocking-pink helium balloons floating above gobsmacked small children, plus deafening rendition of *It's raining men*.

'And how are we today?' Serving wench shrieking in his ear.

'We're starving, dearie. Make it a Margarita and a Coke, and quick!'

Food food food, and yes it would come. But now, oh bollocks and holy shite, snow kicking in outside, vicious gusts hurling it against special offers on windowpane, while out there in the weeld Heeland neet, beyond the inestimable FU, a barbaric neet on a bus-station bench lay in his stars.

Chapter Five

Elena

'Help! Help me, Elena!'

She dreamed of narrow streets of white stone, fiercely lit by a high sun, yet cold like winter. Her mother's screech came from somewhere ahead. She must find her. She must save her. She was running, side by side and hand in hand with Aunt Marisa and pulling a small suitcase.

'Dear God, help me! Marisa!'

At the sound of her name, her aunt pulled back. 'Stop. Come away, Elena. We are too late.'

Death was blazing down out of the harsh white sky. Elena clutched her aunt's hand, but it melted through her fingers. Flesh transparent as a ghost's, the incandescent dust of the street shining through her body, Marisa was dissolving, falling away. 'I must sleep.'

'Oh help me, someone, please help!' Her mother's anguished plea.

'Don't sleep, Aunt! Wake! Speak! You must show me the way!'

For a moment her aunt's eyes focused. She lifted and pointed a finger. Fragile, blue-veined, the pulse as terrible as in a fledgling fallen from the nest. 'That way. But no, don't go. You are much too late.'

'Marisa! Papa! Don't leave me!'

Such desolation in that cry. Elena spun around, desperate to find her mother. When she looked again, her aunt had gone, vanished into the white stones like holy water. Elena put out a hand to touch and stalled in shock. The stones were warm and damp.

'Too late,' they said.

'No! It mustn't be!' She was running again through the choking streets, forcing her limbs to keep moving, though death poured its weight on her shoulders and the stones clutched at her feet. She ran the way her aunt had pointed, following her mother's voice, wordless like the sigh of a roosting gull, a mere squeeze-box lament. And still the street twisted and hurled steps and corners in her path and would not let her see.

And then she was out, where she could not bear to be. Out into the village square, where there was something she could not bear to see. The glare hurt her eyes. An acre of white stone under the harsh white sky. A child, ragged and barefoot, weeping by the well.

There was blood on the stones of the square.

She tried to close her eyes, to turn away, but she could not. The child at the well lifted her head, uttered a dreadful wail and held up her arms to be comforted.

She did not want to, but she went. Across the bloody stones. Towards the child who was her mother. Towards the well.

Too late. No! She started upright on the guesthouse bed, staring in terror from carpet to washbasin to flowered wallpaper.

Nothing here. All done and lost. She moaned aloud.

Her watch showed six-thirty! What was she doing, wasting time in sleep? The library was marked on this map the man at the station had given her. She must go straight there, where her enemy would come tonight, if he still lived. He was old, close to death. She kept his heart beating by the strength of her will. She must find him before death did.

Henry

The spray of heather, 'Springwood White', picked fresh from the front rockery that morning, looked pleased to be in the Highlands. He slid the stem into his buttonhole and grinned into the mirror, determined to see a romantic hero. He saw a middle-aged man rigid with adolescent nerves.

Through the window he noticed it had begun to snow, but with his Barbour jacket and padded cap he was equal to all weathers. 'Proper little boy scout,' Peter always mocked, though Henry couldn't for the life of him see why. Where was the virtue in being ill-prepared?

Damn it, he must stop brooding about Peter. His brother's jibes weren't worth being hurt by. He wouldn't have him on his mind if it weren't for all this ducking and diving. It was Marjorie he should think of—he was on his way to meet Marjorie.

The library was nearby, the map on the flier showed how close, round the block from the station. It was six forty-five.

'Time to go, dear,' said his mother.

He took one last look in the mirror, swallowed the tremor of fear and made himself set off.

In the corridor, Scotland did her best to bolster his confidence. The soft eyes of a stag in the painting opposite his door confirmed the worth of humility in an arrogant world. The subdued light revealed the familiar green and gold covers of Marjorie's novels in a glass-fronted bookcase. And then he was descending the delightful staircase, gliding over the brass stair-rods as smoothly as the leading man in a Busby Berkeley musical.

Yes, he was almost dancing as he crossed the well-upholstered lobby and pushed out through the heavy doors. 'Enjoy your evening, sir.' The young man in reception knew how to make a chap feel good.

He stepped into a blizzard. The snow was settling thickly on roofs and ledges, and on the headdress and shoulders of the kilted stone soldier who guarded the front of the station square. Battling the wind and his nerves, Henry turned right, crossed the first junction, and pressed on past a looming mass of church.

The street was silent, preternaturally white, and deserted except for a hurrying figure ahead. A youngish woman in a smart black suit, without coat or hat or umbrella, almost running through the torrent of flakes, her sharp footprints fading to pearl, to white, to nothing. She turned right and disappeared.

Henry's pace slowed as he approached the corner. Margaret Street. His mother's name. This street contained the library, Marjorie Macpherson, his future. In two more paces, there he would be, a man at the crossroads.

'You'll be fine, dear,' said his mother.

He was there. He turned and looked. There was nothing to see but whirling white, and the hunkered shape of the woman, scurrying ahead. Henry's face was cold—the flakes were beginning to stick, establishing colonies on his brows and lashes. He pulled his cap down hard and started along Margaret Street.

The wind doubled its force. It snatched his breath,

tugged at his ears and bombarded his eyes with stinging missiles. He could scarcely see beyond his feet. He had a sense of narrowness opening out among what might be bus shelters. Then a glimpse of phone-boxes and a parked coach, before, through a gap in the storm like the lifting of a proscenium curtain, a row of bright, tall windows, ladders of yellow light, a startling array of Doric columns, a frieze of stone wreaths and two wonderful, terrifying words. PUBLIC LIBRARY.

The woman had broken into a run. Something about her—the way she moved, her helplessness against the weather—reminded him of his mother.

'Why, it must be Marjorie, dear,' his mother said. 'Don't you think so?'

He stopped and stared. Smart, attractive, in her early thirties, the woman was dressed in unseasonable clothes. She was racing against time as well as cold. Two minutes to seven, she was running towards the library. Towards the workshop.

Yes, his mother was right. This was no Inverness housewife. This was Marjorie!

His woman! His destiny! He was seeing her at last!

Peter

Saoil an robh oidhche na b'fhuaire na seo riamh ann?
Was ever night colder than this?
Fada fada na b'fhuaire. Sin mar a bha.
Far far colder. That is how it was.
Blue ink on worn A4. Stanza one hundred and thirteen of the mystery manuscript. Still too early for rendezvous with wee Scottish prankster, and they wanted this room

for some amateur scribbling group at seven, but meanwhile he had to be somewhere out of the blizzard that had blown up from nowhere bang on cue to make his life a misery. The delights of the Deep Pan Pizza Company's selection of laminated menus had exhausted his budget if not his appetite, and the comforts of the bus station were proving so far less than irresistible. Where better to take shelter from the storm than a library, home to tramps and poets the wide world o'er? Plus this one, Nazi sepulchre without and chunky pine and yellow paint within, was hame from hame indeed, offering as it did and should a passable pile of tomes on Gaelic literature, including *The Complete Works of Calum Calum*. Or so the poor buggers thought, for he knew better, yes, so here he'd come and on he'd travel like Sir Henry Morton Stanley, following the trail that soon would prove him right.

Doctor Livingstone, I presume?

Yes! He felt his fluency return. Racing through the Gaelic, gulping it like equatorial rain. Calum this was, and *genius*. Wonderful stuff. A poet's heart pulsing in his hands. Love and loss, pain and passion, crafted from old gold, lost hope in a lost language, lament for honour carelessly mislaid in the battle of life, cruel with lack of self-absolution—

But hang on! Head jerking in alarm. *Please return it, soon and in person.* Miss Fiona McSquirt was wanting this back apparently, which wouldn't do. He couldn't part with it, he needed proof. Plus it was too marvellous, what was he playing at? Straight into the trap. Talk about curiosity killing the king of the jungle. What in hell was FU's game? And here it was, close on seven, and he'd nearly fallen for it. Vamoose, quick!

Precious manuscript stuffed back in Jiffybag, stuffed deep into the personal jungle of his rucksack, and he careering out of Reference Room at top speed. Only to collide in corridor with advancing gaggle of chest-high Scottish geese, with identikit grey perms, clutching secretarial notebooks, sharpened pencils, thermoses, tray of sandwiches. And help! behind came goose-girl, five foot nothing, with smiling, bright, all-seeing eyes, heading fast this way. And yes, 'Good evening, Fiona,' the chorus rising from the geese. But devil be praised, she let him past without a murmur, let him through into the empty corridor. And *bang* through door into reception, past sign to PHOTOCOPIER. And *bang* again through alarmed gate that registered no alarm. And *bang* right, *bang* left and he was out into the swirling, blinding snow, skidding *slap bang* into some woman—*'Ay!'* 'Sorry!' *'De nada'*— sense of *déjà vu*, and fast across into bus-station bog, where *Sandy loves me* was the most dependable thing he'd seen all day.

Chapter Six

Elena

A soft blanket of yellow library warmth curled itself around her. The pelting cold was behind her, and the brief shock of colliding again with the young man from the train, the one with the fierce blue eyes. A man who was angry when she was angry, fearful when she was fearful. An embodiment of the turmoil in her head.

She paused inside the door, letting the yellow warmth seep into her, muffling the echo of her mother's cries, calming her shudders. How careless she had been to lose her coat. She must guard her strength.

Through the warmth a smile was beaming. A small woman, about her own age, stood behind a heaped and businesslike librarian's table. Her eyes were strong like the young man's eyes, yet neither angry nor afraid. She appeared like an angel in the radiant yellow, with strong eyes, kind smile, calm brow, asking, 'May I help you?'

Elena stepped forward, speaking the words she had prepared. 'The book group, they are meeting here tonight?'

'They're just beginning, in the Reference Room.'

'And Mister... Mister Angus Oor-coo-art?'

'Er-cut. We pronounce it Er-cut.'

'Mister Er-cut, he is with them?'

'No.'

'No?' Elena put a hand on the table to steady herself.

The librarian seemed suspicious—her smile had faded.

'Did you want Mr Urquhart particularly?'

'Yes.' She began the lies, forcing herself to hold this woman's gaze. 'I research to write a book, about the older people's memories of war.' She held out the page from the Internet. 'I see Mr Urquhart on your website.'

The librarian shook her head. 'He's not a member of the group. He only came for that meeting, to talk about Spain.'

'But I need to find him.' Elena was swallowing tears. 'How stupid I am. I travel since yesterday. From Brussels.' Her voice failed.

The librarian leant forward, still unsmiling. 'I'm sorry about that. Perhaps we have books to help you on our lending shelves.'

Henry

What the hell was going on?

The wind was tugging at his cap. His nose and ears were numb and so all at once were his feet. A shrinking ache had taken hold of them. Looking down, he found he was ankle-deep in snow, no footprints visible behind or ahead. Alone in a blizzard, twenty yards at most from the glowing honeypot of the Inverness Public Library, into which an astonishingly elegant Marjorie had run, he was in danger of becoming literally frozen to the spot.

But damn it, what was happening here? Marjorie and Peter. Perishing Peter! Colliding and speaking. Then running in opposite directions.

They knew each other. Henry was sure of it. The way she'd spoken to his brother, then turned to watch as he vanished into whiteout. Their look of startled recognition.

Were they in cahoots somehow? Preparing to wave his love-letters in his face?

Henry's stomach was shrinking like his toes. It was a feeling straight from boarding school. The awful knowledge that some trap lay just ahead and, whatever he did, he could not escape. He would stick his head into the honeypot and be derided for a fool. Or retrace his steps and be scorned as a coward. This was the last moment in which dignity might be grasped, and he had no idea where to look for it.

Six pillars and a portico. A frieze of wreaths. Twelve bright ladders of light. He lifted a foot and took an indecisive step. Humiliation? Was that the worst that could come of this? And the best, what would that be?

Marjorie. Her face turning to watch *him*. With a different expression than the one she had given Peter. It wouldn't be here, it wouldn't be tonight, it would be somewhere else safe and familiar with all the uncertainty resolved. His pub in Guildford, perhaps? Yes! He would be at the bar, ordering a brandy for himself and a... a what for Marjorie? And the coarse new barman, all mouth and trousers, would be winking and whispering, 'Cracking bit o' stuff you've got there, Henry.' And he wouldn't mind, not one bit. He'd be proud to have the locals gossiping. He'd turn from the bar to glance at Marjorie, to check she was really there, and then he would see it, the expression on her face. He would catch her smiling at him when he wasn't looking, like his mother used to do. A beatific smile, it wouldn't fade or falter on being discovered. It would persist, unashamed, and allow him to smile straight back.

He yanked the other foot out of the snow and headed bravely through the door of the Inverness Public Library.

'May I help you?'

No one was laughing at him yet. High-ceilinged, bright with light, the reception area gave no sense of impending ambush. To his left a massive, gold-framed portrait of some benefactor presided benignly. To his right stretched a vista of free-standing, modern bookcases. Ahead he saw a desk, a door, a wall-clock. There was no sign of Marjorie—she would be in the Reference Room—but the smile he had imagined was here. It made him bite his lip to see it. A small woman, emerging from among the bookcases, had taken shape around it and was offering to show him the way.

He spoke the name aloud. 'Marjorie Macpherson? Her workshop?'

The librarian's smile broadened, generously, as though sharing a joke. 'Yes, indeed. I remember you telephoned.' She indicated the door ahead. 'Through there and to the left. The Reference Room is signed. They've only just begun. Do join them.'

Following her directions, he found himself in a low-ceilinged corridor with doors off. Each bore a label. *Staff only. Highland Council Archive.* He explored left, trying to breathe normally. Glancing down, he discovered how wet he was. The snow he'd carried in was melting onto the floor. He took off and shook his cap and Barbour, then smoothed his hair and wiped his face, which felt glowing and fresh from the blizzard, not quite his own.

Last on the left. *Reference Room.* Here he stood. All that was left to do was to go in, and there she would be. Marjorie.

His fingers closed around the handle, which turned smoothly.

He eased the door open, held his breath and stepped inside.

Peter

Gnawing on thumb, fast pacing between basin and bog, the one embellished with nicotine, the other by Sandy's ephemeral mistress, Peter gave this whole business some sensible thought.

The manuscript was his, nine points of the law, deep in rucksack. And why be furtive? Punter in library, incognito, could be anyone. Plus she'd never expect him here so soon.

And library still the more expedient haven. Offering PHOTOCOPIER—good thought—for a duplicate in case the original was confiscated.

Not if he could help it. If she sussed, came over dangerous, he'd up scarper, *bang* right, *bang* left and straight as an arrow through the concealing snow to this municipally-tiled love-nest where she'd never think to look.

So ploughing now through knee-high drifts to library, whirligig of white, Acropolis in paper-weight.

Flash of brilliance! *Angus Urquhart, 1999*. MISSING POET FOUND IN PHONEBOOK! Cut out the middle-woman—trade in dark night of the soul in bus-shelter-cum-igloo for short blunder through blizzard to snug cottage, stocked with finest malt whisky, and Calum grateful to be discovered as a child in hide-and-seek!

Henry

It took a few moments to focus. This was nothing like the

Reference Room he'd fantasised. There were no oak panels or dusty rugs, just stark strip-lights. The ceiling was low where he was, but farther out the room opened up, and high on the wall reared four of the tapering ladder-windows that were beaming light out into the storm.

And here, true to his dream, was a circle of chairs and people.

No one was looking at him. No one had noticed him.

Where was the woman in the smart black suit?

The chairs were royal blue, the people grey and pastel. Grey perms and pastel cardigans. He was looking at a conclave of elderly ladies, plus three younger men. One of these, a bald fellow with a large nose, brandished a piece of string. 'The first big scene. A quarter or third the way in.' The man pulled the string taut and indicated a point on it, with his nose. 'Something has to happen.'

Henry struggled to see clearly. Chairs. People. A table littered with mugs of tea and sandwiches on paper plates. A scatter of playing-cards. Damn it, it was no use, he could make no sense of this.

'So what shall we have happen?' said one of the ladies.

'What sort of thing should it be?' said another.

'Anything we like, Annie,' said a third. 'That's the whole point.'

The pate of the bald man shone under the strip-lights. Looking up, he met Henry's eyes and smiled. 'Hello there. We've only just begun. Were you wanting to join us?'

Fear paralysed Henry's tongue. He felt the scrutiny of a dozen neat, wrinkled faces, but worse, the bald man's smile. First the librarian and now this bloke, offering him Marjorie's smile without being Marjorie. This was an ambush laid by his brother and he was about to ride straight in.

He shook his head, speechless for fear of springing the trap.

The librarian. He would go back to the librarian.

'No.' He shook his head again. 'No, thank you.' He reversed into the corridor.

The door to reception was halfway along on the right. He pushed against it and was almost through when, hell! in the nick of time he spotted Peter coming in from the snow. He dived back into the corridor and looked frantically around. *Staff only. Highland Council Archive.* But he must go somewhere. Any moment now Peter would step into this corridor and the game would be up.

At the end furthest from the Reference Room was an unlabelled set of double doors. He raced towards them and saw, thank heaven, beyond the glass the wide spaces of the lending library. A glance over his shoulder showed the corridor still empty. And he was out, safe, through the double doors and into the maze of bookcases. Half a step ahead of disaster, quivering with anxiety, his mind blank of everything but the need for cover, he dived from shelf to shelf and into the children's section at the far end to the left.

Where he huddled until his panting eased. Gradually his chaotic thoughts reduced to only one: the need to get out of this place. Still trembling, he inched back into the main lending-room, and hovered there, peering around a bookshelf to see if the coast was clear.

It was impossible to tell—all the sightlines were blocked by shelves. The label next to his nose said *Palaeontology.*

Chapter Seven

Peter

Through and in, the door swung shut behind him on the howling wind, *bang,* and there she was, Fiona he presumed, womanning the desk. Woman indeed, no whimpering discarded ex of Sandy this one. Small and plain and bossy-looking, lifting her eyes like radar to examine him, seeing right through to the stolen Calvin Kleins.

Get a grip, she didn't know him from St Michael, yet her eyes unnerved him. And her smile, familiar so as to be uncanny. Surely he knew her, surely she knew him? *Have we met somewhere before?* The cliché was scarcely worth a sneer, yet here, for this little goose-girl, it was true. Except that it wasn't sex. Or fear. What was it, was he haunted?

'May I help you?'

'The photocopier?'

'Behind you there, beside the exit, to the left.'

She didn't know him, it was he knew her, but where and when?

'How much?'

'Ten pence a sheet.'

Times twenty-three pages, holy bovine, two-pounds-thirty! Find machine, empty pockets, position paper. Then watch it clunk and glide, swallowing coins like Smarties.

Fuck it, ten pee and one page short. Never mind, back to FU, facing out her disconcerting eyes. Familiarity waning, possibly imagined.

'A telephone directory?'

'The Reference Room is closed just now for a meeting, but,' watch it! she was after conversation, 'what is it you need? Maybe I can...'

Quick, switch into shoplift mode. Don't pause. Nod and smile, no problem at all, and off away right, away from her, away from Reference Room. Busy himself among the lending shelves.

Henry

Oh God, oh merciful God, there she was! Through a gap in the shelves, he saw her. On a low chair in the centre of the labyrinth. The woman who might be Marjorie.

Her jacket lay folded beside her. Her elegant profile was bent over a book. A ballpoint pen was poised in her fingers. He was barely breathing, barely thinking. He saw sleek, dark hair tapering into the curve of a neck. Strong shoulders beneath a white shirt. The taut, black edge of a skirt meeting the sheen of knees.

This was no ghost. This was a real woman. But not at all as he'd imagined her—was it she? He crept closer, skirting *Medicine,* and *Crime.* Freezing by *Biography.*

Yes. He'd seen it in the snow, and now again: her vulnerability revealed her. In her writing, in her person, a sense of helplessness beneath the strength. The shadow of his mother that he'd glimpsed outside. This was Marjorie.

Yet still he was confused. Why wasn't she in the Reference Room? He struggled to account for it. A three-hour workshop, he reminded himself, and Marjorie by nature inventive and elusive. She wouldn't deliver lectures and trot out answers, one, two three. Maybe she'd given her students a warm-up exercise before withdrawing so as not to cramp their style. Or, better still, she'd left the task on the table for them to find. *Discuss this, please, before I join you.* Industrious as he knew her to be, was she using the time to research her next book?

The sight of her was quelling his fears. It was paranoia, surely, to imagine this woman would plot against him with his brother? He ventured a quickstep across to *Gardening*, where he pretended to browse, while secretly admiring her left ear, so close that he could, if only these ghastly preliminaries were over, reach across and touch it.

I'm Henry Jennings. He had to say it. He cleared his throat. *Hello, Marjorie. I'm Henry Jennings.* The words refused to come.

And Jesus Christ Almighty, here was Peter! Still a few bookcases between them, but sauntering this way, oh help, with the air of insouciance he always wore when he was pulling some scam. Henry hurled himself behind *Arts and Crafts*, then edged along, ready to vanish around one shelf-end as Peter materialised around the other.

But wait. Thank the Lord, Peter was veering off. He was slipping through the double doors into the corridor to the Reference Room. He was gone.

Henry's head swam. He felt quite sick. He leant his head against *A Child's Guide to Macramé*. What in heaven's name was going on?

Elena

Craigston Castle, south-east of Banff. Seat of the Urquhart family. Current chiefship held by American branch of family.

Tartan—green and buff with stripes of darker brown and large squares of thin red.

Her notebook lay forgotten on top of her jacket. For long minutes she had been rigid with excitement, voraciously consuming page after page.

For here he was! She had surely found him. Angus Urquhart, acclaimed SAS hero of World War II, also veteran of the Spanish conflict, gunrunner and yes! eyewitness to the fall of Malaga. Saints be blessed, for no doubt this was he. And here also a photograph, taken on his eightieth birthday in 1996. His beard white, his blue eyes clear and proud, the calves of his legs still muscular below the pleats of the green and buff kilt. With a dog at his side, he stood erect beside a shallow river in a grey landscape of stones, his smile satirical not kind. Capable and alert, with many evil years left in him.

Elena closed her eyes and touched her forehead to the shiny surface of the photograph. 'I will shame you.'

The book was full of praise for his valiant deeds. She skimmed the text again. Parachute drops into occupied France, secret camps, intelligence gathering, carrier pigeons, brave forays against enemy strongholds, and more—

... awarded the Military Cross for courage above and beyond the course of duty... a daylight raid... village swarming with Germans... stormed into the square in a single jeep, leapt out and opened fire... killed ten, leapt back in and drove off... sustained only minor wounds.

Survival miraculous... confusion covered the escape of twenty-six Frenchmen about to be executed. "Foolhardy," wrote his commanding officer, "showing utter disregard for danger, but gallantry of the highest order."

'No, it is not enough.' She sprang to her feet. Somehow, she must find him. The librarian was unhelpful, but the book group, maybe someone there would know the way? And first she must have a photocopy of these pages to wave under his nose—*Yes, my dear young lady, I am he, soldier and hero*—before she unmasked him and found the way to bring him to his knees, begging her absolution, which she would never, ever, give.

Peter

Luck of the devil—U-turn through double doors into corridor behind. All clear. Book group, bollocks, he'd barge straight in. Memory glowing with shelves of Yellow Pages smack next to Gaelic dictionaries beside the door. He wouldn't have to cross the room. FU's eyes might be unnerving, but goosey stares he'd brazen out, no sweat.

Hold on! No! Through other door, here she breezed, the pint-sized guardian of the Reference Room, turning his way, heading straight towards him, smiling her discomfiting smile, fixing him with those canny, uncanny eyes. And yes, she did mean him.

Time to turn and run. But no, the eyes had him, he'd never seen such eyes. Might think in the normal way of things that here was bed for night plus leg-over, but somehow not these eyes. Did she know him after all? What was her game? She had him like the proverbial bunny in a beam.

Henry

When his heart let up thundering in his ears and he

emerged from *Arts and Crafts*, Henry discovered with a new, sick lurch that Marjorie had disappeared. Not even her jacket remained.

Panic swept him. He must find her. He stumbled towards reception, staring wildly to left and right, almost succumbing to the urge to call her name. Where had she gone? Out into the snow? Back to the Reference Room? He mustn't lose her. He couldn't bear it.

Thank goodness—he sagged with relief—here she was, along this little dead-end beside the exit, lifting the lid of the photocopying machine.

He must stop dithering. He would do it. He smoothed his hair, took a deep breath, willed himself to approach and speak.

Elena

Beneath the lid there was a ragged sheet of paper, left by the previous user. She yanked it out and placed *Twentieth Century Scottish Heroes* face down on the glass. She posted coins into the slot, punched the green button and stood back. As the machine began to trundle through its cycle of flash and slide, she glanced at the paper in her hand. It looked like poetry, shakily hand-written in a language she did not know. Her professional eye skimmed, seeking some word or phrase that might give a clue to meaning.

'*Ay!*'

She dropped it in shock, then fell to her knees and stared. Yes. She had made no error. At the foot of this dog-eared page, the writer had signed his name.

Angus Urquhart!

Peter

A bunny in a beam.

Henry

Creeping up on Marjorie Macpherson.

Elena

On her knees.

There was a moment of mutual stillness in which, quite
suddenly, the lights went out.

Chapter Eight

Elena

She remained absolutely still, struggling to make sense of the double shock—the signature on the paper and the dramatic darkness—shock that was fast turning to fear. Her skin felt electric, as though at any moment her enemy would reach from the blackness and lay his hand on hers. She swallowed a cry, and struggled to her feet, bumping against the photocopier. The dark was absolute. It pressed on her eyes like a cushion. Yet through it she felt watched.

Someone had been nearby, she realised. Behind and to the left while she sat reading she had heard a quiet cough. Then someone approaching as she was photocopying. And yes, with a shiver she remembered, the glass of the photocopier still hot when she raised the lid. Was *she* in pursuit of Urquhart, or was *he* the hunter, luring her in like a moth to a web?

But how? No one but she had heard Aunt Marisa's last whisper. No one had watched as she pulled the lace cocoon from the linen-drawer and wept over its yellowing contents. How could *el malo* know that Carlos's granddaughter would come in search of him after sixty-three years? To this library, tonight? Such knowledge was impossible.

Queda tranquila. He could not know she was here. She was the hunter, he the prey. There was no trap. The blizzard had cut off the electricity. Pure chance had put this paper in her hand. She would be strong. She would find the librarian and question her again. Elena let herself exhale, then drew slow breaths, relaxing her shoulders, reassuring herself there was nothing to fear. Out in reception, she could hear subdued voices and see a flickering point of light. People were doing something to end the darkness. There was little point in moving, she decided. She would stay here, safe beside the photocopier, breathing in, breathing out, rebuilding her courage.

Peter

He remained absolutely still, struggling with the after-image of the librarian's eyes. The memory of them glowed through the shroud of darkness, whose arrival seemed natural, like mercy from the devil, the only possible escape from the unnerving power of that smile, that steady gaze heading his way, compulsive and terrible like... like what? Words wouldn't come. Not sexual, not censorious.

Where was she? Shrink against wall and scour the silence with his ears. Not a sound. No breath, no footfall. Had darkness wiped all trace, gathered her up like ectoplasm? Was she a ghost, a shadow cast by Calum Calum, dead as the world believed him, gone beyond grave to purgatory, to scratch out his transcendent poems on a blood-spattered desk three below Keats and one along from poor Kit Marlowe?

The reward will surprise you. FU.

FU! Of course, right in front of him. Too hungry, too engrossed in Gaelic, too jumpy altogether. F fucking *U*. Fiona *Urquhart*, stake his soul on it, same name as on the poem. Calum Calum alias Angus Urquhart, ask at the library, Fiona.

Niece? Granddaughter? Cousin twice removed? Could these be Calum's eyes he'd seen, could still see, strong, omniscient, lighting his way forward? No wonder he was mesmerised. Calum's genius in her genes, the walking echo of a man whose face was hidden from the world. No trick, no con—she meant to bring him straight to Calum, and Calum straight to him. Bards of the old and new millennia, bound together by mutual awe.

Speak her name. 'Fiona?' Was she still here in the blacked-out corridor, waiting for dawn to break in his head? Inch his way along the wall, whispering, 'Fiona? Are you there?'

Henry

He remained absolutely still, struggling with indecision.

He'd opened his mouth, the words were there, he would have spoken them. *Hello, Marjorie. I'm Henry Jennings.* But then, alarmingly, she'd cried out and fallen to her knees.

He'd wanted to rush to her aid, he'd taken the first step, when, damn and blast, the lights had failed.

What to do? Grope his way forward with the offer of an anonymous tweed-clad arm? *Oh, and by the way, I'm Henry Jennings.*

It wouldn't do. Stranger writes love-letters, won't take silence for an answer, then leaps from the dark to offer help? No. Retreat and regroup, that was the thing. He turned and swam in the approximate direction of the librarian's desk, burrowing ahead with his hands.

Then, he remembered. Of course, he had a torch!

Proper little boy scout.

He'd bought it a while ago on a whim. 'The slimmest in the world' it was billed, stacked with its fellows on a shop-counter like a tower of After Eights. Idly curious, he'd picked one off the pile. With not a clue how to make it work, he'd tried squeezing it between finger and thumb and, click, there was light. A fierce little ray from a minuscule bulb on one edge. He'd had to have the thing. He had it now, in his breast pocket. Click and there was light.

'Oh, thank goodness.'

The librarian. He swung the fragile beam in search of her. She was no more than two yards away, but the torch illuminated only a few square inches at a time. Her kind smile, and then her eyes, large and serious, searching the darkness to know who he was. He swivelled the torch to his own face and cleared his throat.

'Do you need help?'

'Yes, thank you. Please,' her disembodied voice, 'it may be a power line down, but there's a chance it's only the fuses. I've seen them in a cupboard out back. And candles too. If you could light my way?'

'Of course.'

Damn. *Damn.* DAMN! It meant leaving Marjorie. But how could he refuse? The librarian stumbled against him. She took hold of his sleeve, redirecting the torch, then edged away towards the bookshelves, following the dancing Tinkerbell beam. He went with her reluctantly, twisting his neck to stare behind, straining to see. The only discernible shape was a faint grey ladder of light, window onto the snowbound world. There, unguarded, lay the exit, through which, at any moment, Marjorie would slip away, into her forever separate life. He groaned.

'Are you all right?' said the librarian.

'Yes.'

They had threaded their way through the bookshelves to the back wall of the lending room. The needle of light was discovering the jamb and handle of another door, *Staff Only*. The librarian opened it and led him inside.

Chapter Nine

Elena

The returning light restored her confidence. The shock of the signature on this stray bit of paper had passed. Now it seemed a gift, proof that the spirits of her mother and aunt were guiding her. The poetry was in Gaelic, she decided, the ancient language of Britain's Celtic fringes. She photocopied it, along with pages from *Twentieth Century Scottish Heroes,* then took time to squeeze every drop of meaning from it.

Though the language was unintelligible, the handwriting, blue from the nib of a fountain-pen, was eloquent. A tremor marred the antiquated script—*el malo* was less strong than his photograph pretended. Yet defiance remained, a pressure on the page and a filling of it from side to side that allowed no contradiction. *I am powerful and decisive. See what I can do.* Here was a man still mighty in his own eyes.

Only the final line—*Mar sin leibh*—and the signature faltered. Less weight, less character, and the last few letters—*a-r-t*—a timid mark. There was pride in the writing, but not in the name.

'I *will* shame you,' she whispered again.

She folded the photocopies into her bag, then picked up her jacket and returned to the librarian's desk. No one was here except the young man with whom she kept colliding, the one whose eyes mirrored her emotions. Now he looked determined. She nodded, and he nodded. 'Have you seen the librarian?' he said.

'No. I wish to find her also.'

'You try that way. I'll cover the Reference Room.' He vanished through the door beside the librarian's desk.

Elena wandered back into the lending room. She replaced *Twentieth Century Scottish Heroes* on the shelf, then stretched up on her toes to see beyond the bookcases. Nothing moved. But then, yes, a door was opening in the back wall and through it were coming two people. The librarian, and a man with a brown coat over his arm and an expression of great anxiety.

Henry

'No, really. Not at all.'

The librarian was thanking him, but Henry couldn't concentrate. He wished he could, he must seem rude, but he was gripped by his need to find Marjorie. The librarian was intolerably relaxed, while his feet fidgeted and his mouth stammered platitudes. Slowly, too slowly, they were making their way towards reception.

Then his heart leapt. The jolt in his chest spread outwards in an exquisite flood. Marjorie hadn't abandoned him in the dark. She was here, heading straight towards him, holding a piece of paper. 'Please, you excuse me. You know what this is?'

The paper flapped under Henry's nose. 'Marjorie?' he said.

She took no notice. She was looking at the librarian. 'I find it in the photocopier.'

Adrenaline rebounded on him like a hose-jet from a

wall. This wasn't Marjorie. The woman had only rudimentary English, some kind of foreign accent. It absolutely wasn't her.

The librarian seized the paper. 'I don't believe this!'

'Neither do I,' he said fiercely. He made a point of never losing his temper, but he could feel it slipping.

'Please. What do you not believe?' She was still ignoring him, this woman who wasn't Marjorie. Addressing her questions to the suddenly incensed librarian. 'Why are you angry? Tell me, is Mr Urquhart here?'

Two angry women, both ignoring him, neither of them Marjorie. Where the hell was Marjorie?

'That young man!' The librarian spun round, looking. 'He must be Peter. How unbelievably careless!'

She had to mean his brother. Henry's head was churning. Nothing was making sense.

The woman who wasn't Marjorie showed no more interest in Peter than in Henry. 'Urquhart,' she repeated. 'The man who signs this. He is here?'

'No! I've told you, no.' The librarian was growing more hopping mad by the second. 'How could he? It's so precious.'

Nothing was clear except, surprise, surprise, Peter had messed up. Henry exploded. 'Marjorie,' he demanded. 'Where's Marjorie Macpherson?'

The librarian took no notice. She was marching off with the paper clutched to her bosom and the foreign impostor hard on her heels.

'MARJORIE MACPHERSON,' he yelled after them. Then stared wildly around, in the desperate hope that Marjorie would hear and come running. She had to be somewhere in this impossible place. Hidden around a corner, wearing, not a sharp black suit, but a long red skirt and tartan sash, with golden buckles on her shoes and a halo of bright hair.

His bellow brought the librarian to a halt. She turned to face him, frowning. 'The workshop, you mean? They're still there, I expect.' She pointed. 'The Reference Room. Along the corridor.'

'*NO!!!!!!*'

'No?' She blinked at his rudeness.

'No,' he said despairingly. 'She isn't *there*.'

'Who isn't?'

'*MARJORIE* isn't.'

'Marjorie?' said the librarian.

Was the woman obstructive or stupid? He could hear himself shouting. 'YES, DAMN IT. MARJORIE. THE WRITER. THE WORKSHOP. MARJORIE MAC-PHERSON. WHERE IS SHE?'

'Oh dear me. I see,' the librarian said. 'I do apologise. I thought you knew. It's been a secret, but now he's such a success.'

'Hold on. What are you talking about? Where's Marjorie?'

The librarian came nearer. She had an intense, earnest expression. Her voice was filtering through the tumult in his head. 'Michael McCoy,' she was saying. 'Women used to write as men, but more often these days it's the other way around.'

'What?' He couldn't understand. He couldn't be hearing right. 'What are you saying?'

'The writer. His name is Michael McCoy.'

The truth slammed into him. He let out a long, low

moan.

'I'm so sorry.' The librarian had her hand on his arm. There was a look of pity in her eyes. She knew.

Somewhere nearby, beyond the librarian's intolerable kindness, Henry heard the foreign impostor laugh. She knew too.

Chapter Ten

Elena

Her laughter was unforgivable—she immediately repented it. She was tense, hysterical perhaps, but nothing could excuse such rudeness. There was no remedy—to say more would make things worse. The unfortunate man, white with shock, was backing away among the bookcases despite the librarian's efforts to guide him to a chair.

'I'm fine. No. Fine. Leave me alone, won't you?'

He was panting. He looked as though he might faint. But he threw the librarian's hand from his arm with such violence that she had to concede. Then he turned and almost ran, between the bookcases, disappearing among them.

Elena stood side by side with the librarian, staring after him. She hated herself. 'It is wrong to laugh. Unkind. I do not mean—'

'Of course you don't,' said the librarian.

There was no censure in her voice. Elena felt absolved as by twenty Ave Marias. For a blessed moment she was free of anger.

'Will he be okay?'

'I don't know,' said the librarian. 'He needs to be by himself.'

Elena felt unreal, as though someone else were having this conversation. For days she had been silent, confiding in no one, and then she had been travelling.

Mikhail. She had wanted to speak to Mikhail. Or simply to be held by him.

'The poor man,' the librarian was saying. 'But there's nothing we can do, I think. We only make it worse by knowing.'

Her steady eyes held Elena's. The man's mistake was humorous, but his suffering was not. Elena decided that she liked this woman.

She remembered the paper in her hand. 'Urquhart.' The name was sharp as steel in her mouth. 'The man who signs this poem.'

The librarian shook her head and looked away.

'But please. I have to find him.'

'He's a very private man.'

'You know him, then?'

The librarian met her eyes reluctantly. 'Well yes, I do,' she said. 'I know him very well in fact. He's my father.'

Peter

Plenty of Urquharts in the phonebook, but nary a one with initial A. No option left but trust in sweet FU, who wasn't here, only the geese and two ganders, all of a flutter from the blackout. Plus their gooseboy, a limp-wristed wanker with no hair, settling the flutters and recapping on some erstwhile spout about motivation and big scenes, before launching a goosey brainstorm. 'Choose three objects. Anything you like. But careful, these will be clues or plot connections.' Then turning, all gay smiles, to Peter skulking by the door. 'Do feel free to join us.'

Desperate for more male members? Whoops, no thanks mate. Must skedaddle after fair Fi and Calum.

First, yank Jiffybag from rucksack. Need her note. Want to present her note, not poem. Hold tight to poem until her game was clear. Take one last look at miraculous manuscript, touch Calum's signature for luck.

Pages muddled.

No, where was it? Fuck! where was it?

Shit and double-shit! Searing vision of page face down on hot glass, left in the machine!

Grab everything and outta here, galloping along corridor again, *bang* right and—

Curses! four accusing female eyes, Fiona and the Spanish dame, and worse, the lost, last page of lost, last work of Calum, tight in Fiona's mitt.

'Peter Jennings?'

'Yes.'

'I'm Fiona Urquhart—'

'Yes, I know. Daftest thing. Been looking for you everywhere, and here you are.'

'May I have the rest of it, please?'

'I was just coming for that. Left it in the photocopier, don't know how. No damage, eh?'

Her outstretched palm as flat and unforgiving as Loch Ness. 'The rest of it. Please.'

'And then you'll take me to meet Calum?'

Bulls-eye. Her face amazed. 'Calum?'

'Yes. The man who wrote this poem. You'll take me to him?'

Mouth open. Blinking. Speaking. 'Yes.'

Yes! The word was yes! Calum alive! Her palm still up and empty.

'But his name is Urquhart, no?' Spanish dame cutting in, eyes aglow, fretful as a prima donna. 'I also, please. *I* need to meet him.'

'Why?' He and FU the opera chorus.

'He is a hero, no? The SAS? In France? In World War Two?'

Fiona frowning, nodding, yes. Amazing, who would credit it? Good old Calum in the SAS.

'Permit me to explain. My name is Elena Martínez. I am researching for a book on war heroes like your father.'

Her *father*? Calum's *daughter*? Quantum leap from flesh and blood.

'But a different kind of book. I want to meet them, to hear their memories.' Señorita droning on.

Take good look at Calum's daughter. No more than thirty-five. Calum twentyish in nineteen-thirties, eighty going on ninetyish now. Long in the tooth when he sired this one.

'... how heroism feel to them. Not battlefields and glory, but close up, inside the head.'

Far far colder. That is how it was. Echo of Calum's poem. Keep shtum, keep listening, with twenty-two of twenty-three pages still in rucksack, and Fiona's empty palm forgetful by her side.

Henry

He struggled like a leaf above a storm drain. He was lost beyond imagining, drowning in the laughter of his vanishing ghosts. His idiocy seared his mind in flashes. Marjorie a man. A man reading his love-letters. Smiling. Slipping a flier into a dark-pink envelope. The images made him yelp and hop, trying to escape, trying to make them not be true. His mother, he needed her comfort, her arms. Please, Mother. But her smile shimmered out of reach. Cool, aloof, as mocking as Marjorie Macpherson, she refused even to look at him.

His mother was dead.

The thought concussed him. He dropped like a shot deer. Marjorie was gone. His mother was gone. Loneliness was spreading through his veins. Silence bombarded his ears and he could scarcely see. He hugged his knees and held on grimly, down the drain and into the darkness.

Time passed, and the storm. He wasn't a leaf, or a shot deer, or a lost soul. He was a middle-aged financial adviser cowering with eyes tight shut in *Palaeontology*. He would have to prise his eyelids open, straighten creaking knees, brush himself down and make some kind of exit from this hellhole.

His eyes stayed shut. The flashes began to return. Marjorie a man. Oh Christ, he couldn't bear it. He fought off the thoughts with images of the Royal Highland Hotel, the staircase, the tartan carpet, the soft, sad face of the stag in the painting—

No, even Scotland mocked him.

Guildford then? His house.

Where a romantic hero leered from the hall mirror.

His garden.

Where 'Springwood White' smirked in the front rockery.

The pub, of course, the pub. *A double brandy, Henry? Coming right up. Cracking bit o' stuff you've got—*

Oh God, was there nowhere to hide?

Bump, thud. The breathy sound of a microphone. Henry opened his eyes and read the nearest book-spine. *Rocks from lost civilisations.* An immense, aching sadness reached from his chest, up through his throat, and insinuated its fingers into his nose and eyes.

'May I have your attention, please.' The librarian's brisk voice came through the tannoy. 'The weather's so bad, there's a risk we may be snowed in. I have to close the library.'

Henry looked at his watch. It said five past eight.

'I'm so sorry to inconvenience you. I hope you get home safely.'

Bump, thud, click. The announcement was over.

Chapter Eleven

Peter

Watch geese flock around FU honking, 'Such a pity, such a pity.' She and camp gooseboy soothing and persuading, edging them through gate to exit. Some refusing the snow, waddling back through entrance door, beaks outstretched and feathers ruffled. 'Fiona, Mr McCoy, the storm is done.' 'Mayn't we stay?' 'Mayn't we finish the workshop?'

Gooseboy smiling, nodding gamely, murmuring solutions, steering them patiently out through gate again.

Feathers ruffled here too, though not a goose, an eagle. Rucksack in talons, eyes locked on paper still in FU's hand, then meeting her disturbing gaze.

'Tomorrow, Peter.'

'What? Tomorrow, what?' He must be sure.

'I'll bring you to my father tomorrow.'

Such eyes, what else to do but trust them? And yet, 'Why not tonight?'

'Snowploughs take time. Come morning, I'll ring my brothers to check we can get through.'

'Your *brothers?*'

'Yes.'

'Your *father's* sons?'

'Yes.'

'How many?'

'Four.' Calm answers blowing him away.

'And where? How far?'

'The hotel at Loch Craggan. Thirty miles west of here.'

'Please, you permit me,' Spanish fly-in-ointment buzzing in, 'you allow me to come there also.'

'No.' Too right. Three a multitude. 'I'm sorry, but it simply isn't—'

'But please, Miss Urquhart, I am begging you.'

Fiona shaking head.

'I come here especially from Brussels.' Spanish histrionics. Don't weaken. Tell her no. 'What your father does. So much courage. To save so many men.'

FU reluctant, barely smiling.

'I need little time only. Little, little. Only what your father wish to tell. If he say no, okay, you send me away, yes?'

Fuck it, fuck it, no.

'Oh dear. All right. Tomorrow morning then.'

'Thank you, Miss Urquhart. You have much kindness. Where am I meeting you?' Fucking Spanish bull-at-a-gate crasher.

Fiona vexed, voice clipped. 'Back here, at ten. My car's outside, but I'm walking home—the snow's too deep to drive.' Rounding on him. 'So please, Peter.' Eyes on rucksack, palm afloat. 'Give me the poem. For safe keeping until tomorrow.'

Talons tightening in panic, almost a squawk escaping. Without poem, all might vanish—FU, Loch Craggan, brothers, Calum Calum—vanish in the snowdrifts, not a trace, no proof at all. Starting awake, icicle on nose, alone and empty-handed in a bus-shelter.

Wham! The answer. Keep the poem, lose the Spanish fly. 'Of course, you're right. But first, I wonder.' Flash blue eyes at fine Fiona, dish up abject grin. 'Nowhere to stay.

Completely skint. Mortgaged my soul to get here. Is there a hostel, do you know?'

Bingo! Straight in! FINE SCOTS LASSIE SAVES THE DAY. 'I'm so sorry, I didn't realise. And all my doing, how remiss of me. Please, you must be my guest.'

Henry

Hat pulled hard over eyes, collar up round ears, Henry was heading for the door. He wanted no more than to be out of this nightmare, barricaded safely in his hotel room with a bottle of brandy, a large tumbler and only four walls to witness his tortured descent into oblivion. He hovered by the last shelf—*Sport and Travel*—seeking an opportune moment to dash for the exit.

The crowd of elderly ladies was thinning and with it his cover. The little librarian would surely be last out, but Peter and the foreign woman were circling her like predatory birds, showing no sign of leaving.

Peter's presence was unfathomable. Bizarre coincidence, nothing to do with Marjorie it seemed. Some business with that piece of paper. The librarian still had it. Peter's eyes were fixed on it.

The minutes were ticking by. Peter's fixation was the only cover Henry was going to get. Head down, he scuttled across and made it through the gate.

The librarian saw him. He glanced sideways as he went and met her eyes. She didn't betray him by a flicker. He was out.

But still not free. Against a startling backdrop of moonlit snow, the elderly ladies were thronging round the bald man with the large nose. Henry ducked behind a pillar.

'Mr McCoy. Mr McCoy.'

Michael McCoy. The name the librarian had spoken. Henry closed his eyes as the awfulness seized him like the whirling pits of drunkenness. On the other side of this sham-Doric column was the person whose prose had captivated him, who had read his bared soul, seen his foolish grin through the lens of Trevor's Pentax, then summoned him here to receive an answer that needed no words. A bald man with a large nose whose name was Michael McCoy.

Were you wanting to join us? He shuddered, remembering the words. Cruelty he might have expected. Scorn, or anger even. But no. As Marjorie would have done, this man had lifted his head and smiled. *Were you wanting to join us?*

Damn it, this man *was* Marjorie. Marjorie didn't exist. Another tidal wave of loss threatened to break over his head.

He must hold on. He mustn't go under until he was back at base. Reality check. His forehead was numb from the frosted stone. The women's voices were receding, sounding happier. He stepped clear of the pillar and saw them moving away, clustered around Michael McCoy, trampling a path with the soles of their stout boots.

The snow had stopped falling. It lay in deep drifts, reflecting the streetlights and a high, racing moon. Henry set out after the group, glancing back in fear of seeing Peter. The mocking ladders of yellow light all at once went out. There was no time to lose and nowhere to hide. Nothing to do but press on, staring in anguish at the unprotected pate of the stranger who had enticed him here and now was leading him away.

Elena

'Fine. All gone. I can lock up.'

The librarian pulled keys from a drawer. Her manner was cool, her eyes refused to meet Elena's. She did not wish her to accompany them tomorrow.

Urquhart's daughter. Elena must give meaning to her stares. She pointed towards the lending shelves. 'Should we check? The man who—'

'It's all right, he's gone. I saw him leave. But what about you, Señorita Martínez? Do you have far to go?'

The librarian was buttoning a sheepskin coat and stepping into fur boots. The young man had a ribbed sweater under his denim jacket. Elena glanced down at her black suit. 'Not far. Ness Bank.'

'But you'll be frozen. I've a blanket in the car. Please, you must borrow it.'

Falsely generous like her father, her courtesy abhorrent, yet a blanket was impossible to resist. 'Thank you, Miss Urquhart.'

The librarian offered her hand. 'Now that you're coming, do please call me Fiona.'

Elena accepted the hand. She must control her feelings, must give the appearance of trust. 'Thank you, Fiona,' she repeated. 'So, also, you will call me Elena?'

Trust. *Trust me, Carlos.* Remembered in blood on the stones of the village square. Again it was happening, Carlos's granddaughter and Urquhart's daughter, stepping out into another bright, white square. But this time, she the traitor.

'I was going to doss in the bus station.'

She had almost forgotten the young man—his words made her jump. He seemed as mesmerised as she was by the librarian. His eyes, ever a mirror for Elena's moods, were fixed on Fiona Urquhart's small, gloved hands, which were scraping snow from the roof and door of a Deux Chevaux. The roof was yellow for cowardice, the door red for blood. Fiona had it open and was reaching inside.

The blanket was tartan. Green and buff with stripes of darker brown and large squares of thin red. Fiona shook it, folded it corner to corner, then reached to drape it around Elena's shoulders and put the fringed edge into her fingers. 'I hope this will be enough to keep you warm.'

Elena could not speak. Urquhart's tartan, light on her shoulders, pressed dark and heavy on her soul. She clasped it to her breast and nodded dumbly.

Fiona pointed. 'The book group have beaten us a path.'

The young man snorted. 'Not completely useless then.'

They set off along the trail of compacted snow, Elena following behind, clutching the blanket round her, blinking at the cold. At the end of the street, the beaten path veered left towards the station.

'We go ahead here, Elena. Your way looks clear.' Fiona lifted her feet and ploughed into a virgin drift. 'And ours is no distance, Peter. Down this lane and over the footbridge.'

'Please. Call me Mr Jennings. Only jesting, Fi, I'm with you all the way.'

'So,' Fiona turned and smiled, '*buenas noches,* Elena. *Hasta mañana.*'

'*Si. Buenas noches.*'

She watched them go, small and tall against the snow.

Urquhart's daughter and the young man with blue eyes like mirrors. Cheerful, impregnable, a pair of lovers in the making, while she remained alone. The empty street was as desolate as the one in her dream.

She found her mobile and pressed redial.

'Thank you for calling. Mikhail Kilvanev is not—'

She cut off his voice, blinked back the tears. She concentrated with all her strength on Angus Urquhart. *Hasta mañana*. Face to face with him, everything would change. Poet, hero, and evil traitor! She, ushered in by his daughter, introduced as admiring biographer. And then...

Elena shivered. Her teeth chattered and her feet shrank from the snow. Was this only cold that she was feeling? Too terrible suddenly it seemed, to denounce a frail, old man. The smooth surface of another's life impossible to challenge. The habit bred in her that she was the outcast.

Not so! An end to self-pity and disgrace! To the stain that stunted her life! It was Urquhart, not she, who was the sham. Urquhart who hoodwinked the angels to be given sons and a daughter, adulation as a hero and a peaceful old age. While Carlos, his betrayed friend, was flung into hell. Honour lost, life cut short, daughters and granddaughter left fatherless, cursed and shunned.

'*Maldita sea*! I will shame you!' cried Elena at the moon.

She pulled the hateful blanket tight, wriggled her frozen toes and picked up speed towards the station.

Chapter Twelve

Henry

'Hell and damnation!'

He paced the outer lobby of the Royal Highland Hotel and cursed aloud. He wasn't sure he could take much more of this. Beyond the etched glass, the tartan-carpeted, wrought-iron and gold-fronded staircase swept gracefully aloft. The glowing tulip-shades of the chandeliers beckoned. The receptionist came and went, smiling and nodding, bearing his clinking tray of wine and whisky. But Henry could not bring himself to step inside.

For Michael McCoy was there.

Complete with his gang of hangers on, dangling his piece of string and shuffling his pack of cards, throwing back the booze and soaking up the fickle receptionist's soothing courtesies. Michael blasted McCoy.

Henry retreated impotent and seething into the station square. Anger helped, but it wouldn't last. Only alcohol was going to douse this surreal pain. A pub, damn and blast it. He would have to find a bally pub.

Best keep a weather eye open for Peter. He shot a glance back towards the library. No sign of the pest, but here came the foreign woman, teetering in her silly shoes, shrunk inside a blanket like a gypsy.

He retreated into the shadows, bracing himself for a new seizure of mortification. With relief, he found it didn't come. To see this stranger bedraggled in the snow was oddly consoling. Not an hour ago he'd invested her with infinite capacity to cure his ills. Her failure to do so had been a cruel blow. But her power to injure him was gone, and his torment eased. She wasn't Marjorie Macpherson, but that was scarcely her fault. And she'd laughed. Okay, she'd laughed. Henry shrank several sizes in his skin to avoid a replay of the awful moment. But she wasn't laughing now—she looked damned sorry for herself. Come to think of it, she looked as much in need of a drink as he was.

What the hell, misery made him reckless. He launched himself into her path. 'Hello there.'

'Oh!'

'Forgive me, did I startle you? It's just, you look so very cold. I wonder, may I lend you my coat?'

'Oh...' The woman's face crumpled. She was crying suddenly, shivering and unable to speak.

Henry's anger evaporated. 'Please. Let me. It has a padded lining.' He whipped off his Barbour and helped her into it. He replaced the blanket round her shoulders, then found her frozen hands and pushed them into the Barbour's warm pockets. 'A drink. A brandy? May I buy you a brandy?'

'No. Truly.'

She didn't mean no, he could tell. She needed a drink. And kindness, she needed kindness. 'Look, please, don't be alarmed or embarrassed. I'm more than a bit beset myself. I could do with the company.'

She was finding her voice, her earthy, foreign, can't-possibly-be-Marjorie voice. 'I am so sorry. In the library, I was unkind. Discourteous.'

He managed a smile. 'No, really, I was making a

complete spectacle of myself. So please. But I'm sorry, I haven't introduced myself. Henry Jennings.'

'Elena Martínez.'

'So please, Elena Martínez. Won't you share a brandy with me?'

She was nodding uncertainly. He was steering her away from the station, in the direction she had been going. With luck, and it was high time he had some of the stuff, they would find a pub before she changed her mind.

Peter

Long suspension footbridge bouncing like a trampoline from kids up ahead, leaping and whooping, zipping snowballs past each other's ears into the river. Feet aslide, grab frozen rail, cold spreading like a slow burn through palm and fingers. Warm himself with vision of bossy wee Fiona, leading him on, Good Witch of the North.

'My house.' Her finger outstretched over moon-splashed water. 'We'll soon be there.'

'It's good of you to take me in. Mad axeman for all you know. Or have we met before?'

Pink cheeks, a glimpse of smile. Answer reaching him in puffs of icy mist. 'No, not at all. Though in a way. We're not altogether strangers.' Speaking in riddles.

'How? *How* do you know me?' Panting to keep abreast, to keep those eyes in view.

'My father. He told me about you.'

Punch air with joy. '*He* knows me?'

'Yes.'

'And he's Calum Calum?'

'Yes.'

Melodious sound, this woman's 'yes'. Her father, Calum Calum, knowing, knowing. Struggle to catch her up. 'And so, your dad says to you, "Fiona, daughter mine, send Peter Jennings my poem. Bring him to me."'

'No.' Halting, turning, showing him those eyes. Sad eyes. At centre-bridge now, face to face, strung out on steel cables over rushing water, kids yelling and jumping, iced footpath bucking like a boat-deck.

'Which bit no?'

'He didn't ask me to send it.'

'But he didn't stop you?'

'I didn't tell him. He would have forbidden me. He would have taken it back.'

Holy moly! Twenty-two pages safe in rucksack, one in her bag. Kids away now, bridge silent, only the sound of water. Fiona staring out across the racing current.

'So you sent it without telling him?'

'Yes.'

'Why?'

Silence. Not answering.

'To save it?'

'Yes, perhaps. In a way.'

'Because you want the poem to be read?'

'Yes. But more.' Eyes averted, moving on across the bridge, tugging at the collar of her sheepskin.

Hurry, overtake her, block her path. 'What sort of more?'

Stalling. 'It's hard to say.'

'And why send it to me?'

'Because I wanted *you* to read it.'

'Me especially?'

'Yes, you especially.' Lifting those melancholy eyes.

'And I wanted to meet you.'

Excitement numbing the brain. What piece was missing here? 'Calum Calum is my muse. My thesis is about him.'

'Yes, I know.'

'You do?'

'My father has your thesis.'

Oh joy! 'But it's unpublished, not even finished.' Fiona nodding. 'So how did he come by it?'

'I'm not sure.'

'And my poems? Has he read them too?'

'I think so. Some of them.'

Warm rush of glory, stifle whoop of triumph, swoop instead to scrunch a snowball, send it flying into Moon River.

Fiona watching, grave eyes bright and clear. 'My father's poem, Peter. Have you read it?'

'Yes!' Nod wildly, clap hands to kill snowball cold, rejoice in imminent fame and fortune. No use—calm eyes extracting truth. 'Well, most of it. A good half anyway. The Gaelic was a touch rusty yesterday, but it's oiled and spinning now.'

'It's woesome, Peter, don't you think?'

Brought up short. Calum's poem. *Far far colder*. This was the truth she wanted. 'Yes, too right, a palpable lament. But more than that, it's *great*, Fiona. A miraculous poem. The best he ever—'

Shaking her head. 'I found him weeping over it. He told me its story. He said to write again after so long, to confess, helped him.'

'Confess?' A poet resurrected. Mystery in Peter's hands like Ariadne's thread. 'What story? Tell me.'

'No. I see now. That's why I wanted you to come. I want him to tell you himself.'

Elena

It was impossible to speak in this bar by the river, into which they had come to escape the cold. There were so many shouting red faces. Three bearded men were attacking their guitars and violin with the gusto of Flamenco players.

Nor was there anywhere to sit. There was barely room to avoid touching this eccentric man, Henry something, who had pushed back through the crowd with two bright globes of cognac.

Tears sprang again in Elena's eyes. This was a mistake. She did not want to be here. She needed to prepare herself for tomorrow. She took the cognac, nodding her thanks. The man was speaking.

'Excuse me?' She leant closer. Saw the pain from the library still in his eyes. Turned an ear to catch his repeated words. There was too much noise.

'Why are you crying?'

The question unlocked her tears. She was sobbing stupidly. She bent her head, fighting to recover control.

His breath came hot on her ear. She turned sharply, fearing lechery. But no, his eyes were closed as though he were fighting tears himself. Then they opened. 'Forgive me,' he shouted above the music. 'None of my business. Drink up. We'll both feel better.'

Chapter Thirteen

Peter

Steps up to door, cherry red, framed by pink granite. Glow of light behind closed curtain, cheeky dormers peeking through meringue topping. Fiona's key turning, releasing bloody great hound, all wag and slobber.

'Hannah likes people.'

'Dogs are funny that way.'

Pat animal, take in clues. Bicycles in hall. Roar of TV from front room. Football match. Door opening on fat, trousered thighs and lager cans.

'Hi, Hamish. Hi, Greg.'

'Hi, Fiona.'

'This is Peter.'

'Hi, Peter.'

'Hi.' Who the fuck Hamish and Greg?

'This way.' Fiona's sheepskin swinging from newel post, boots abandoned in hall, voice calling him on. 'Would you like some soup, Peter? Or, sorry,' coming back, 'did you want to watch the game?'

Like hell, what did she take him for? Pull full poetic height and follow, pausing only to extract Hannah's nose from arse. 'Soup. Whatever. Great.'

'Woof!' Dog still bustling and barking, must have decided fair Fi lost at sea, while she, busy with pan, hoicking bowls from cupboards, wiping oilcloth table, clattering spoons, sawing bread, women in kitchens never still. 'Tea? Wine? Whisky? Or maybe Hame and Greg can spare a lager.'

Sudden thought. 'Are they your brothers?'

'No, my lodgers. What'll it be?'

'Whisky, ta.'

Whirling off again on her woolly, red-socked feet, unscrewing bottle, splashing two fingers, handing it over, stirring soup, rumpling dog's ears, tossing her head. 'I need one too.'

Waft of soup and hit of whisky. Fine Fiona, guardian of holy secrets, priestess to the Muse. Touching her golden glass to his—'Cheers, Peter'—then to her lips. Confronting with those upturned eyes. Daring him... to what? To make a pass?

'Cheers, Fiona?'

Stepping back, lowering her eyes, shaking her head. 'Peter, this is difficult.'

Follow close, touch her hand.

'Woof!'

'No, Peter, really. Stop.'

Try full, blue, abject beam. 'But why? Why not? You're gorgeous.'

Hyperbole working, Fi smiling, but jumping out of reach. 'Trust me. Till tomorrow. Finish reading the poem, Peter. Meet my father. It's the only way.'

Elena

She was safe, her body shielded by a robust coat and her brain by a mist of cognac. Her feet in their thin shoes on the trampled snow still remembered the warmth of the bar. After the deafening music, her ears were opening to the stillness, to the chatter of the Ness from its pebbled bed. Beside her, wrapped in the borrowed blanket, a benevolent stranger was walking in silence. Stars glimmered through branches wind-whipped with snow. They were passing a line of glowing guesthouse windows. Her key was in her hand.

There was no wind, or sound of gulls, or tears.

'This one is mine.' It was difficult to recognise. The low-walled garden lay cloaked in snow, the frosted ivy hung heavy as Aunt Marisa's lace. 'Will you come in? To be warm before you go?'

The man retreated a step. He shook his head solemnly. 'It's kind of you to offer, but I understand. It's no problem, really. You'd prefer to be alone.'

She started to unfasten the coat, to return it to him. Immediately she was trembling, the cold was so intense. In his hand was Urquhart's tartan.

'No!' The word burst from her. She did not want to be alone. 'It is you who are so kind... Henry,' she remembered and spoke his name, 'and unhappy. Maybe you tell me a little of this? And it will please me also to recount my story. Truly. The bar was loud.' She led him into the hall. A pink lamp burned on the proprietor's desk beside the bell. The clock showed nine forty-five. 'They have more cognac here perhaps?'

He nodded. She rang the bell. There was the sound of feet approaching from hidden rooms. The proprietor arrived, smiling. 'Cognac? No problem. Not vintage or nothin, but should 'it the spot. What weather, eh? In your room would you like it, or in 'ere?' He threw open a door, revealing an empty sitting-room with more pink lamps and a gas fire. 'Make yourselves at 'ome. Let's turn it up, eh? You look like you could do with a bit of 'eat.' He adjusted the fire. 'Back in a tick.' He was gone.

Elena dropped Henry's coat and sank into an armchair. 'The Scotch people, they are kind also.'

He was smiling at her. His face was pink from the cold air. She liked his face. 'Scott*ish*, they prefer to be called. But that one's not a Scot. More Thames Estuary, I would say.'

Henry

He was attempting to be calm and sensible. He hoped he seemed so. An attractive woman was about to cry on his shoulder.

She wasn't Marjorie Macpherson. She wasn't his mother. She was Spanish, good lord. Elena Martínez, her eyes and voice dark and deep, her English halting. She was quite unlike any woman he knew, or any fantasy he'd ever dared have. Was that the attraction? Frying pans and fires—steady on, Henry.

Essex man was flapping round them, doling out the cooking brandy and asking, would they like the bottle? Henry proffered a twenty-pound note, which did the trick. 'I'll leave you to it then. Don't hesitate to ring if you need anything.'

'Thank you so much,' Elena said firmly. 'I am sure we will be okay. Goodnight, *señor*.'

How self-possessed she seemed. Henry steadied his nerves with a swallow of brandy before daring to push his luck. 'So, do you still feel like telling? Why the tears?'

The ferocity in her brown eyes was unnerving. 'I tell nobody. I need to tell somebody. Maybe I am mad?'

'No, no,' he said. 'I'm sure you're not.' He thought of himself and added, 'Or else we all are. It's a mistake to assume anyone is sane, don't you think?' She was frowning. He hastened to revise. 'Forgive me, I mean, you're not mad, of course you're not. But maybe *I* am? Mad, I mean.' A short silence. 'Though not dangerously.'

Her frown gave way to a smile. But he had lost the plot. What had she said? Oh yes.

'I'm sorry. Please. You need to tell somebody. And I am somebody, I suppose, even if, right now, I'm not altogether sure who.'

The smile was still there. His courage put on a spurt of growth. 'So, how about it? Shall we give it a try? Will I do?'

Chapter Fourteen

Peter

Stomach full and Calum spread on the oilcloth table—
one hundred and twenty stanzas down, eighty to go. Hard
work under FU's exacting eye. Show proper scholarship,
catch wave of fluency, leave lexicon alone.

Recap: love destroyed, honour mislaid, intolerable cold,
da-di-dah, something something. Yes, but what story?
What confession?

'Three nil.' Greg or Hamish reporting glumly. 'Any
soup left, Fi?'

'Plenty, Hamish. In the pot.'

'Me too.' Greg drifting in behind, slumping down,
wolfing last slice of bread.

Snatch up Calum, shake off crumbs, resume later with
dictionary under blanket.

'You're home early.' Brown hair. Hamish.

'The blizzard, you berk.' Red beard. Greg.

'Woof!' Pooch. Hannah.

Hugely inconsiderate of brown, clean-shaven Hamish
to snaffle ginger, hairy name.

'Yes.' Fiona passing time of night with oiks. 'And the
lights went out for a while, so I thought it best to close up.
I feel bad about it. The weather's okay now, and the book
group weren't best pleased.'

'Of course! The group!' Chin excited for some reason.
'How did they react?'

'Were they shocked and horrified?' Beard adrip with soup.

'No, they were thrilled.'

'Fancied him, did they?'

Losing thread here. FU dissolving into giggles. New dimension, not in keeping. She'd better not be shagging one of these losers.

'Maybe they did. He was charming, and they were flattered to be the first to know.'

What was she on about?

'So was it you who spilled the beans?'

'Or did he leap out at them, no warning? Surprise, surprise?'

Chew finger, and exchange long look with Hannah. Not a clue.

'I did it. He said he hoped I wouldn't mind, he was a wee bit shy. I broke it to them before he went in.'

'Bloody wonderful. And they didn't laugh?'

'Or lynch him?'

'No. They plied him with sandwiches.'

'Woof!'

Time to sigh and remark wearily, 'I suppose there's zilch chance of your letting me in on this one either?'

'Oh Peter, I'm sorry. The man with the book group tonight. He publishes under a woman's name. Tonight was his coming-out. They thought they were going to meet "Marjorie Macpherson."'

Flash of geese milling around gooseboy. 'They fancied him all right.'

'Well, they would, wouldn't they?' Beard upending soup pan into mouth. 'Author of their romantic dreams turns into handsome, charming prince.'

'Not handsome.' Fiona giggling again, pleasingly uncharitable.

Chip in, quip irresistible, 'And more queen than prince.'

All eyes on him. Fiona's serious. 'Yes. You may be right.'

'Not a doubt in hell. A definite fruit.'

Frown from Fi, uplifting roar of mirth from chin and beard.

'Your poor ladies.' Beard oozing malice. 'One kiss and, wallop, Prince Charming is a frog.'

'But still,' Chin, 'it's gotta be an advance on a woman.'

'Mmm,' Fiona sighing, 'but it is dangerous, pretending to be what you're not.'

Pause.

'Why d'you say that?' Chin.

'No, I shouldn't.'

'Shouldn't what?' Beard.

Fiona squirming, about to spill some gossip. More imp than angel, bless his stars.

'Oh, all right. There was a man who arrived late, after I'd told them. Not a member of the group, a fan of Marjorie Macpherson's. He rang a couple of weeks ago, asking could he come along. I don't know how he'd heard about it, but, well, of course, I said. And when he arrived, I don't know why, I assumed he knew. Anyway, it was awful when he realised. And when he saw *we'd* realised.'

'Realised what?'

'About "Marjorie Macpherson". Why he'd come. You see, he didn't know she was a man. I think he'd hoped—'

'For a bit of sexual intercourse?'

'Well, yes. Romance and—'

'Fucking hell!'

'Woof! Woof!' General merriment and barking.

'No. Stop it. All of you. It isn't funny. The poor man. He was a nice man.'

Chin, beard, dog, Peter, all shouting her down. Poor man bollocks, it was hilarious as hell.

Elena

'He promise he will return—one day, or two, no more— with the guns. He leave in darkness. The sun rise and set, rise and set. The village is waiting. Young men, women, children.'

'And he doesn't come back?'

In the soft, pink light, the stranger's eyes as he leant towards Elena were swimming. Cognac tears, showing his own grief as much as hers. But genuine. Of this much she was sure.

'No, he does not return. First they believe him dead. Or captured by Franco.'

'But he isn't?'

'No. Word come. He is elsewhere in the Sierra. He take our money, but he bring no guns.'

'But that's dreadful. Wicked. Your village was in danger.'

'Yes. The front, it hold for many months. But who can say when Franco will break through? And my grandfather, he is the *alcalde*.'

'What's that?'

'The leader. The principal socialist. A farmer, but they elect him *alcalde*.'

'The mayor?'

'Yes.'

'So he felt responsible?'

'He is responsible. He give Urquhart bed and food. He call him brother. Make him a friend of the village. Hand him their money.'

'But how do you know this?'

'My aunt, Marisa. In November—this last November—she die. And as she die she tell me. She show me.'

Sobs overwhelmed Elena. She struggled to stifle them, expecting the man to leave his seat, to touch her. But he did not. He splashed more cognac into her glass on the low table and waited for her tears to stop. When they did, she picked up the glass and smiled at him, this good, kind man. 'Thank you, Henry.'

'So tell me. Your aunt. What did she show you?'

'Papers.'

'Papers?'

'A message from the traitor to my grandfather. A postcard with four words. *Trust me, Carlos. Urquhart.*' She took a sip of the cognac and closed her eyes. 'And a diary.' The cognac numbed her mouth and nose, blocking the tears. 'My mother's diary.'

'A diary she wrote in nineteen-thirty-seven?'

'Yes. She was seven years old.'

'That's young to write a diary.'

'She has no one to tell her feelings. Only Marisa, two years younger.'

'What about her own mother? Your grandmother?'

'She died before. And afterwards, no one speak or smile. So many dead, and only my mother and Marisa to hold the blame.'

Her anger grew. It gave her strength, she realised, to

speak this pain aloud.

'Do you want to tell me what happened? What your mother wrote in her diary?'

'Yes.' She took another sip of cognac. 'It was February. Like here it is cold in February in the Sierra. For months nothing, then all at once Malaga fall. Franco's army, they come with guns. They kill the men. The boys also. My mother's cousins and her playmates. They shoot them in the square. Between the stones of the square the blood, it lie in *charcos*. Puddles.'

She bit her lip and stared for a moment at her glass. 'November, I am there. We take Marisa's body to the graveyard. There is no blood now. The stones are white.'

Her voice was sounding strange to her. Flat and cold, like the stones.

'So. Franco's men, they shot your grandfather?'

'No, they did not shoot him. He is away. Seeking Urquhart.'

She hid her face in her hands. She was following Marisa's coffin again, over the white stones, past the well. She was turning her head to look into the well. The pulley and rope hung loose, stirring in the cruel November wind. Only in her dream did the rope strain at the knot on the iron ring, and stretch taut as a guitar-string into the blackness.

'He hang himself.'

Chapter Fifteen

Henry

He was back under the frozen stars, striding coatless towards the Royal Highland Hotel, no need of the tartan blanket under his arm, powered by brandy and by the conviction that things were looking up.

Thank you, Henry.

Her eyes in that moment had shone so dark, the pupils dilated and bright with tears. A real woman confirming his humanity. And when her story was done, and his, and it came time to leave, again she bestowed her trustful gaze, so even as he spoke he knew she would say yes.

'Forgive me, I realise you're an independent person, more than capable of looking after yourself. But if you would like, if you would like company? I have to be back in Guildford by Monday. My neighbour, Trevor, I've promised him. But tomorrow's no problem. We could meet up, I could come with you.'

'Yes, Henry. You have so much kindness. I *would* like this. Also Fiona, the librarian, she is not wanting to invite me. But you please her, you help with the light. Perhaps she will be more happy if you come.'

Her voice made him shiver. It was so deep, so substantial.

Elena Martínez. He let the name form in his mouth, hearing her speak it—'Elena Martíneth'—with her lovely, lisping, Spanish zed. Tomorrow he would see her again.

Peter would be there. A pang shot through him. He nearly missed his footing in the snow, remembering her words. 'Your brother? The young man with the blue eyes, so expressive?'

Damn his brother's blue eyes. Plus he would have to suffer Peter's derision over Marjorie. The librarian would show she knew him, it would all come out. Though maybe not. She was good-hearted, he sensed. If he dived in fast, turned the spotlight onto little brother, maybe she would take the hint. 'Good heavens, Peter,' he would say, 'We must have missed each other by inches. So how come you're in bonnie Scotland?'

Elena had thrown no light on the conundrum. Peter was keen to meet this Urquhart character too, apparently. Something about the poem in the photocopier. Peter was always banging on about poetry, usually to some unsuspecting lass. Don't be fooled by the blue eyes, Elena. The young man has a cold heart.

Henry's buoyancy persisted. It was his eyes, not Peter's, that Elena was looking into. He'd damn well show his brother he wasn't a write-off.

Steady on there. Slow down. Elena was in need of a friend, that was all. He mustn't presume, and he certainly mustn't imagine. He'd done more than enough fantasising to last a lifetime. He would stick to reality from now on, nothing but reality. It was all there was, and it was what he would deal with.

Here was the station square and the welcoming portal of the Royal Highland Hotel. Brandy and reality marched him smoothly towards it. *Goodnight, ladies.* It was all he needed to say as he swept through the foyer and up the stairs. *Goodnight, ladies.* Michael McCoy could think what he liked. Marjorie Macpherson wasn't real and Michael McCoy didn't bloody matter.

He was almost disappointed to find the foyer deserted. Only the charming receptionist remained, dismantling the circle of chairs and returning them one by one to their places.

'Good evening, sir. Is there anything I can get you?'

He needed to sober up. He needed to be as good as he could be tomorrow. Not a romantic hero, no, not at all. Just as good as he could be.

'Yes, please. A bottle of Highland spring water, flat not fizzy, in my room. Would that be possible?'

'Of course, sir. Yes. At once.'

Elena

Sleep refused to come. Her brain bubbled with cognac and new resolve. Confessing to Henry had eased her guilt and confusion.

Wicked. That was his word. She was not mad. She was not alone. Urquhart, *el malo*, Henry had affirmed it.

She sat up, switched on the bedside light and pulled from her bag the pages she had photocopied. Here was the traitor's photograph, reproduced in shades of grey. Eighty years old, upright and proud, smiling the same self-satisfied smile as his daughter. But in his eyes she could see it—the lack of confidence she had perceived in his signature. Here stood a man who knew he was a fake.

She propped her head with pillows and began to read, more carefully than before.

Angus Urquhart was born in Inverness-shire in 1916 into a family of crofters. Wayward and foolhardy from an early age, he liked nothing better than to disappear into the mountains for days at a time carrying little more than survival rations. At school he astonished his teachers with his first-class brain and with their encouragement applied for and won a scholarship to Trinity College Cambridge. It was here he met the lazy, charming David Stirling, who was later to found the Special Air Service (SAS).

Elena had heard of this British SAS. They appeared from nowhere, swinging on ropes to dive, feet-first like James Bond, through embassy windows. They shot terrorists and rescued hostages.

Stirling and Urquhart were frequent companions, renowned less for scholarship than for drinking and gambling, and also for style: each six-foot five-inches tall and immaculately got up. Urquhart was never to be seen other than resplendent in dress kilt and glengarry, which he wore stubbornly throughout the war, disdaining disguise on even the most dangerous missions behind the lines.

So her mother's diary had described him. A gigantic man, full of wine and laughter, whose pleated skirt flew out when he threw little Marisa in the air and spun to catch her.

In 1941 Churchill agreed the establishment of the SAS despite the inertia of high command, who pooh-poohed it as a meddlesome suicide squad. The generals shrugged their shoulders. If it worked, fine. If it didn't, it hardly mattered. A ragbag outfit that attracted the mavericks and misfits who wouldn't take orders. At least in the SAS they risked only their own necks, and with luck they might confuse the enemy in the process.

Angus Urquhart was the ideal recruit. Aged 21, while Stirling set off to attempt Mount Everest, Urquhart

119

graduated straight from Cambridge to gunrunning for the Republicans in Spain, mastering the high passes of the Sierra Nevada as readily as those of his native Scotland. Alas, his efforts were in vain. Franco's forces prevailed and Urquhart found himself eyewitness to the fall of Malaga. Evading capture, he returned to Britain, where before long the outbreak of the Second World War offered a new arena for his restless energy.

Elena spluttered with rage. She could not read on. Was this all they could find to say of events that had ruined her life? Restless energy? Alas? In Spain Urquhart had risked more than his own neck. In Spain he had done more than confuse the enemy. Alas, her village massacred! Alas, her grandfather's neck broken in a well! Alas, his daughters cast to the mercy of embittered widows and vengeful priests!

She flung the pages violently to the floor. The sobs were rising again. She clenched her fists, switched off the light, stuffed the pillow into her mouth and howled.

Peter

A' bhliadhna seo thàinig geamhradh fuar agus móran sneachda,

There came one year cold winter and much snow,

le cur is cathadh.

with fall and drift.

Alone now, warm and fed beneath duvet, nothing keeping him from Calum but haze of sleep, soup, bread and whisky—and Gaelic, never as easy on the page as in the melodious air back then, singsonged by Ma while Pa away. All these lenitions, slenderisations, epenthetic vowels, preaspirations and hiatuses, insinuating themselves between spelling, sound and meaning. But mustn't weaken, must plough on from page to dictionary to page, push himself forward.

For tomorrow, they would meet. Muse and disciple, mislaid and undiscovered, revered and soon to be acclaimed, Calum Calum and Peter Jennings, poets and heroes of the past and future.

Calum's stamp on every stanza—frank to the ear, but thread soon lost in allegory. Some dame in plot: sultry eyes, splendid tits, definite hit in the sack. Won and lost, found and lost again, coming and going like nobody's business. Sometimes a ghost, more often X-rated real. Good old Calum, no holds barred, Gaelic answer to Henry Miller when that way inclined.

Plus line after line of unrelenting cold. No escape but in those eyes, between those palpable tits, and when dame gone or ghostlike no escape at all, cold as an Inverness bus-shelter.

And honour, honour, honour lost. Lost and never found. Searched for in the bowels of hell. Glimpsed—*Tha e agam fhathast*, I have it still—and lost again.

Sleep, soup, bread and whisky, dream of hot, dark holds. Mind losing grip, hand on prick, dictionary thump on floor. And anyway he couldn't finish it tonight cos bossy wee Fiona—great eyes, and tits acceptable though not a patch on Calum's ladylove—yes sweet, sad Fiona—did she have a man? where was he?—still had final page.

Henry

Straight-backed, dry-eyed, and anaesthetised by brandy,

Henry sat on the edge of his bed in the Royal Highland Hotel and allowed himself to think about Michael McCoy. His mind touched the subject gingerly at first, like a wet finger to the surface of an iron, but gradually his fear eased.

He was alone. His mother wasn't here. There was no one here but him.

Beside him, beneath the bedside lamp, gleamed the green and gold cover of 'Heart of the Glen'. He'd been contemplating it a while, daring it to speak. From time to time he was on the verge of speaking himself, moved to interrogate it, to demand answers. But he stopped himself each time, renewing his vow to give up imaginary conversations. With Marjorie, with his mother, with the fates, with God. Reality was all there was. He must confront it head on.

He took stock of himself. He was a forty-one-year-old financial adviser, somewhat overweight, wearing blue-striped pyjamas he had ironed himself—how sad was that?—and sitting, altogether alone, on an anonymous hotel bed. The world wouldn't so much as blink if he were to leave it. Only Peter would grumble at the chore of having to dispose of his corpse as the price of inheriting Pa's money at last.

Before tonight, such thoughts had had him quivering with self-pity, but now somehow they did not. Had public humiliation numbed him? Was he building new fantasies around Elena? Was he still in shock? He didn't know, and yet he grew in self-esteem. Alone and crisply pyjama'd in the Royal Highland Hotel, he faced facts as squarely as he could manage, and self-pity missed its cue.

Still he gazed at 'Heart of the Glen'. Three-hundred-

and-odd pages of bulk-produced paperback, his place marked with a dark-pink envelope addressed in a strong italic hand. He didn't need to open the envelope. He knew the words by heart.

SHAPING THE STORY. Spend three hours with Marjorie Macpherson and discover her secrets.

It was exactly as he'd thought. A personal invitation from the author. *You say you love me, Henry? Whoever and whatever I am? OK. Come to Inverness, and I will show you who and what.*

Cruelty or kindness? He couldn't decide. Cruel it felt, cruelty he suspected, but another possibility was nagging at his mind. *Were you wanting to join us?* How politely Michael McCoy had greeted him. With Marjorie Macpherson's smile, as shyly welcoming as in his dreams. *At last we meet. How good to see you. So, Henry Jennings, now you see me, who I am, now what do you say?*

Henry let his hand move. He picked the book up and opened it at the marked page. Put the envelope aside on the bed and began to read.

Through the last night he stayed with her, Maggie lay awake and watched Fergus sleep. At rest, his face wore a smile that invited kisses, but she did not kiss or touch. Sometimes the smile deepened, while his eyes trembled beneath their lids and the muscles in his limbs twitched. Happy dreams visited him, private visions of peace and light. Maggie's heart near burst with love and grief. Then, for long hours, he slumbered more profoundly, motionless save for the drawing and release of the breath that kept him alive, kept the heat and smell of his sweat spreading through the bed towards her. With each breath his chin was drawn chestwards and the blanket rose with his ribcage. Then, as he let go, the blanket subsided and his head relaxed. For a fragile moment he was completely still, empty of air, and effort, and life. Then came the next breath, each one a return from the dead. Two days ago, had he died, she would have mourned him beautifully, believing in his love for the rest of her life. Widowhood was kinder by far than this. But it was too late. And she did not wish him dead. Fergus had the right to live, to withdraw his love from her and bestow it on another.

Towards morning, her husband's sleep became fitful. At any moment his eyes would open and meet hers. She could not bear to witness his awakening, to see his smile freeze at the sight of her whom once he had claimed as his own and only Maggie McConn. She slid silently from the bed and padded barefoot into the kitchen, across the cold stone flags. She pulled on wellingtons, threw an overcoat over her nightgown, lifted the latch and stepped into the dew-hung garden and the mocking welcome of the dawn chorus.

There was no more to do, there were no more words to speak. Her own and only Fergus was lost. Knee-deep in the wet grass beneath the apple tree, she gazed clear-eyed, up at the purple mountain. She began to let him go.

Henry sighed. Despite everything, the ghost of Marjorie Macpherson still had power to move him.

Cold turkey, he promised himself—he would read no more of her. Not now. Not ever. When he got home he would take the whole lot to a charity shop. He snapped the book shut, picked up the envelope, strode across the room and stuffed both into his bag.

She began to let him go.

She. Him. It hadn't struck him before, but the love object in these books of Marjorie's, wasn't it always a man?

He cast his mind back. Yes, invariably it was Maggie McConn, or her daughter, her mother, her girlhood friend, who was in love. Scarcely surprising from the pen of a woman. But Marjorie Macpherson was not a woman.

Was this the answer to the riddle? Had Marjorie refused *him*? Or was he refusing—dared he think it—Michael?

One more time he opened the door of the Reference Room. The shy smile of a bald man hung in the air before him. *Were you wanting to join us?*

'I'm sorry.' Henry forgot his vow and spoke aloud. 'I'm truly, *truly* sorry.'

He paused, remembering his admiration for whoever wrote these books. He tried his best to return the smile. 'I'm sorry, but no can do.'

Chapter Sixteen

Elena

Just after eight-thirty the next morning, wretched from lack of sleep, Elena put on Henry Jennings' coat, settled her bill, and, escaping the proprietor's intrusive smiles, stepped from his gloomy hallway into a world so white it made her eyes water.

There was the hush that snow brings—the air seemed motionless, but the breath she drew was mild, the cold had lost its spiteful edge. As she crossed the road blinking, the murmur of the river asserted itself like the voice of a friend. The rippled, glassy surface bore a scatter of gulls bobbing quietly in the current, their faces and tails black as though dipped in ink. For a moment her mind was empty of everything except birds, water, and benign, soft air. All over her body the tension fell away, and she surprised herself with an involuntary smile.

Just to notice this was enough to rewind her muscles and her brain. She stared at the gulls, hoping to catch the moment, yearning to inhabit its elusive serenity. It was only this she wanted, she told herself. Not revenge on an old man, not to prove her worth to a censorious world, only an end to anger and anxiety.

But it was impossible. She could not turn back from Angus Urquhart. The shame she had carried all her life belonged to him, she could discharge it into his hands alone.

She was much too early. She would have to wait at the station or in Henry Jennings' hotel. She began to wheel her suitcase slowly along the line of guesthouses.

From the town, couples were strolling towards her on the riverbank, some with arms linked, their eyes bright with sun and snow. As they passed, each nodded and smiled. 'Good morning. Lovely day.'

Of course, it was Saturday, their time for *el paseo*. In her village at such times, the streets became thronged with people arm-in-arm. But her mother and aunt had remained silent behind their shutters, and Elena had never learned the art. In Brussels Mikhail had begun to teach her. 'At weekends we will dawdle together, Elena. We will look in shop windows, drink coffee with our friends. You will cease from running everywhere, except, once or twice, unexpectedly, to kiss me. Okay?'

Okay. And she had begun to understand how it was done. How she had no need to race every minute to prove herself. How time could linger and caress, not challenge and threaten.

She passed the last guesthouse and a church. Ahead, the riverside road skirted a hill, topped by a castle she had not noticed before. Built of pink granite with castellated towers, it looked fine against the snow. Yet it lacked the romance of Castle Urquhart, the ruined fortress she had viewed many times on the internet screen in Brussels. A name and the touch of a button had summoned the image. Always technology impressed her, she had come to it so late.

She had carried her mobile to the breakfast table this morning, willing it to ring, but she had not pressed redial. Technology worked. Her messages had arrived. Mikhail had been angry, and now he was beyond anger. In his warm bed, happy with his new companion, he had forgotten her.

She paused to gaze up at the pink castle, obscured by snow-hung trees and bushes, and by her tears also. She had pushed Mikhail too far. 'You are wrong! I am right!' In the indifferent murmur of the Ness, she was hearing his reply.

Among the bushes she saw a rabbit. Then another, two, three... and yes, here, two more. Brown against the snow, their noses and whiskers trembling, they seemed anxious, jumping uncertainly. One, landing too deeply, struggled in panic to recover itself. Another was digging, here then there, abandoning each hole until finally it found grass and began to feed. Its companions quickly joined it. The patch of green grew. Soon all five were eating busily. They had seen Elena, but they paid her no attention, accustomed to the safety of their walled bank.

'Only when you love your home country will you be happy.'

Mikhail had been so sure of this, but he did not understand. In Spain she would find no patch of green.

She reached the road-bridge that led west. There was no traffic—would the way be clear to Loch Craggan? A bird—*un cuervo*—huge and carbon-black, crossed the empty street ahead of her, twisting from hip to hip like a man with wooden legs. She followed, mimicking as she would have done for Mikhail to make him laugh.

She must stop thinking of Mikhail. Perhaps she must never think of him again.

Urquhart. She must think of him, not of Mikhail. She must plan what she would say and do. But it was too difficult. Urquhart, Urquhart. Her exhausted mind was stuck, like a needle on her mother's old gramophone, unable to get beyond the name.

El cuervo opened big wings and laboured into the sky, filling her at once with longing and despair. A cold breeze had begun to blow, making her cheeks and fingers ache. Turning up the hill from the bridge, tugging the suitcase with one hand, she thrust the other deep into the warm pocket of Henry's coat.

Of course. She would think of Henry Jennings, whose childhood, like her own, was unhappy. Sent away to school while his mother's affection went all to her new baby. Elena quickened her step up the high street.

Then widowed, poor man, a blood vessel bursting in his wife's head. One minute here, the next gone. The wheels of her case rattled over the stones behind her. She swung left towards the station.

'Truly, you must think me mad,' he had said.

'Why?'

'You know why.' His gaze dropping. 'What you saw in the library.'

'Your mistake about the writer?'

'Yes. Marjorie Macpherson. Michael McCoy.' Lifting his eyes to hers again. 'I've been obsessed with a ghost, Elena. In love with a woman who doesn't exist. Writing her letters, for God's sake. If that's not mad, tell me what is?'

She had seen the misery tugging him down. She had reached to touch his hand. 'You are not mad, Henry. You are too much alone.'

His pain had eased. His face was not handsome, but it was open. 'Thank you, Elena. It helps that you understand.'

She could not accept his gratitude. 'It is not that I understand, Henry. More it is that I know.'

She had reached the station square. On the inside corner, as he had described, was the Royal Highland Hotel. And there in the doorway, looking extremely nervous, he stood.

Henry

'Better weather for you today, sir.'

A new, bland-faced receptionist stowed Elena's case behind the desk. It fitted snugly alongside Henry's Gladstone, from between whose hinges a corner of the tartan blanket showed.

'Yes. Indeed. Thank you.' Henry prolonged the exchange, trying to steady his pulse and control his rampaging hopes before turning back to Elena. In the subdued light of the hotel lobby, her face seemed sallow with fatigue, the dark eyes lack-lustre.

'You managed to get some sleep, I hope?'

She shook her head. 'No, almost none. And you?'

'Oh, you know. Enough.'

It was true. A kind of unwinding had come from saying no to Michael McCoy's ghost, and that, plus the brandy, had done the trick for a few hours, before yesterday's events had come swirling through his head in luminous dreams.

He had woken in an icy sweat, and for a moment, as the memories slammed into him, his need for his mother had been overwhelming. Her ghost had hovered nearby, eager to resume as though nothing had altered. With huge effort he'd managed to refuse her, turning his head away and closing his ears to her sympathy while he took breakfast in his room, then braving the lobby to escape her.

There, while the other guests came and went beneath the tulip chandeliers, he'd battled to overcome his dread of meeting Michael McCoy. He was damned if he would hide. An exchange of nods would suffice, of 'good morning's perhaps. He would decline any further conversation with dignity.

But McCoy had not appeared, thank heaven, and as reward for his courage, Elena had turned up early. She looked warm but awkward in his Barbour and her shoes were no use at all. He gestured at them. 'Look, I don't know what you think, but we have an hour. The shops are just opening. May I help you find a coat. And something warmer for your feet?'

Her face was hard to read. 'You mustn't worry if you're strapped for cash. It would be my pleasure, if you'd allow me.' Oh dear. She was looking surprised. 'What am I saying? I'm so sorry.' How crass to ply a woman he barely knew with offers of expensive gifts.

'No, Henry, please. I have money. But if I had not, you are generous, thank you. Let us go shopping.'

She slipped her fingers into his elbow, which he bent instinctively to support them. She was beside him, allowing him to guide her across the ice of the station square, towards the kilted stone soldier on his plinth.

A real woman on his arm. How long had it been? His mother, he supposed. After his father's death, he'd taken her to restaurants. Encouraged her to try the more expensive dishes, taken care of the bill, then escorted her to the car or for a post-prandial stroll. How good it felt to be allowed to take care of a woman again.

'In Spain, they call this *el paseo*,' Elena said.

'I thought that was in the evening, before dinner.'

'Yes, or before the lunch on Sunday. They walk, we walk, to be with our friends. But why not in the morning also?'

Henry looked about him. There was a shopping centre along to the left—M&S, that sort of thing—but that didn't seem right for Elena. Across the road he saw an entrance in monumental style. Corinthian arches, animal carvings. "Victorian Market", it announced itself.

'Let's have a look in here.'

He couldn't have chosen better. The morning light streamed through high windows into a charming interior of stained glass and wrought iron. An arcade of small shops stretched ahead. The shopkeepers were setting out their pavement displays and two wholesome-looking children were busking on a fiddle and a flute, playing a Highland reel that had him quickening his step, and Elena quickening hers in time beside him, so that in his head they were almost dancing, and he dropped a pound into the fiddle-case before spying exactly the shop, piled high with oilskins, fleeces, socks and boots.

'This looks the thing. I hope there's something here you like. We'll soon have you cosy and warm.'

Peter

Kippers afoot—stench luring him down to busy kitchen. Chin and beard dab hands with fish-slice at the Aga, swathed in daft scarves and headgear for some away game in Arbroath. Fair Fi blithely stirring cauldron of porridge. Bow-wow tucking into Meaty Crunch.

'Hi, Peter. Sleep well?'

'Yes, ta.'

'Hannah'll come with us to Loch Craggan today. She likes the car.'

Jumbo rush of glee. 'We're going then? The road is clear?'

'Yes. My brother William says the blizzard wasn't too bad up there. The postie got through all right.'

Nothing but time and miles between him and Calum. Severe attack of heebie-jeebies. 'Did you tell your father I was coming?'

'No. These last two months he's been mostly in his croft. It's up the hill a way. I'll have to fetch him down or take you to him. And… Peter…'

'Yes?'

Wooden spoon aloft and beckoning, solemn as a miniature Statue of Liberty. Slide past chin and beard, snouts in plates, minds on kippers, chewing and grunting. Heat-seek wicked thrill of FU's whisper. 'Listen. Only the family know he's Calum. You mustn't let on I've told you. Okay?'

Wonderful! Was he in or what? Gifted protégé in the know!

FU loud again, her glutinous oats aswirl. 'I explained to William about Elena,' hell's bells, he'd altogether forgotten the Spanish mare, 'and I said a friend of mine was coming too.'

'Meaning me?'

'Uh huh.'

Better and better. Close friend of great man's edible

daughter. 'So may I hold your hand and call you "darling"?' Flash eyes and make her giggle. Good giggle Fi's, throaty soft, not one to make you wince and run.

'No, you may not. Behave yourself.'

'Oi oi?' Chin tuning in, mind a quagmire of conjecture.

'Grow up, you berk.' Beard plating last kipper as he spoke.

'Hang on, Greg.' Damsel to rescue. 'Did you want that kipper, Peter?'

Fight own battles, thanks. 'No thanks.'

Greg grinning between ginger, hairy cheeks, shovelling in forkloads of juicy, orange flesh. Grin back with malice. Graciously accept Daddy-Bear-sized bowl of porridge.

'So what'll it be, Peter? Bacon? Sausage? Mushrooms? Egg? Tomato?'

Bloody marvellous. Catch jealous quiver of Ginger's chubby chops. He fucking loved this woman. 'Now you're talking, Fi. The works!'

Chapter Seventeen

Henry

It was hard to think straight. A boisterous yellow Labrador was thumping its rear end against his knees while rummaging nosily under Elena's new coat. She was struggling with the dog and failing to make introductions. Peter was scowling, no surprises there, but, oh dear, the librarian was looking distinctly miffed as well. And her car, red and yellow, was one of those French tin-can affairs, embarrassingly small. Thank heavens there was a harness arrangement on top for luggage.

But worst of all, the library was here. It had given him a shock when he turned the corner of Margaret Street, to see it lying in wait. Without Elena's hand on his arm, he didn't think he would have been able to approach it. It towered over him, its grand Doric portico unforgiving against the turquoise sky. And the librarian was staring at him, open-mouthed. Oh God, was she about to spill the beans?

'Hannah. Stop it. Be good.' She seemed flustered. She'd been so level-headed yesterday.

'Henry! What the fuck are you doing here?'

'Do you two know each other?'

'Yes, worse luck. He's my brother.'

'Your *brother?*'

'Yes, Fi. My turn to have brothers.'

'Brothers?'

'Just the one. Just this banana here.'

'I am full of apology.' Elena, bless her, was struggling to recover the situation. The story they'd agreed on was gushing from her as from a fractured pipe. 'It is my fault completely, I meet Henry last night and he lend me his coat, I tell him about the book I am writing, he is kind, he is interested, he ask will he come with me.'

How implausible this sounded. Henry grimaced in what he hoped was a jolly way, squeezing Elena's hand tightly in the crook of his elbow.

'And you are Peter's brother?'

'Yes.'

The librarian, bewildered, looked from him to Peter and back again. She was about to say 'Get lost', and who could blame her?

Elena streamed on. 'But I not realise, Fiona, about the dog, perhaps we are too many?'

Fiona seemed to collect herself. 'No. Forgive me. I'm sure we can squeeze in, if no one minds. You in front, Elena. Or perhaps... Henry, is it?'

'Yes. So sorry. Henry Jennings.'

'How do you do. I'm Fiona Urquhart.' Glory be! She wasn't going to tell. 'Perhaps you, Mr Jennings, in the front, seeing as you're...' She stopped in confusion.

'The largest,' completed Peter sourly.

Elena

She was crushed in tight with Henry's brother and the dog, breathing the new coat's dark-brown sheep-smell, and following the dog's avid eyes through the car window. They were climbing through a forest of conifers, heavy with snow as in a land for vampires. Beside the road, water cascaded over a staircase of giant rocks. She could hear its thunder above the roar of the engine, which carried them relentlessly up towards Angus Urquhart.

Her stomach contracted. What would she say? How would she greet this man? She should be preparing herself, but she could not. She could only anticipate and fear.

The hill eased and with it the noise. In a gap of pasture, three cows with wide horns and dense, red coats lifted their heads from a hay-bin. The dog's bark made Elena jump.

'Hannah. No. Shush,' said Fiona Urquhart.

Then they were climbing again. A van emblazoned 'Daily parcel service—Glasgow, Inverness, Skye' was parked where the road widened for the first zigzag. Fiona sounded the horn and dropped a gear to pass it. The car laboured and complained. From her window, Elena saw *un altro cuervo*, calmly meeting her eyes. Its stare unsettled her.

'Fiona. Please. That bird. You know it? Big, black, solitary—'

'A raven.' Henry's brother stopped biting his fingers to answer her. 'As hymned by Edgar Allen Poe.' He met her eyes without a smile. *'Desolate yet all undaunted, on this desert land enchanted.'*

'Stories of murder and horror,' Fiona shouted above the noise of the engine. 'My father likes Poe.'

Elena frowned. Of course he did. The car toiled around another curve above a torrent of water. Peter's elbow pressed sharp against her arm. She tried to move away but the elbow followed her. His face loomed close, his blue eyes malevolent. He began to declaim as if to her alone.

'*Leave no black plume as a token of that lie thy soul hath spoken!*

Leave my loneliness unbroken! Quit the bust above my door!

Take thy beak from out my heart, and take thy form from off my door!'

He meant he did not want her here. His stare was icy. She managed not to blink.

Henry was twisting his head, trying to see. 'Are you all right, Elena?'

'Yes, Henry. Thank you.'

'Yes, Henry. Thank you,' Peter echoed. Then, '*And his eyes have all the seeming of a demon's that is dreaming—*'

'By the way, Peter,' kind Henry interrupting, 'to answer your question, I'm in Inverness on business. So how come you're here?'

To Elena's relief, Peter's eyes left hers and seemed instead to seek Fiona's in the driving mirror. The pressure of his elbow eased also. He extended a hand to touch Fiona's shoulder. '*Tell me what thy lordly name is on the Night's Plutonian shore—*'

'Oh, please yourself,' said Henry.

Anger filled the air. The hatred of brothers. Elena's knees pressed hard against the back of Henry's seat, and the dog weighed so heavy she could barely move. It turned and panted in her face. Recoiling from the stink, her head bumped against the canvas ceiling, fat with luggage. She fought a wave of nausea, then wrestled her arms from the sleeves of the coat.

Fiona was yelling above the engine. 'Do either of you two like poetry? Mr Jennings? Elena?'

How condescending. Elena answered with impatience. 'I do not know the English poets.'

'Poe's American,' Peter sneered.

'I know this,' she countered. 'I mean I do not know poems in English.' She was weary of explaining herself in this alien language.

'Or Gaelic?' persisted Fiona.

Elena struggled to rise above a sea of nausea. This was more than idle conversation. Fiona meant the poem in the photocopier, the one by her father. She was exchanging glances with Peter in the driving mirror.

'No, I have no Gaelic.'

'What about you, Mr Jennings?'

'Me? No. I'm useless at languages. Music too.'

'And poetry?'

'Definitely not your man, Miss Urquhart. Wouldn't know Shakespeare from Shirley Bassey. Peter's the poet in the family.'

'Whereas Henry's the pudding-head with all the money.'

'I offered you your share, but you wouldn't have it.'

'He didn't leave it to *me*. I wouldn't touch it with a lavatory brush.'

The dog barked again. They were speeding along a valley between two great mountains, the car bumping on its overloaded springs. The air was far too hot, thick with the smell of dog—why did no one open a window? Elena saw Fiona nod at Peter.

'You asked why Peter's here, Mr Jennings. My father has written a few songs in the old language, and Peter wants to meet him. That's all.'

No, this was not the truth. Or not the whole of it.

Elena struggled to think with an aching head as the car swerved to avoid a pothole. Last night in the library: Fiona angry, Peter anxious, both of them agitated about that poem. She turned to Peter. 'Why?' she said. 'Why do you want to meet this man?'

His blue eyes slid away. He addressed the dog.

'Then upon the velvet sinking, I betook myself to linking

Fancy unto fancy, thinking what this ominous bird of yore—

What this grim, ungainly, ghastly, gaunt, and ominous bird of yore

Meant in croaking, "Nevermore."'

Fiona was grinning. 'Peter, stop teasing.'

'Right you are, Fi.'

He gave Elena another insolent stare. More bully than tease, she knew the difference. She met the stare until he was forced to smile. 'So. Why?' she repeated.

'I'm on a bit of an odyssey. In search of poetic inspiration.' He told his lies smoothly, this Peter. 'Back to my childhood. My Ma sang Gaelic lullabies.'

'Did she?' Fiona seemed enchanted.

'Not to me, she didn't.'

Elena heard sadness in Henry's voice. She wished she could touch his shoulder, as Peter had touched Fiona's. Or could say to him 'don't beat yourself', as Fiona had said 'don't tease'. She and Henry had shared secrets, yet still they were too much strangers for such intimacy. Were Peter and Fiona lovers already?

As if to answer, Peter leant forward and squeezed Fiona's arm. 'I think Hannah may be a poet,' he said. 'Doggerel. That kind of thing.'

Elena did not understand. Was this a joke? Not

funny—Henry was not laughing. But Fiona Urquhart began to giggle, and for a while seemed unable to stop.

Peter

Fuck it, he adored this woman—wasn't she superb? Savvy with subtext, sure in subterfuge, good with grilled bacon, great eyes, okay tits, nibblable ears. And Calum's daughter! Try to hide it as she might, she liked him, he was in. Grinning at him in the driving-mirror, thrills around the corner, always the way, talk about luck of the devil, his from birth, while pathetic Henry, for all he'd landed Pa's loot, trundled along totalling columns and clipping his tedious front hedge.

Pain in the arse his turning up. Here on business—really?—and now looking set to seduce the Señorita. Thrills and spills for Henry too, well who'd have thought it? Eyeball to eyeball, Ms Martínez no pussycat, way out of Henry's previous league.

From urban sprawl and wretched no-man's land, view out to Beauly Firth, horizon blighted by endless Scottish bridge—tuning forks, bowstrings of wires—and Henry sighing 'beautiful', sad git. Then up through tracts of pop stars' tax-deductible fir-trees, up and up. Past the raven, bless him, *Thing of evil, prophet still if bird or devil.* Track burbling burn through rocky pass to, turn the corner.

Wowee! Wide-slung valley, walled on three sides by peaks, footed by untroubled loch and ersatz mansion, all wings and turrets, afloat above its own reflection. Excitement rising in his throat like fire. Calum 'up the hill a way' said Fi at breakfast, but these were mountains! Best stay shtum on Calum, keep Spanish Inquisition quiet, but afire with questions, not to mention rampant lust. Raring to be alone with glorious woman. 'So what are your brothers' names, fair Fi?'

'James, Owen, William and Gavin.'

'Older or younger?'

'Older. I'm thirty-five,' as he'd guessed, 'and they're forty-four, forty-two, forty and thirty-eight.'

'No letting up till they got a girl, eh?'

Her mirrored smile again. Boy, what a girl they got!

'And they run this hotel?'

'Well, it's Owen and Janet's business. But James is the chef, and the rest of us often come for weekends. It's the only place for miles. Fishing and hiking. We're in the Good Food Guide. We get a lot of Americans.'

Road running out. Rutted gravel track. House swelling in size, odder and uglier on close acquaintance, as though cobbled together from unwanted parts. No trees in sight, just snowy slopes closing in, blocking out the sky.

'Of course,' Henry starting up a witter, 'a hotel. I should have said before, Miss Urquhart. Elena and I, we mustn't presume on your hospitality. You will let us pay?'

Fiona turning to reply, glancing back and crying, 'Oh, dear me!'

What's up? Follow beam of beloved's eyes to find, oh bloody hell, the Señorita, face like curdled milk, beads of sweat, whole deal, out cold.

Chapter Eighteen

Henry

Oh God! No! Poor Elena! As they guided her inside, her knees gave way, and only his and Peter's efforts kept her from the flagstoned floor.

What kind of place was this? Henry's skin shrank a size in horror, though he didn't know why. The hallway was full of running children, whose shouts echoed up a cantilevered staircase. A few of them stopped running. 'Who are you?' 'What's wrong with her?'

Henry realised why he was afraid. The hall, the staircase, the odour of wood-smoke and mildew, the children's shouts and stares, the clattering echoes, all reminded him of boarding school.

'Oh look, it's Hannah! Hello, Hannah! The dog had got down to serious bustling, patted by many small hands. There were no dogs at boarding school.

'Elena,' Henry said anxiously. He struggled to support her weight. This was his fault entirely. He'd seen how tired and strained she was. He should have insisted that she sat in front.

'Be more helpful, children. The lady's unwell.' Here came Fiona, thank goodness, carrying Elena's coat. 'Where's Owen? Owen's the chap we need. Jeannie, run and fetch your father, quick now.'

Jeannie set off. She was a nice-looking child, nine or ten years old. There were no girls at boarding school.

More children assembled to stare. Henry counted five, plus Jeannie made six.

'Sit her here.' Fiona grabbed magazines from a massive chair—carved oak the colour of ebony—and dumped them on a table. She arranged Elena's coat like a sheepskin nest.

'Get a move on,' Peter growled. 'She weighs a ton.'

They got her to the chair, then Henry crouched on the floor, tugging at her limp hand. 'Elena,' he pleaded.

Her head lolled. Her eyes rolled. Dear God, she looked terrible.

An enormous man arrived. 'Hello folks, I'm Owen. What's up?'

'I think she's worn out,' Fiona said.

Owen knelt beside Henry, dwarfing him and exuding an aura of comfort. He had hair like tweed and wore thick green corduroy trousers. 'What's the lassie's name?'

'Elena.'

Owen's huge hands drew Elena's head to her lap. Of course, thought Henry. Why didn't I think of that? 'Elena, lassie. Can you hear me?'

'Yes.' Her hand was stirring in Henry's. She tried to raise her head.

'No, keep your head down. I'll carry you.' Owen picked her up and swept her away. She was a child in his arms. Henry battled unworthy feelings of envy. It was easy to be a romantic hero, built like that. He stooped to pick up Elena's coat.

The hall was emptying. Children, dog, even Peter, all trailing after the remarkable Owen. Only Fiona remained. She seemed anxious, almost secretive. Oh God, of course. She'd be wanting to ask him about Marjorie.

She came close, raising her serious eyes to his and speaking fast in a low voice. 'You mustn't worry, Mr Jennings. Owen's a doctor, she'll be fine. And please, I won't hear of your paying. I'll speak to Owen. You mustn't be embarrassed, the hotel's almost empty at this time of year, more family than guests.'

He gathered courage to interrupt. 'Miss Urquhart—'

'Fiona, please.'

'Fiona, I haven't yet thanked you.' He stalled.

'Thanked me?'

'For not mentioning. You know. About last night.' He could feel himself blushing crimson. She seemed at a loss. He blundered on. 'You can't imagine. And Peter. My brother. He would laugh mercilessly.' She must think him some kind of lunatic.

'No, no. I can. And I know he would. But really, you mustn't thank me. I'm so sorry. When I saw you this morning, I...' She stopped short. Then continued. 'But it's all right, thank goodness. And of course I wouldn't. I mean I won't.' She looked as flustered as he felt.

'Hey. Fi. What are you two yakking about? Come on.' Peter stood framed in the stone archway through which the procession had passed.

Owen was there too. 'Henry, is it?'

'Yes.'

'You're wanted. The lassie's asking for you.'

Elena

She was in Angus Urquhart's arms. He was spinning her as he had spun Marisa, the pleats of his kilt whirling like knives. He bore her away, fast, beneath a stone lintel into bright light.

The village square! She struggled to fight his strength and speed, but it was useless. 'No, lass, no.' His false care crushed her protests. He was carrying her to the well. To throw her in! She tried to scream, but her throat was dry. It was too late. She was falling, falling.

Into cushions.

She opened her eyes. He was here still, gigantic and falsely smiling, but so too were children, and a dog. She remembered the dog's name. 'Hannah?'

It pushed a wet nose into her hand. Through the crowd she glimpsed a young man with impatient blue eyes, and heard his voice. 'What's keeping Fi?'

Henry's brother. The world reassembled itself. 'Henry. Please. Where is Henry?'

'I'll fetch him for you.' The gigantic man strode off, followed by Henry's brother.

How stupid to be like this, scarcely able to think or lift her head. She stared about her, trying to breathe more calmly. She was alone with a dog... two dogs, and many children. She was lying on a grand sofa whose cushions smelled of smoke. The room was panelled floor to ceiling with books, the doorway was an arch of stone, and yet the light was bright as day. Turning her head, she was amazed to see a wall of glass, beyond which lay snow and water and blue sky. The glare hurt her eyes.

'Hello, Lena.' She turned back in alarm. 'Do you play Snap?' A small boy was offering a pack of cards.

'Not just now, Georgie. The lady's ill.' A new voice. She swung towards it, terror draining blood from her head and sight from her eyes. She clung to consciousness, struggling to identify the figures in the archway. Fiona

146

Urquhart, luminous as an angel in the bright light, was returning with the giant and Henry's brother.

Beside them, almost running, carrying her coat, came Henry. 'Elena, here I am. Are you all right?' He sat next to her and squeezed her hand. 'Well I'm blowed!' His eyes had found the glass wall. 'How bizarre.'

She must not be ill like this. At any moment an old man with a white beard would appear. She tried to sit up. 'I am so sorry. I cause much trouble.'

'Hush.' The giant's cheeks glowed red, his eyes were blue as the sky spilling through the glass wall. 'It's food you're needing and then sleep. Let's ask James what he can whip up for lunch. Come along, Georgie.'

The boy's head barely reached the giant's knee. They left together hand in hand.

'Fiona. Please. Your father?' Elena hardly dared to ask. She dreaded his coming. 'He is here?'

'No, he's fucking not.'

'Hush, Peter,' said Fiona and Henry.

Elena moaned with disappointment. She could not help herself.

'I'm sorry,' said Fiona. 'I should have explained better. He lives up the hill. After lunch, while you have a nap, I'll go and tell him you're here.'

Peter

'And I'll go with you.'

'No, not yet.'

'Why not?' Pull face at fair Fiona, why delay?

'Peter, I need a word. Come with.'

At last. Abandon Henry to his fancy woman. Pursue

FU from human aquarium into baronial hall. Track her white sweater through the gloaming. 'In here.' Small, leathery room, dust-covered computer, ledgers. Fiona spinning on her heel to face him, brow furrowed, fluffed up with secrecy.

'What? *What*, Fiona? What's the deal? *I* don't need lunch. *I* don't need a sodding *siesta*. Why not take me straight to Calum?'

'Hush, Peter. Calm down. And please, don't call him Calum.'

'Why are you whispering? Why not?'

'Because, I've told you, it's a family secret. I mean it, I'm not joking.'

Fuck it, small was beautiful. Grab her hand, and swoop down for a snog.

'Stop it, Peter!'

'Why? You know you like me, don't pretend you don't.'

Struggling and smiling like a virgin. 'Yes. In spite of everything, I do.'

'So kiss me then.'

'No, stop it. Stop it, no! Sit down. Sit right down here, and *listen*.'

Wonderful, masterful woman. Rush of blood to head and hard-on.

'You have to wait. I have to see my father. He's been in low spirits awhile, shutting himself away from us. I have to break it to him gently that you're here, that you know he's Calum. Ask him if he'll see you.'

'Ask him? He has to see me!' Telephone on desk. Grab receiver, toss it to her. Neat catch, Fi. 'So ask him. Now!'

'He has no phone up there. I think he will agree to see you. But first he'll be upset, and cross with me. I have to

148

talk to him, okay?'

'Okay, okay. But you do like me, yes?'

She smiled, she couldn't hide how much. Those great, grave eyes could only speak the truth. Must be a handicap. 'We'll talk about it later. After you've met him. After Elena's met him.'

'To hell with Elena. *Mañana, mañana.*'

Taking his hands, preventing them from wandering. 'Peter, I promise. Whatever happens we will talk. So please, just now, be patient.'

Chapter Nineteen

Peter

'So will you help me with the luggage?'

Sure thing, slave for the day, anything for fucking Fi. Except he wasn't. And not alone in servitude, in model canine company, for here came Hannah, plus moth-eaten lookalike last seen comatose, sprawled on hearthrug, now engaged in stiff-legged scuffing of hall flagstones, wagging and sneezing at embraces denied to bad dog Peter.

'Meet Mabel. She's Hannah's mum.'

A stickler for introductions, Fi. 'Well Mabel, how do you doggy do?' And off we go. Strait-laced Red Ridinghood and three panting wolves. One mutt and three bitches, out into the midday thaw.

Porch-ice adrip like glass-bead curtain, parting to reveal Highland amphitheatre, set for a slave sacrifice. Marble-white crags, footed by glittering loch and gravel arena where—splash of blood and bile—red and yellow Dinky toy, roof festooned with entrails. Ban-the-bomb rucksack, Red Ridinghood's casket, and fucking Henry's fucking Gladstone bag. Unhook bungee ropes and yank them down. Wrench boot open, tip out Spanish wheelie. Seriously pissed off.

'Oh good. My blanket.' Fiona opening Gladstone, extracting tartan and stowing it in car. Exposing Henry's smalls—oxymoron if ever one was—in M&S grey, stacked like cucumber sandwiches, not a crust in sight. And, wouldn't you know it, blue-striped jimjams and some naff novel.

'Oh dear! *Ow!*' Fiona in sudden boomerang from car, horrid clunk of her skull on doorframe. But barely pausing, snatching Henry's bag and dumping it on wet gravel, fighting to refasten it, hand closing on paperback, shoving it from view.

Oi oi, in Chin's immortal words, what new game afoot? Zoom in to help. Fi's grip tenacious, eyes aslide, untouchable cheeks afire. Not content till Henry's modesty restored.

'Hey, slow down. What's with you, FU?'

'Nothing.' Inane grin and slippery eyes. 'Let's get these things inside.' Raising hand to head.

'Nasty crack you dealt yourself.'

'Yes. No. I'm fine. I'll carry these. Are you okay with those?' Fi charging off through sea of dog-flesh, superglued to Henry's handles, and hefting Señorita's suitcase, wheels or no wheels.

Close car door thoughtfully. Swing half-empty rucksack to shoulder, scoop up Fi's bag and follow, back through glass-bead curtain and massive, iron-studded door.

'Come on.'

Heel, boy. No let-up in obedience training. Drop bags in hall, track unfair mistress into crazy living-room. Human aquarium as busy as Barrier Reef: all the small fry plus shoal of bigger fish seething round the Spanish Main Attraction, with Henry billed as Francis Drake. Colossus Owen here again, plus more Rob Roys and two of their harem. One quite doable at first shufti. Legs a mile long, explosion of red-gold hair, shoulders and arms bare above pink boob-tube. So watch it Fi, the name ain't Fido.

'I've fruits of the sea to tempt you, meat to build you, vegetables to put roses in your cheeks, and puddings to make you purr.'

What wanker was this? Face jewellery, shaven head, down on one knee alongside Henry at Señorita's feet, chef's hat doffed and flourished.

'And so, for starters what is your desire, my lady? Pan-fried scallops, translucent with taste.'

'Who he, Fi?'

'Or poached wild salmon, spiced with lime and ginger?' Tracing culinary patterns in the air.

Fiona back on message. 'He's James. My eldest brother. He trained in Paris. Cordon Bleu.'

'*Un peu précieux, n'est-ce pas?*'

Intake of breath, seraphic brow apucker. 'Yes, Peter.' Decidedly frosty. 'James is what I believe you call "a fruit."'

Fi turning her cold shoulder, drawing closer to her holy family. Well bugger you too then, darling.

'And so, to follow, what's your fancy? Prime Aberdeen Angus steak, or pink and tender Highland lamb?'

Enough. Tedious. Food was food, not poetry. And Fido was off the leash, so, yes, melt through archway into hall. Sidle up to Henry's bag and smoothly does it—less haste more speed, Fiona—hand straight in, under jimjams and haul it up and out. Henry's bedtime reading. 'Heart of the Glen' by Marjorie Macpherson.

Big Ben bonging away in bonce. What? When? Press rewind. Back to soup and bread and whisky. Fiona furtive, spilling gossip. *There was a man. He turned up late. I think he hoped...*

Henry! It was Hooray fucking Henry!
Stuff fist in mouth to stifle shriek of glee.

Henry

The dining-room was confusing to say the least. Tubular like a London Underground station and papered in the same green-and-brown tartan as Elena's borrowed blanket. It lacked windows altogether—a series of glowing crystal chandeliers, slung low over two rows of tables, stretched away and away to vanishing point. How could it be?

'All done with mirrors!' James executed a leap from a Russian ballet. 'Look behind you.'

Henry turned. Beyond his own reflection, he found another tunnel of lights and place settings spinning away to infinity.

'We can seat fifty at a pinch, but after a good bottle of wine it feels like five hundred. We have to take care the punters don't collide with themselves on the way to bed.'

James was even more impressive than Owen. Physically of normal size, but compensating with a flamboyant personality and startling appearance. He was shaven-headed and pierced—it was hard not to stare at the spikes that protruded from eyebrow, nose, lip and ear—and his white double-breasted chef's jacket hung open to reveal a tattooed slogan above a nipple—*What big teeth you have!*

'Here. Sit here.' The extraordinary man ushered them to a large, circular table midway between the mirrors and lit by a double-sized chandelier. Henry helped Elena to a place and sat beside her. The Urquharts—Owen the doctor, two conventional-seeming brothers, two women he hadn't yet put names to, plus the six children—were busy pulling out chairs or fetching them from other tables. Fiona and Peter took seats opposite Henry. Peter was sporting an uncharacteristic grin. Henry saw the scene reflected again and again—it seemed that no direction lacked a mirror.

'Leave space for me,' bellowed the chef.

'Round!' the littlest one began shouting. 'Round, Uncle James.'

'Hold your water, Georgie.' James knelt again at Elena's feet, doling out the charm. '*Cómo está, Señorita?*'

'*Muy bien, gracias.*' She looked pale but determined. She smiled, first at James and then at Henry, insisting it was true.

'Okay, Georgie. But gently. Hold on to your sporrans. And Señorita, you must say if this makes you the least bit giddy.'

He spun like Nureyev to the side of the room and pressed a switch. For a moment nothing happened. Then, slowly, the vistas of chandeliers and Urquharts began to revolve. Good lord, they were on a turntable!

Peter was still grinning, straight into Henry's eyes, and Henry ventured to smile back. He felt an unaccustomed glow of pride. He had endured humiliation, pressed on through storm and night, and here he was, for his brother and whoever cared to see, gallantly escorting a glamorous woman with a dark secret through a world of mystery and surprise.

'Scallops and steak it is then,' said James.

'*I* want a burger!'

Georgie banged the table with a spoon.

'Chips, Uncle James,' chipped in another child.

'Ketchup,' another.

'And all shall have what they desire.' James bowed low, then vanished through a tartan-papered door.

Henry ventured to address Goliath. 'Are all the children yours, Owen?'

'Nae, only the eldest. Mary, Charles and Jeannie. The three wee bairns are William's.'

Another brother, cursed with a florid complexion, completed the roll-call. 'Adam, Debs and Georgie. It's ever the way, we haven't explained ourselves.' He seemed irritable for no obvious reason. Each nodded in turn as he snapped out introductions. 'Owen, our medical man, and Janet, his better half. Gavin, the mountain guide. Kim, who was Gavin's girlfriend at the last count.' Gavin, with ginger crew cut, scowled, while the young woman with the riot of auburn hair fluttered her fingers and eyelashes across the table. 'Plus James of course, our virtuoso chef. Which leaves me. Will,' he concluded belligerently. 'Entrepreneur, builder, decorator. I trust you like the house.'

'Yes, indeed,' said Henry. He wished the room would stop revolving.

'Owen and crew are in residence here,' William continued. 'Plus James of course. Gavin and I share a house-cum-building-site in Inverness. A filthy death-trap for my kids I'm told, so they continue to abide with my lovely ex-wife.' He hissed and made a crucifix with his fingers.

This easy sarcasm impressed Henry, who felt his own divorce as a badge of shame.

Gavin, still scowling, chipped in above the chatter of

the children. 'William, you've missed out our busy wee sister, who owes us some introductions of our non-paying guests.'

Oh dear. That must be why they were cross. Henry looked questioningly at Fiona. Should he offer again?

She shook her head firmly. 'Elena. Peter. Henry,' she said. 'Elena wants to talk to Father, Gavin. She's researching a book about the war.'

Elena nodded. 'I meet Fiona in the library. She is so kind to invite me.'

Henry beamed corroboration.

'That's good,' said Owen. 'For let's hope it will cheer him up. You're more than welcome here, Elena.'

'And Peter?' persisted Gavin.

'Peter's an old friend of mine,' Fiona said smoothly. 'And he'd like to meet Father too. He's interested in Gaelic poetry.'

Henry opened his mouth, then shut it again. An old friend? It wasn't true. 'That young man,' she'd said last night. She hadn't known his brother. But she was honourable, he felt sure of it. She must have good reason to lie. So they wouldn't have to pay? But why?

The reflected smiles bewildered him. Fiona was lying, Peter was lying, Elena was lying. Was anyone here telling the truth?

'Quite a pilgrimage,' said Gavin. 'And Henry?'

A dozen pairs of eyes scrutinised him, while Elena, bless her, found the strength to trot out his own lies. 'I am cold in the snow. I meet Henry and he lend me his coat. I ask he come with me today. You pardon me, I hope. It is presumptuous.'

'Not at all,' said big Owen. 'The more, the merrier. So

Henry's—'

'My good friend,' said Elena.

'Not to mention my complete idiot of a brother.' Peter's intervention was so loud that the children fell silent.

'Your brother?'

'Yes.'

Gavin shook his ginger head. 'I'm confused. So you were both in Inverness, and—'

'No,' Henry jumped in. 'I'm up here on business. I happened to meet Elena, got invited along, and blow me, there's Peter. None of us can figure it out. It's one of life's amazing coincidences.'

'So what line of business are you in?' demanded red-faced William.

'Financial advice.'

'What have I missed?' James erupted through the tartan-papered door, pushing a hostess trolley.

'Only introductions,' said Fiona. 'That smells good.'

'We'd just got to the interesting part,' said Peter.

'Oh, splendid. Do tell. I am agog!' James was dishing up burgers, chips and peas at the speed of light. Briefly he juggled three sauce bottles, then set them on the table.

'Henry's business in Inverness.' Peter's voice was sugar-sweet. 'It's amusing. I'm sure he won't mind sharing it.'

Henry froze in panic. Peter had bloodlust in his eyes.

James lifted the lid from a steaming dish and began doling scallops onto white plates.

'I said,' Henry managed. 'Financial advice.'

Peter hooted. 'Oh yeah? And who was your client? Mzzz Marjorie Macpherson?'

His heart stopped dead.

'Peter!' Fiona hissed. She had betrayed him. She had

told Peter.

'I've heard of her,' said Gavin's girlfriend. 'She's an author, isn't she?

'Yes.' Peter rolled on like a Sherman tank. 'She gave a talk at the library last night.'

Henry stared at Fiona, imploring her to save him somehow. But she had shrunk in her seat, her eyes cast down. Wretchedness overcame him. He ducked his head and waited for the trap to close. Elena's hand fumbled for his under the tablecloth. He grasped it and clung on tightly.

'Shut up, Peter!' Elena said. 'You completely bad young man.'

'"Shut up" is rude,' said Georgie.

'So what's the joke?' said Gavin.

Peter was flying. 'My brother is. He spends his life reading penny dreadfuls. Gets the hots for some old ladies' pin-up novelettist. Arrives at her talk angling to get his leg over, and—fucking shock of his life—discovers she's a he!'

'"Fucking" is really rude,' shouted Georgie joyfully.

'Well I never. Is it true? Marjorie Macpherson's a man?'

Henry dared to look up. No one was laughing. The children were still tucking into their chips. It was Kim, the girlfriend with the auburn hair, who was asking.

'Yes.' Fiona found her voice. 'His name's Michael McCoy. His publishers thought he would sell better under a woman's name. But now he's coming out.'

'I read one of hers... his... last year,' said Kim. 'It was good, it made me cry. I would never have guessed he was a man.'

Elena gave Henry's hand a squeeze. He found courage to speak. 'Yes. They *are* good, the books—they're really very good. Accomplished. Sensitive, I think and, well,' he dared to say it, 'attractive.'

'I'll say.' Kim nodded and waved her bare arms about. 'Great sex scenes.'

It wasn't what he meant, but it would do. He held fast to Kim's eyes and to Elena's hand and headed for the safety of confession. 'But it was rash of me. Unbelievably foolish,' he grinned to prove the point, 'to form an attachment, so to speak, sight unseen.'

Peter whooped, but there was no other laughter. James lobbed the last plate of scallops onto the revolving tabletop, then straightened up. 'Love is blind,' he pronounced blithely. 'And nobody's perfect.'

Elena

'Why you are so disagreeable?' She was trembling with fatigue. She could barely reason or lift a fork to eat this food. But she found Peter odious and wished him to know it.

Still he was grinning like a stupid little boy. He refused to look at her, or at Fiona, who also was glaring at him. *Hipócrita!* Elena almost spoke the word. Peter had exposed Fiona's two faces. She who resembled an angel and behaved as a saint, she had laughed in secret at Henry's suffering. But of course, treachery was in her blood. 'Peter Jennings,' Elena insisted. 'Are you so much a coward that you cannot answer?'

'It's all right, Elena.' Henry was pleading with her. He wished her to stop. But she was furious at such injustice. She could not see it and say nothing.

Peter's blue eyes joined hers across the spinning table.

'Me, coward. You, cow.'

'Peter! Behave yourself!' Fiona pretending goodness again.

'And you fucking bossy-boots,' said Peter.

'Excuse me,' the wife of Owen intervened, 'but would you please mind your language in front of the children?'

'I'm so sorry,' said Henry. 'This is all my fault.'

'Nonsense,' said Fiona.

'I hate to interrupt the fun, but I'd welcome views on the scallops,' said James. 'What do you think? Do they merit promotion to the punters' menu?'

'Come on, Elena. Loosen up.' The blue eyes still held hers. 'You gotta laugh. SADDO STALKS SEX-CHANGE SCRIBE.'

'This is not humorous,' she told him. 'Have you no care for your brother, who loses his wife so tragically?'

'Please, Elena, stop!' Henry was gripping her hand so hard it hurt.

'My heart bleeds.' Peter was all disdain. 'Fancy-free for seven years and all he can find to fancy is some fairy. And just how tragic is it to have your wife decamp with an effing stockbroker?'

'Is "effing" rude?' asked Georgie.

Elena did not understand. 'Henry's wife die,' she told the table. She leant forward to give force to her words. 'It is very sad. She—'

'No, Elena! No!' Henry was loud with desperation.

'He told you *what?*' The triumph on Peter's face frightened Elena. Had she said something wrong?

Henry was tugging at her hand. She turned to him. 'But yes?' She was certain of this. 'Your wife. Suddenly, with no warning. From blood in the brain.'

'Wh-hooo!' Peter banged the table. 'Would you credit it? What a chat-up line! Ingrid never dropped dead. She sussed the pillock in a couple of months and scarpered before she died of boredom.'

Henry's face was scarlet. 'I am so dreadfully sorry, Elena. I've no excuse, no explanation. I told you a lie. Only one, I swear. Please forgive me. It's a fantasy, that's all. Another idiotic, habitual fantasy of mine.' His hands, clutching hers, were slippery. 'It's the truth, God help me. Ingrid didn't die. She lives in Torquay.' His voice grew loud. His face was filled with self-disgust. 'She left me, just as Peter says, for a richer, cleverer, vastly more attractive man than I am.'

Elena stared at him. The table, revolving amidst myriad reflections, was completely silent.

'A—nd CUT!' said the brother with spikes. 'Great stuff, guys, it's a wrap. And now, please, can you hold the next scene while I go cook the steaks?'

Chapter Twenty

Elena

The air began to pulsate and hum, the sunlight dazzled her, the seat beneath her was hot stone.

'Whoa!' she heard Urquhart cry. He towered above her, gigantic and without pity. He blocked the light and the village voices as she slithered into the well.

She tried to save herself, but her strength was gone. She was weary beyond caring. It was tranquil to slide and fall through the suffocating air. The well opened its black mouth and swallowed her. From air into water, she sank peacefully, gently, relinquishing her fear, until warm mud lifted itself to claim her, swallowing her softly in its turn. Down she drifted, deep into the mud, each moment more slowly, until at last she lay still. Peace embraced her. She rested safe in the earth beside her mother and Marisa. She saw their faces, clear and bright, not old as before. A smile from the angels was growing around them. *You can stay here*, the smile said. *There is no need to think or worry, no need to move or open your eyes.*

'Sleep now, lassie.' Urquhart's voice echoed inside the angels' smile. 'Close the curtains, Janet. Let's be leaving her to sleep.'

Henry

'Please. Henry. I need to speak to you.'

He faltered at the foot of the cantilevered spiral staircase, up which big Owen, competent and kindly, had just disappeared with Elena's limp body in his arms and his nice wife, Janet, at his side. The staircase wound into darkness above Henry's head. Not even the echo of their footsteps lingered.

He had lied to Elena. He had lost Elena. In one wretchedly small and unnecessary detail he had broken faith with reality, and bang, he had blown his fragile chance of winning a woman of his own.

Fiona Urquhart bobbed at his elbow, wanting to speak about things that didn't matter. Nothing mattered any more. And here came his bloody brother, smirking.

Fiona followed his despairing eyes. 'Peter,' she said. 'Will you take Elena's case up? And her bag?' She paused. Then, 'Henry?'

What? She was touching his fingers. He looked down and saw the handle of Elena's handbag clenched tightly in his fist. 'Yes, of course.' He let it go.

Fiona took it and held it out to Peter. Peter pulled a face. He slung the bag to his shoulder, lifted Elena's case and executed a clicked-heel salute. '*Ja wohl, mein Führer.*'

'You never relent, do you, Peter?' said Fiona.

'I will if you will, so will I.' Peter set off up the stairs after Henry's forfeited chances. Henry watched until he was out of sight.

Fiona's anxiety lapped around the wreck of his hopes. She still had her pointless speaking to do. 'Please let me apologise, Henry. I have no excuses either, but I want you to know I never once laughed at you, or felt like laughing.'

He dragged his eyes away from the dark spiral of steps and tried to cut her short. 'Whatever you say. It hardly matters. Elena was there, Elena saw. And she laughed, why not? But then, later,' he took a breath, remembering her tearful, trusting gaze, 'later she didn't laugh. She completely understood. It was my lie. Mine was the lie that counted.'

'Oh dear me!' Fiona became agitated. 'Have I lied to you, Henry? I didn't mean to, really I didn't. I thought the danger was past, that Peter wouldn't realise. But yes, I suppose, you're right. I am so dreadfully sorry.'

Henry's mist of self-pity lifted. For a brief moment, he felt vengeful. 'Are you saying you never knowingly tell untruths, Miss Urquhart? About you and my brother being old friends, for example?'

She looked startled. He felt like a cad. 'Henry,' she said. She had the tone she used for his brother. She was about to tell him what to do, and he was powerless to gainsay her. 'Henry, I'm going up the hill just now, to speak to my father. Will you come with me?'

Peter

Up, up and up, shouldering Señorita's effects, pissed-off as hell with the lot of them, thwarted robot powered by Duracell, programmed by FU, audience with Calum interminably postponed.

More than one exit from this escalator—where did Rob Roy get off? Sod it, Spanish mare scarcely in urgent need of toothbrush, let rage propel him upwards, into some turret, some eagle's eyrie, whence he could espy Calum Calum scratching out his golden Gaelic. Up and fucking up.

Spiral narrowing, stairs creaking, breath short and legs aching. Trapped twixt dizzy corkscrew down to unforgiving flagstones and gnarled door by brothers Grimm. Cold draught beneath. Bend ear to oak—what's this? Low, intermittent female moaning, plus DIY supply of spooked violins. No key, be bold, try handle. Yes! with Hammer-horror creak, door opening stiffly, inch by inch, into castellated thin air.

Wind upping ante from moan to wail. Step through into surround-sound space. White peaks fast vanishing in lowering cloud. Growl of thunder, snow turned to rain falling straight from the freezer. Banshee howl. Squall slamming door behind, wrenching hair-roots, tearing suitcase from shoulder and flinging it against battlement. Elements trying to kill him. Rise like Lear to yell at sky, '*BLOW, WINDS, AND CRACK YOUR CHEEKS!*' Fuck them all with poetry.

Beethoven joining in—Ode to Joy—scarcely in keeping, what in hell's name? Phone chirruping away in Señorita's bag, ruining mood entirely. Dig in, pull it out, hit talk to stop the thing. '*What?*'

Shriek of gale dumping him—'*Ow!*'—on knees, phone to lughole, chin on granite ledge. Stare out through castellations at Highland wilderness, wild-eyed and disembodied like Urquhart clan trophy, some deep-voiced foreigner girning in his ear. 'Elena?'

'Yes, mate.'

Next bit lost in whirlwind.

'Come again.'

Phone droning protests. 'What is happen? Where is Elena?'

Movement on mountainside below. Fiona it was! dogged by dogs and climbing into imminent cloud-line, side by side with some brother or other. Fuck it, *his* brother! Henry! Fiona, the double-crossing witch, leading the jammy creep straight to Calum.

Anxious crackle in his ear. 'Hello. You there?'

'Yes, mate, more fool I. The fool on the foul, fucking heath.'

'Who is this? Where is Elena?'

'Not here. I'll tell her you called.'

'Yes, tell her please, my name is—'

Storm lashing face with ice, inflating jacket, halfway to lifting him over parapet.

'Mick, you say?'

'No—'

'Look, Mick, now really *isn't* the best time.'

Punch off-button. Glare through tempest at Fiona and Henry, heads down, battling through. Beethoven kicking in like mocking, clockwork jester. Stupid phone, hurl it at Henry's head. Watch its impotent, parabolic dive, down towards gravel, disappearing, grey on grey.

Whoops. But something had to give. Do this, do that—what was he, a fucking factotum? View gobbled by racing curtains of iced fog. Nothing to see—storm crashing like South Atlantic round cabin-boy in crow's nest. Crawl on hands and knees to wrench door open, drag bags through, clamber after them and let it slam behind.

Collapse on top stair, hair raked, face scoured by cold, shivering, dripping, muttering curses. Replay of creaking woodworm silence, haunted by wailing ghost. And nothing still to do but wait.

Chapter Twenty-one

Henry

The weather had ferreted out gaps at Henry's neck and ankles and was insinuating icy dribbles onto his bare flesh. The wind kept trying to steal his cap. He pulled it down hard and bent into the torrent of rain. Beneath his feet, the path had transformed itself into a stream. The dogs gleamed wet as otters.

He could hardly see Fiona—he stumbled against her and then away. In his head she was not Fiona, she was his mother. He gave in to the old comforts, took refuge from the storm within and without, and became a child, battling up hill and down glen to save his mother from some evil villain.

A touch on his arm interrupted his reverie. Fiona wanted to speak. In yellow sou-wester and gumboots, she looked like Christopher Robin. 'I'm sorry,' she yelled. 'This is no fun in winter, but lately he's insisted on hiding himself away up here.'

Reality startled Henry. He had almost forgotten that the man they were battling up this hill to see was an *actual* villain. A man who took money from a friend and brought no guns, who threw peasants to the mercy of Franco's army.

Nothing had altered. What did it matter that he had blown his chances with Elena? He would still risk himself for her. He would remain her cavalier, if not her suitor.

Ouch! He stubbed his toe on a rock and nearly went headlong. Fiona made a grab to save him, and his anger against this inscrutable little Scot resurfaced. She hadn't explained her lie, he noted—thought she was going to get away with it, no doubt. She might yet if he didn't smarten up. For Elena's sake and his own, he must be level-headed.

There was a flicker of lightning, then thunder built and rumbled round them, bouncing off the unseen mountainsides. The dogs came close, their tails between their legs.

'It's not far.' Her face, framed by the sou-wester, was whipped pink by wind and rain.

'Yes, but what's the real story with you and Peter?'

She stopped and stood quite still, meeting his eye with no hint of embarrassment. She spoke deliberately through the storm. 'It's more a secret than a lie. You'll know it soon. Today, if my father agrees. But please, Henry, do believe me when I say how badly I feel for gossiping about you. I'd no idea Peter knew you.'

The wind tugged relentlessly at Henry's cap. His anger found no words. He was a useless cavalier.

They ploughed on through the rain, skirting a giant rock to their left. There was a roar in the air, steadier than the storm, the sound of falling water. They were up past the rock and onto level ground. The cloud lifted, the wind dropped and hushed, and the rain stopped battering his face.

Henry gasped. He was standing practically on the lip of a hanging valley that reached deep into the mountain. A river was bowling along it and, a few yards from his feet, a mini-Niagara dropped sheer through a belt of mist to Loch Craggan far below.

'Beautiful, aren't they?' said Fiona. 'My father's falls.'

He nodded dumbly, mesmerised by the water's transformation from rain-pocked silk to white havoc. As he watched, his spirits lifted.

Was he romanticising Scotland again? He stole a glance at Fiona, but she too was smiling at the falls.

'Yes,' he said. 'Incredibly beautiful.'

His eyes were drawn past her, along the valley, where the dogs were running. The snow was gone, there was nothing to see but grey. Boulders, stones and water, no tree or patch of green. Only a croft with a chimney at either end and a porch centre-front, behind a dry stone wall. A makeshift retreat for a shepherd.

Fiona turned and followed his gaze. 'I know. We've been worried about him. But this is all he seems to want just now.'

Elena

She dreamt she was strolling with Mikhail, arm-in-arm on a curved, sandy beach, beneath the Mediterranean sun. They smiled and recited English tenses together. 'There was no problem, there is no problem, there will be no problem.' The waves fell with a sound like thunder. Or was the thunder from the sky?

'Is there a storm, Mikhail?' She knelt to put her ear against the sand.

The sand was warm and damp. Mikhail stroked her hair. 'There will be no problem,' he said.

She opened her eyes into a pillow. Mikhail was gone but his touch remained, and his voice. *There will be no problem.*

Beyond the pillow, she saw a room covered with roses. The walls, the closed curtains, the bed-linen, the carpet, the framed prints. Everywhere she looked, pink blossom clustered and twined.

Loch Craggan! Her heart accelerated as she remembered. But her head was free from fear.

Mikhail was lost. She gasped to think of it. She must not think of it. She must find her anger again.

Her mother's diary. Yes, she had only to remember and her body sprang alert. How foolish she was to be ill. In place of food she had drunk cognac. In place of sleep she had wept with rage. How stupid. She must not waste this anger.

Angus Urquhart. She must find her enemy with no more delay and hear his lying histories of heroism. His wickedness had soaked through the generations and stained her heart. She hated the old man he had become. She hated him and all his smug, smiling, Scottish family, born of lies and treachery. Before night came, they would look into the eyes of Carlos's granddaughter and know their shame.

Her watch showed two-thirty. She left the bed, searching for her luggage.

Her jacket and the new sheepskin coat were hanging in the wardrobe. Her new boots lay on the rose-patterned carpet. But where was her suitcase? And her handbag?

She refused to panic—the anger had concentrated her mind. She put the boots on, crossed to the door and opened it. The hotel corridor was empty. Slipping the key into her pocket, she hurried to the central stairwell and saw the stone floor of the hall below. Henry's bag lay beside a huge, carved-wood chair. Fiona's small suitcase was there also, but her own was not.

Who had taken them? She could feel her fear returning. Worse than fear, her terror. She clung to the stair-rail, trembling, as she went down.

And then she realised, it was the smell that was making her afraid. The dusty odour of old wood was evoking the shuttered house of her childhood. Spain was so near in this hallway. Hated, rejected, feared, it followed as many miles as she could run.

She must not be foolish. Here was the stone arch through which Urquhart's giant son had carried her from shuttered house into sun-brilliant square. Perhaps in the salon with the glass wall she would find her bags. She entered bravely.

Only the disagreeable young man with the blue eyes was here, Henry's brother Peter. With relief she saw her case beside his feet. He was crouched on the sofa, chewing his fingers and studying pages hand-written in blue like the one in the photocopier. Urquhart's poetry. He noticed her and made a defiant face. 'Hi, Señorita. Your things.' He pushed them with his foot.

He was not worth fighting. 'Thank you. But where are Henry and Fiona?'

'Gone without us, the sods.' He jumped from the sofa to point through the glass wall. 'Up that path, to see her dad. Jack and Jill, up the fucking hill.'

The view was grey with rain. 'So come,' she said. 'We follow.' Her anger was pure and pressing. She must find Urquhart.

Peter's blue eyes mirrored her urgency. She did not like him, not at all, but always she found herself reflected. 'You're right. Why not?' He was pushing the poem into his bag and heading for the hall. 'No more *mañana*. Look, there are some cagoules here. Let's go.'

'Wait.' She ran after him with her luggage. 'Five minutes only. I will get my coat and meet you here.'

Peter

'Well hi! Where y'from? Ain't this place just grand?'

No time for idle chat. Cagouled and in cahoots with Elena, bulldoze through sudden plague of sodden, sodding Yanks, back from huntin, shootin, fishin, oil-prospectin. 'Sure. Yeah. Seeya layder. Godda fly.'

Onto gravel, whoops! swerve round broken phone in puddle—'Here's the path'—and set about it, Mohammed at the mountain.

Climb and climb and climb. Steep as hell and savage gale, but rain stopped and clouds parting, shaft of sun from Hollywood epic, and Calum up here somewhere, holy Moses with tablets of Gaelic stone.

Interminable track, steps cut into bedrock, up and up. Hammering heart, aching muscles and skewered ribs—keep it going, one-two one-two, squaddy with backpack, Sisyphus with deadline to meet.

Catch breath, glance back, check progress. Señorita way behind. Valley and loch in massive bas-relief, swept by giant cloud-shadows and searchlight of sun, gold on charcoal, wow, and bang, it got him, Icarus in solar beam. Godda fly before his wax wings melted.

Señorita waving, shouting, 'Peter. Please.'

Sun swallowed by black sky and icy gust. Must stick together, for sphinx minx Fi might bar his way, *Peter be patient*. 'Sorry. Too fast for you?'

'Yes. Thank you. Too fast.' Panting and pale, cagoule aflap round face like yellow flag.

'Sure thing. Take five. Admire the fucking view.'

Heart banging in mouth, plus earache from wind, and stab of stitch, an eagle at his liver, Prometheus now. Press elbow into side, pull up hood, glare down at Urquhart pile. Granite fist with central 'up yours' tower. Ring of gravel, sporting Land-Rovers around Fi's little car, like break-out at Jurassic Park.

'Peter. I have a question.'

'What?'

Ominous Spanish scowl. 'I notice how you speak.'

'Oh yeah?' Grit teeth for lecture, female censorship.

'Is difficult to understand, but I not complain.'

Match scowl: eye for eye and tooth for tooth, hood to flapping hood.

'You are brief, but you invent. I am impressed, though many times confounded.'

No answer to that but 'Charmed, I'm sure' and wait for the 'but'. Yes, here it hailed, slap-bang on cue.

'But Peter, I am wondering. Why the bad words and—how do I say it?—*la malevolencia?*'

Why, she wants to know. Here's why. Strung out on a cliff in vicious gale, where better to bellow truth? 'BECAUSE I'M FUCKING ANGRY, THAT'S WHY.' Great surge of freedom, snatched by wind and hurled against the sky.

Señorita, mouth open startled, had it coming. But hang on, what was this, a laugh? And yelling as loud as he? 'YES, PETER, I SEE THIS, BUT WHY? WHY ANGRY?'

Double the volume, let his fury fly. 'WHY NOT?

AREN'T YOU? WHAT IS THERE *NOT* TO BE ANGRY ABOUT?'

Truth shared, Señorita's hood snatched by howl of wind. 'YES. I AM ANGRY ALSO. JUST AS YOU.' Voice of a diva in his face.

So kiss her, yes! Her tongue right there, hot and hungry. Gobble it up, cagoules acrackle, hands a-roaming. Fi wouldn't kiss him, *Stop it Peter,* frigid Fi with unhinged Henry. Calum waiting, godda fly, but Señorita tugging at his hair, clash of teeth and hard against his hard-on, good angry kisser, angry woman, eating his anger up.

Chapter Twenty-two

Henry

'Sugar?'

'No, thank you.' Henry smiled politely. He was trying to imagine this old stick of a fellow roughing it through the Sierra Nevada with a pack of rifles on his back. Only he hadn't, had he? There had been no guns.

'Guid,' the old man said, 'for I've nae sugar to offer ye.' He dumped the mug in Henry's hands. The rim was chipped and stained. 'A biscuit, though? Ye'll be having a biscuit?'

Henry nodded nervously.

Urquhart was levering the top off a rusty tin. 'They're auld, mind ye. I don't bother with them. I keep them for the dogs.' Hannah and Mabel milled round his knees expectantly.

'Father.'

'Or the meece when they gang hungry.'

'Father, don't tease.'

'Nae, Fiona. The wee mun wants a biscuit. Dinnae ye?' The tin was under his nose.

'Be brave, mun. Have a biscuit.'

They didn't look too bad. Henry took a chocolate digestive. 'Thanks,' he said and bit into it. It was a touch stale, but nothing he couldn't cope with.

'Sae, "Henry" is it?'

This was harder. Hearing his name pronounced in this

way that accused him of being English or worse. 'Yes. I'm—'

'Father,' Fiona intervened. 'Henry is a good man, and you're to treat him kindly or I shall be cross with you.' She turned to Henry. 'Whereas my father is a vexed *old* man, with nothing better to do some days than pick on other people.'

To Henry's relief, Urquhart smiled. 'That's ma wee lass. Keeping her faither in order.'

'Sit down, Father. I have things to tell you.'

He did as she said, sinking abruptly onto the edge of his unmade, wood-framed bed with knees well apart. This Scotsman wore navy underpants, thank God.

Henry was perched beside Fiona on a low, foam sofa, covered in the familiar tartan. The only other furnishings were a table and stool, a bookcase, a ragbag heap of clothes, a sink unit with a camping stove on the draining-board, a shelf for crockery, and a paraffin heater.

It was chilly in here. The dogs had settled close together near Henry's feet. The older one, Mabel, was snoring already. He leant to pat Hannah, and she licked his hand.

Where was the loo? The cold was making him want to go.

'There are others below I want you to be kind to, Father. They've come especially to see you.'

Henry finished the biscuit. The door beside the sink was probably the loo. He cleared his throat, and Fiona and her father looked at him. 'Excuse me, but do you have a lavatory?'

'Nae, laddie, I don't,' the pressure in his bladder increased a notch, 'but there's a privy oot the back, with soft paper from Tesco.' The old man guffawed and walloped his knee.

Henry struggled up from the sofa, his ears burning. 'Back in a tick then.' How banally English. He was definitely off on the wrong foot here. As if to confirm it, he tripped over the dogs and then had trouble getting the door open, one of those lift-the-latch affairs. He stepped out into the rain.

A hut housed a seat above a pit. He emptied his bladder, then lingered, gathering himself against Urquhart's gibes. Old age was no excuse for bad manners, he always thought, though everyone conspired to pretend it was. He was glad this was Elena's enemy, he felt mild enmity himself.

'Constipation, laddie?' Urquhart said brightly as he let himself back in. 'Or haemorrhoids, have ye?'

'No.' He was bolder now, more equal to this game. 'Do you suffer from them yourself, sir?'

Urquhart played deaf, but Fiona smiled. It was okay to do battle. Henry retrieved his mug of tea and withdrew to the stool by the table, near the paraffin stove, keeping his distance from both of them.

'Sae, Fiona. Who else hast thou brought to bother me?'

She hadn't told him then. She'd waited for his return.

'Two people, Father. A lady from Brussels. Her name's Elena. She came to the library yesterday, looking for you. She's read about you on the Internet. She wants to hear about your time in the SAS, for a book she's writing.'

'Och aye?' The old man sat straighter and his blue eyes focused.

'She's been unwell today. Fainting. She should be recovered later, but it will be much better if you come

177

down, Father, rather than she up.' Fiona scrutinised the room. 'And you've run out of proper food again. Father, please don't worry me like this. You must take more care of yourself. When were you last down?'

'Nag, nag, nag. Tis all thou'rt guid for. There are plenty of tins below here.' The old man pointed under the bed between his knees. 'And who's the other body?'

Henry paid attention. Fiona's lie about his brother. Would it now be explained?

Yes. Fiona seemed tense and very small. She glanced up at Henry on his stool, then back to her father. 'Henry's brother. Peter.'

The old man waved a dismissive hand. 'Och well. Henry's brother. And what would Henry's brother be wanting with me?'

Fiona leant to touch her father. 'I sent him your poem.'

He sprang from the bed. 'Thou didst *what?*' He seemed beside himself with anger.

Fiona had risen with him. He was tall, she was small— her head level with his chest—yet she spoke carefully, as though to a child. 'He's reading it, Father. He's Henry's brother. This is Henry Jennings. His brother's name is Peter. Forgive me, but I thought it might make you happy.' She stopped speaking.

Henry felt compelled to rise to his feet too. For a long, disconcerting moment, Urquhart stared at him, before erupting into incoherent sound. Spluttering, looking from Fiona to Henry to Fiona, fighting to find breath for words. Fiona held his hands and soothed him. 'You'll like him, Father.' Hannah pushed her nose between the pair of them, trying to join in. 'He recognised the poetry. He wants to meet the man who wrote it.'

She seemed about to cry, and the old man was moaning wordlessly. Henry was embarrassed. This was none of his business. He headed towards the door to the yard.

'No. Please. Henry. Stay.' Her cry halted him awkwardly by the sink, where he put his empty mug. She turned back to her father, pleading with him. 'He loves the poem, Father. He says it's miraculous, the best you ever wrote. He knew who wrote it without my saying a thing. "Calum," he said, and how could I deny it? But that's all I've told him.'

All this fuss about a poem. Tears glistened on the old man's face. Fiona had whipped out a hanky and was wiping them away. 'It's all right, Father. I'm sure it will be all right.'

Peter

'We will forget this. We do not like each other.'

Fastest turnaround in history, Señorita icing up again. Though maybe not, who knew? Not unknown for harsh words and violent kisses to keep on flowing from one mouth.

But now was not the time, not now. For flowing from this mountain mouth, harsh rock and violent cataract, was poetry!

Path of stones, patter of rain on cagoule hood, nearer to Calum with each step. Valley of stones, croft a mere incidence of stones, poetry a mere incidence of words. Heart battering like genius to be out—cruel, alien spawn fighting, biting its way out, hammering to join its Gaelic fellow. No fun for human host, but here he was and had

179

no option—must carry his genius to meet its muse.

Woman trudging alongside, silent. Cast a glance: face white, eyes staring, fixed on cottage door. Grab another kiss for luck. No resistance, lips tasting of rain, parting to receive his tongue and letting him grope this time through cagoule and sheepskin, shirt and bra, to billow of breasts, heart pumping away like his. Gasping, 'Enough. Not now.'

Catch that? Later then, more to be had, words never mere incident.

Gripping his wrist, white-knuckled. 'Because now we meet Urquhart.'

Urquhart. Calum. Yes. Uptight Señorita a hit in the sack, no doubt about it. Hard-on had violent homing instinct. Heart and hard-on tearing him limb from limb, yet Calum's pull was greater.

Path of stones. Door to his destiny. Bleached wood with iron knocker. Raise it and let go.

Rush of ecstatic Hannah. Fiona's face, wet as Señorita's, puffy-eyed. 'Peter?'

Quick, step back, act gallant. 'Sorry Fi, but couldn't let Elena come alone.'

Peer past her into shadows. Henry. Other dog. And yes! Calum, for it must be he! Tall, and wiry, etched with time, fan of white hair and beard, and pale-blue orbs as wide as wide, fixed on him in startled cognisance, and the clamour of their two hearts silencing the world. Push past women, dive to take his hand. 'I'm Peter Jennings. And you, you're—'

'Calum. Aye. That's who I am.'

Yes! Known from the poem, but always known. Never believed this man a goner. Heard the verdict spoken, read it between learned covers, knew it wasn't so. *Believed dead*, never believed, not once.

No one speaking. Only he and this man, standing heart to pounding heart, aching with grief of genius lost and found.

No words, no easy incidence of words to speak, with here, on shelves beside them, Calum's hard-won couplets leather-bound, plus files of papers and—REJOICE, REJOICE!—his own draft thesis! circa 1996, red cardboard folder with *Calum Calum: Man Or Legend?* inscribed in his own hand!

Elena

There he stood! The old man from the photograph, blue-eyed in his kilt of Urquhart tartan, his withered cheeks disguised with a white beard, his fear concealed behind a smile.

El malo.

His fear was not of her. Not yet. He did not see her, only Peter.

She had no pity for him. She had feared she would feel pity.

She was in no hurry to be seen. The room was loud with people and excited dogs. Their breath made clouds despite the smell of burning paraffin. The old man was holding Peter's hand.

'Are you all right, Elena?' Henry's question startled her. So good a man was Henry, so unlike his brother. She glanced down, straightening the yellow anorak. There was a taste of Peter in her mouth, a tremble of desire still in her throat.

'Thank you, Henry. Yes, I am.'

'Father.' It began to happen. Fiona was steering the old man past Peter's hungry stare. 'Father, you must say hello to Elena. You remember, I mentioned. The lady from Brussels who wants to hear about the SAS?'

Yes, he was crossing the room to give her his hand. Yes, she was taking the hand and meeting his lying smile. His bones under the loose skin were as fragile as Aunt Marisa's. If she chose, she could snap them in pieces. She squeezed hard, too hard, until he pulled away.

He was examining her face. 'Is it Spanish ye are?'

Did he begin to be afraid of her? She could not tell. 'Yes. I am Spanish.'

'*Así. Hola, Elena.*'

'*Buenas tardes*, Mr Urquhart.'

'Nae, pretty lass, dinnae be fussing with all that. I'll be Angus to ye.'

No, he had no fear. Beneath the white brows, his eyes grew bold. *El malo* was flirting with her! How much she hated him. 'Angus then,' she said.

'And if ye insist, I'll tell ye ma stories of France.'

She was strong and unafraid. She smiled into his lascivious eyes. 'I read how you save a village. It please me to hear you recount this.'

'But not now, Father,' said Fiona. 'It's getting dark and there's no food here. Come with us. For a hot dinner and a warm bed.'

Still his odious face pressed close. 'Aye. Thou'st persuaded me. I will.'

The shiver ran from Elena's throat to her knees, then spread in ripples along every nerve. Her mouth tasted of Peter. Her body still quivered at the thought of Peter's greedy hands, the urgent press of him against her. Yet this feeling was more than desire, more than disgust at the old man's smile. It was the thrill, scarcely to be believed, that soon she would shame *el malo* and be free.

He was gone—the door swung open. He was leading the way through the failing light, with Peter, Fiona and the two dogs close behind. She hurried after them, leaving Henry to follow and close the door.

Chapter Twenty-three

Henry

He had lost track of what was happening here. No one cared a damn for him. All he could do was stumble down this hill after the others, like one more foolish Labrador hoping to be thrown a stick to fetch.

He should go home. What the hell, he had to be home by Monday anyway, for Trevor's leg. He could ring for a taxi and leave at once, take the first train south and spend a good part of tomorrow in the pub, calming himself and putting all this humiliation behind him.

Definitely a good plan. Yet something prevented him. Was he a masochist? He hoped not. It felt more like curiosity, some mystery eluding him.

Everyone was lying: this was the truth he'd briefly grasped at lunch, before the balloon went up. And it was how he would get a grip on things, he decided. He would go through the lies, one by one, get them itemised like a list of dicey investments and watch for movements in the market.

He would start with Fiona. She looked straightforward, but she confused him most. He observed her, marching down the mountain path ahead of Elena in her Christopher Robin get-up. He still believed her honourable. Faced with her lie, she hadn't denied or attacked or confessed. She'd commanded, 'Come with me.' Spoken of a secret, belonging to her father. And then—had he imagined it?—she'd seemed to want him as witness. Why?

No use, he could get no further with it, he'd have to await developments. He shifted his thoughts to Peter, way ahead, racing hell for leather after the fleet-footed old man. Peter's were lies of omission. Colluding in Fiona's fib that they were friends. Not explaining his eagerness to meet her father. All because of that poem, apparently.

He recognised it, Father, said it was marvellous, knew it was yours.

No mystery. It was obvious. Urquhart was just some versifier his brother hero-worshipped. Hadn't it been written on his face as he rushed in declaiming, 'Yes, I'm Peter Jennings', then stood there like some dumb chump in love?

Bulls-eye! Henry grinned. Damn it, he wasn't the only idiot in the family who fell in love sight unseen. This snide old goat was his brother's Marjorie Macpherson! Good thinking, he must remember *that* the next time the knives were out.

And maybe this was Fiona's secret too—had Peter been pestering her father? Upsetting him somehow? Had she brought him here to teach him a lesson?

Excellent. Market analysis was paying off.

His attention came round to Elena, a few steps below him on the mountain path. He already knew her secret of course, though he'd almost lost sight of it. And what a secret. She was going to confront this vain old bastard with his original sin. All his medals and poems wouldn't tip the scales. His account didn't balance. She was here to declare him morally bankrupt, to nail his lies for good.

Brilliant. And of course, no question, he must stay here

for Elena—he had pledged her his support. Plus there would be the bonus of watching his brother's fantasy brought down, as his own had been. Problem solved. Henry straightened his back and found a new spring in his step.

He began to watch Elena's hair. He liked the way it bounced, sleek and dark above the yellow windcheater. Close behind her on this stairway cut into the rock, he could see into the parting, where the hairs sprang from her scalp like bristles on a soft brush.

No good. He was feeling troubled again, almost as badly as before. But why? What had he missed? What hadn't he faced up to? It must have to do with Elena. He was watching her left ear, as she negotiated a steep bend. He remembered admiring it in the library, imagining it to be Marjorie's. How small and white it was. He feared for Elena: that was his unease.

But no, not true. She had recovered from her fainting. She was surefooted on this path. And the Urquharts were benign enough, all told. There was no reason to be afraid for her, nothing to harm her here but her own obsessions. Yes, but wasn't that equally true of him? He must face whatever this was and deal with it.

Suddenly he understood and blushed for shame. Again it was his own lie that was eluding him. The truth was he still had hopes—his anxiety was for his chances with Elena.

Damn it, the habit of fantasy died hard. He tried to stand outside himself, to face and name and understand his feelings for this woman. What did he know of her actually? He could not say he loved her or even be certain that he would love her. He was on the rebound from a ghost, and he hoped... yes, he hoped to love her.

This was what was holding him here. He had lost Marjorie Macpherson. He had turned his back on ghosts. But he needed a woman. He craved the love of a real woman. And the shiny roots of Elena's bouncing hair were real as real could be.

Peter

Words multiplying like stones underfoot, all questions, why, why, why? Keep close at Calum's elbow. Hellish difficult—old man galloping downhill like mountain goat, kilt bouncing, white hair flying, arms winging, outrunning the pack. Watch how he does it, eyes intent, each foot placed square, movement smooth as thought. Follow in his footsteps, page to Good King Wenceslas. Written pages would surely follow, spondees and dactyls square, images freewheeling. Getting the hang of it, left, right, that stone, that rock, flexing knees, gaining on Good King—'Calum! Slow down and tell me *why?*'

Old man bounding onwards, eyes afire. 'Why what, lad?'

Hard to speak, words jolting staccato, panting, nearly falling. 'Why disappear?'

'Ma poems dried. Twas they that disappeared.'

'And now?'

'Now what?' Pausing. Turning. Frowning.

'Your poems. They're back?'

'Nae laddie, just the one.' Hurtling down again.

'The one Fiona sent me?'

'Aye.'

'But it's brilliant. You must write more.'

'Nae. It is ma last.'

'Your greatest!'

'Aye. Ma last and greatest, aye.'

Fragments of Gaelic rattling in brain. 'About lost love? Lost honour?'

'Aye. What else is there to lose?'

Off path onto gravel. Whoops! Elena's smashed phone. Giant obstacle to leg-over, she'd have his balls. Or then again, good move—some foreign git in competition. Quick, scoop it up and stuff in cagoule pocket.

Glance back. Elena way behind with dogs, and plodding Henry, and fair Fi who brought him here, but why?

'You have my thesis. *Man or Legend.*'

'Aye, I have.'

'And do you like it?'

'Tis nae bad.'

Glow of glory! Under porch, through iron studded door to hall. Calum whirling to face him, kilt spinning.

Sudden hit of *déjà vu.* Those eyes, Fiona's eyes, this place, dark stairway, carved oak chair. Mind grasping at thin air, struggling to remember... what?

'Aye, Peter lad, and thy verse too, nae bad at all, though thou'st a way in life to go.'

Hang on! His verse? Nae bad? Panic rising in throat. Frantic for relief. 'It's no good? Is that what you mean to say?'

No answer. Calum's eyes soft, and fixed beyond his shoulder. Spin round to look—nothing but place remembered from a dream. Spin back, find Calum striding into shadows, head bent and hand to brow. Follow him. Nothing to do but follow Calum through cobweb of memory. Remembered voices out of reach, but whispering, you know, Peter, yes, you know, there's something, something, nothing you don't know. But what?

Elena

The path was difficult, but she went with scarcely a glance at her feet. Her eyes followed the old man, careering ahead with Peter in pursuit. The pair of them were off the mountain and across the gravel, Peter stumbling briefly, hand to ground. When they disappeared into the house she tried to go faster. So did Fiona, and Henry also. They all moved more rapidly.

The light had died. The night had swallowed the outline of the house, black against the black mountain, leaving its windows like a golden mosaic, with the glass wall of the salon the biggest and brightest piece. As they came near, Elena looked for Urquhart inside, but saw only the Americans and a corpulent waiter dispensing drinks from a tray. The Americans nearest the window waved, like passengers from an ocean ship.

'Where is your father, Fiona?'

Fiona hurried ahead of them between the parked Land-Rovers. She threw words over her shoulder. 'Our sitting-room's at the back. The evening staff have come on duty. The family will be having tea. The dogs need feeding.'

They were at the door. They were inside. The hall still smelled of Elena's shuttered childhood, but she refused the memory, she had no time for it. She concentrated on staying close to Fiona, across the stone floor, beneath the stairway and into an unlit passage, with Henry behind and the dogs panting.

Suddenly Fiona stopped and turned. Elena nearly collided with her. 'I'm sorry, Henry. Your bag's still in the hall. You don't have a room yet.'

'It doesn't matter. Later will be fine.'

Elena met his eyes and, yes, he understood her urgency. They said no more. The three of them raced along the passage. The door was opening into a room full of chairs and sofas and Urquharts. The dogs ran to greet the children, barking with excitement, then found bowls of food and began greedily to eat.

And there stood *el malo*, in silhouette against a blazing fire. She had him—he could not escape. She stepped back, behind Henry. She closed the door and leaned against it. Her haste was gone, replaced by readiness.

'Here they are. For shame, what kept ye? Can ye not keep up with an old man?'

One of the brothers, the younger one with short hair like copper wire, answered. 'For shame yourself, Father. You know no one can beat you up or down the hill. I believe you practise at night to tease us.'

The old man laughed. 'Aye, Gavin. Maybe I do.'

The room was hot and dry. Elena began to shed the yellow anorak and the sheepskin coat beneath. Her shirt was unbuttoned, reminding her of Peter. She looked for him, wanting to consult the mirror of his eyes.

He was close by, standing, his shoulders to the panelled wall. Briefly his eyes burned, in memory of their kisses. But then they returned to Urquhart. Peter was changed, yes, as she was. Intent, curious, focused. More handsome without his anger.

'Come in, Elena. Sit near the fire.' Janet Urquhart rose from beside her giant husband. 'We've been anxious about you.'

'Thank you, but I am better.'

'You're right, the fresh air has done you good,' Owen declared. 'You have some colour in your cheeks. Sit here.' He tipped two boys off a sofa and patted the cushion. 'Well done for tempting the old man off his mountain. Have some tea and scones.'

'With home-made Highland blackberry jam,' cried the brother with spikes. 'We're to have Angus's war exploits for cabaret, we gather.'

'We're the Germans! Let us be the Germans!' The two boys were shouting and jumping, making Hannah bark.

'Me too!' said Georgie.

Urquhart's eyes fastened on Elena as she went forward. She felt the insolent weight of his old man's lust as she took her place by the fire. She returned his gaze without fear, as cold and calm as an avenging angel.

He nodded. 'Aye. Ye must eat, then whatever ye would know I'll tell ye.'

A cushion was put on her lap and a tray on top of it with plate, food, knife, and a mug of tea. 'Thank you.'

Henry sat opposite her, smiling his support. Fiona, beside him, seemed anxious, glancing at Peter, who remained alone by the door, only he and Urquhart standing.

A hush was visiting the room, as in a theatre. Angus Urquhart was swelling his chest to speak, swelling his arrogance to meet her sharp pin of truth. The words of the library book came back to her. *Utter disregard for danger. Gallantry of the highest order.* She sank her teeth into a scone, waiting to hear these vanities from his own mouth.

Chapter Twenty-four

Peter

Clink of crockery and crack of burning logs, yet riddle uncracked and panic unsoothed, brain racked to breaking point. Old Calum playing hard to get in rent-a-crowd of Urquharts, his ancient, blue eyes seeking Peter's, now and now again. Hold stare unblinking wide to catch his glance. Away... then back, away... then back... and hold it, those eyes, hold steady. Shoot question along the beam. My poems, are they bad or good?

'Sae tell me, Elena. Tis the tale of ma Military Cross ye're wanting to hear?'

Watching Peter. Speaking to Señorita. About to spill French beans on derring-do. Listen up—some clue to poem to be gleaned perhaps. Keep ear ajar for cold weather and hot lips.

'Yes, Señor. For the book I am writing about war heroes.'

Calum frowning, gaze wandering to hot-lipped Señorita's cold-lipped smile.

'From reading, I know what happened from the outside. But not how it *feels* to do these things. This is what I hope to know from you.'

Yes, too right. Ravenous to witness bard in action, to watch words fall like moonshine, history distilled to happening, heroism to heroic verse.

'Sae lass, tell me what ye know already.' Calum's eyes

aflicker over upturned faces.

'You drive a jeep, Mr Urquhart.'

'I told ye, call me Angus.'

Deep Spanish breath. 'A jeep, Angus. Into a French village. One jeep. You were alone.'

'Ack ack ack.' Boys behind sofas, leaping and ducking, firing machineguns. 'Germans! There were Germans!'

Señorita undeterred. 'And Frenchmen also, I think. Men whom the Germans mean to kill in the square?'

'Aye. Forty or more.'

'So many?'

'Aye.'

Good old Calum, ayes to cool diva, nose to hot disciple hooked on his heroic, hoary gaze.

'You stop the jeep. You shoot. The Germans shoot. The Frenchmen, they escape.'

'Aye. Not all of them, just twenty-six.'

Señorita nodding. 'That is the number I read. You shoot and shoot. You kill, how many Germans? Ten?'

'Aye, thereaboots.'

'They fire at you. They hit you.'

'Aye.'

'So you stop firing.'

'Nae, the gun jammed.'

'You drive away, with small wounds only. Your general, he say—'

'Nae "general", lassie. We were all one band.'

'He say you fear nothing. You are valiant. They give you the medal.'

Children cheering. Hannah barking. Urquhart frowning, shaking head, quieting them with a hand. 'That's it. Ye have it all.'

'No, I need more. Angus. Much more.' Cop Señorita's solemn face, drawing all eyes and holding them. 'The book is words only. Tell me please, what you remember. The colour of the sky, the sound of gunfire and of shouting, the smell of blood, the feeling of the bullets hitting you. These I can imagine, but what is real?'

Bravo, Elena. Calum gathering breath to speak. Existence gathering to a point. 'It was nineteen forty-four. I was twenty-eight years old.'

His poems dried in nineteen thirty-eight, but Calum carried on.

'There were four of us. The sky was... black.' Sarcastic poet's wink at Peter. 'No moon. No sound. They dropped us between Paris and Orléans. Five jumped, but Buster's chute didnae open. Four was enough. We buried Buster. We built a sleeping platform in a tree. It couldnae be seen from below. We dug a pit for the equipment. Is this too much for ye?'

'No. Please. Continue.'

'A rifle and a pistol each, the radio, some Lewis bombs, the pigeons—we kept these things o'erhead. The tree was... green.'

Winking at him again. Oh praise the Lord, and pass the ammunition. More! More! His poet's voice alive and singing, even in English each cast-iron syllable ringing true, the Gaelic Hemingway. Calum's genius hadnae died—he'd just stopped sharing it.

Elena

She had imagined how she would feel, to hear *el malo* tell his story, and this was not yet how. He was in no hurry, but neither was she. The moment she waited for would come, it could not fail. From this room, packed with his children and his children's children, his words would carry him and her alone, Carlos's killer and Carlos's dead child's only child, into that other village square. Let him speak first of parachutes and pits. The pit was opening for him.

'The *maquis* found us easily enough. They came up the track from the next village in a cart. They were nae bad. They gave us food, wine, intelligence—aye and women too. The wine was red and smelled of wine. The women were brown. Their petticoats were silk, from parachutes. They smelled of woman.'

The little girls giggled. The old man winked again across the room. Elena had wanted his arrogance, and yes, here she saw it, small and mean, an old man's arrogance.

'Sae, there we were. Set to do as much mischief as we could.'

'Don't forget the jeep, grandfather.' It was the eldest of the grandchildren who spoke. She had Fiona's serious eyes. 'You've missed out how the jeep arrived.'

'Aye, Mary, thou'rt right, I have. Tis a good tale in itself. It came from the sky, of course.' Urquhart's gaze passed through the panelled ceiling. A smile was spreading in his white beard.

Elena leant forward, willing his pride to grow. Yes, he began to be transported. Yes, he was twenty-eight again, standing in a wood between Paris and Orléans, staring at the sky. She watched him now, as Carlos's ghost had watched him then.

'It was near midnight when we heard the Halifax. We lit the bonfires. We flashed the recognition letter. The plane passed us, then turned into the wind, low o'er the fires. The noise was infernal. Then, bonny sight, there came the jeep, on four parachutes, gliding down.'

'Like a flying saucer,' said Mary.

'Nae, Mary, like a jeep. We cheered. The plane was gone. The fires were out. The steering wheel was under the seat, the machinegun in the back, a Vickers, mounted, ready. And in a line, more parachutes, six of them, silk for petticoats. Containers crashing through the trees. Cylinders with codes painted on them. Codes that told us petrol, spare wheels and tools. Guns, mountings, ammunition. Rations, rum and cigarettes. Medical kit. Baskets bursting, spilling tents and sleeping bags and clothes. The *maquisards* helped us hide the jeep with branches. We had the wood tidy in twenty minutes.'

His eyes shone with memory. She took care not to break the magic. She spoke no more loudly than a whisper. 'So. Angus.'

He looked at her and smiled, still faraway.

'So, now, in France. You have all you need?'

'Aye, lass. Twas time to kill some Germans.'

Henry

The little boys yelled and fell dead across the sofa-back, then resurrected themselves and charged around doing their machinegun impressions. Everyone seemed engrossed, and Henry supposed he should be as well. This was Elena's big moment after all. But he was hot, and bored actually, and sleepy. Urquhart's doings might be real, but they had nothing to do with Elena's grandfather so far as he could see. It was only a story, and it didn't have him gripped.

196

He'd never seen the point of war yarns, shoot-outs and escapes and whatnot. They offered romance of a kind, he understood that, but not the kind that appealed to him. For where was the point of romance without women? The sex in Urquhart's tale was too basic and offhand—little Jeannie and Debs were still smirking about it. Wine and women, indeed. Just bodies served up—real women didn't get a look-in.

'Ack ack ack. You're dead!'

That was the other thing. All this shouting and leaping from behind chairs reminded him of childhood. The wrong bits of childhood. The boarding school ambushes, the horrid little brother back home.

But he had to listen, for Elena's sake. She looked marvellous. So intent.

'We knew the score from the *maquis*,' Urquhart was saying. 'Things were plenty bad in the villages around. The Germans were swarming like cockroaches.'

Maquis. Orléans. The old man pronounced these words in an easy French accent. His Scottishness was thinning as he spoke. He was forgetting it, Henry realised. The ascetic Highlander was role-play—for this story it no longer suited the sly old bugger to be a Gaelic hermit.

'They had a policy. For each bombed tank, for each dead German, they took Frenchmen in reprisal. Straight from their homes, the first they found, they marched them out and shot them in front of their women and children. Sometimes a whole village paid the price.'

'Yes,' Elena said.

Of course. The air seemed to chill as she spoke the word. The hiss of it lingered. The point of Urquhart's tale was suddenly as sharp to Henry as an unsheathed rapier.

'The *maquis* didnae lose heart. The people neither. They wouldnae give up killing Germans. They would fight till they were free!'

Henry's eyes were fixed on Elena. 'Yes,' she whispered. 'So, take me with you. Angus. Into the village that day.'

'It wasnae planned,' he said. 'I was bringing the jeep from the railway line, before dawn. The line was ready to blow. Hiding the jeep there wasnae safe. I saw the light of flames in the village. I met a French lass on a bicycle, weeping and afeared. Germans were in the village, the SS, killing the men. I drove straight in, as fast as the jeep would go.'

'You are wearing your kilt on this day?'

Strange question.

'Aye lass. I wore it every day.'

'So the book tell me. But this is dangerous, yes? In disguise you would be safer?'

If she was prompting the old man to boast, she certainly succeeded. 'I didnae care a hoot for ma safety!'

But *was* this boasting? To Henry's ears, the old man seemed more angry than proud. He seemed to mean the words he spoke, without bravado. In the thick of action, at the age of twenty-eight, not caring if he lived or died.

'The Germans were expecting nae trouble. It was dark. The dawn hadnae begun to break. Their backs were to me as I drove in. Their guns were idle or towards the Frenchies. They turned as I braked, like men in a dream. I was out of ma seat and had the Vickers raking them before the dust cleared.'

Elena leant forward. 'Darkness. Dust. Germans. Men waiting to die. Tell me, in the square is there a well?'

Her lovely Spanish voice was low and concentrated.

The hairs prickled on Henry's neck. Even the little boys were silent, held by the story.

Urquhart laughed. 'I didnae see, lass. Next time I'm there, I'll remember to look for ye. All I saw were two staff cars with their headlights on and a gang of Jerry. That was what I was noticing. I was firing the Vickers. The cars went up, whoompf, one after the other, their fuel tanks ruptured and catching fire. Then I was dodging bullets and taking care to miss the French. Ye ken?'

'Yes. And then?'

'And then the Vickers jammed. I grabbed a carbine from the jeep, emptied a magazine of fifteen rounds and tried to change it. A bullet slammed into ma right hand, and it went numb. I used ma fingertips to take another magazine from ma pouch and reload. Ma hands were slippery with blood. I took aim. Nothing happened. Two rounds were jammed in the breach. Another bullet hit ma shoulder. Twas time to go, or try to. I didnae expect to live. I was in ma seat, the engine running still. I aimed the jeep at the road out. I put ma foot down. I put ma head down. I didnae raise it till I reached the corner.'

'The corner of the square?'

'Aye, lass. And out between the houses, to rolling hills, and Frenchmen diving into fields of cabbages.'

'Great,' cried Peter. Some Urquharts clapped their hands. The little boys dropped their machineguns to cheer, then wriggled on their stomachs under a coffee table, where Hannah showered them with slobber.

Henry sat still and tight, watching Elena's face. Now surely she would tell the story of *her* square, *her* men, the scenes her mother saw.

A movement caught his eye. The rotund waiter who'd

been serving drinks to the Americans out front hovered in the doorway, coughing deferentially behind his hand. He seemed to fancy himself as Jeeves. His pomposity made Henry want to smile.

'Yes, Gordon?' said Janet Urquhart.

'A new guest has arrived, madam. A gentleman. A single for one night.'

'I'll come and see to him. What's his name?'

'McCoy, madam. Mr Michael McCoy.'

The name sliced through the air. This was how bullets felt. Too fast to dodge or comprehend. Too late to remedy.

Chapter Twenty-five

Henry

He couldn't move. His thoughts would not join up.

What was McCoy doing here? What did he want?

Around him people were reacting. Fiona turned to him as if to speak. Peter punched the air and shouted, 'Wonderful!'

'Isn't that amazing?' The girlfriend with the mass of auburn hair seemed thrilled. 'The man we were on about at lunch.'

'The man who broke my brother's heart.'

Oh God. There was no time to lose. He must leave. He lurched up from the sofa, but his knees buckled. 'A taxi,' he croaked. He made it to his feet again.

This time Fiona pulled him back. 'I'm so sorry. How terrible. I keep doing this to you.' She had tight hold of his arm. 'Last night—before the meeting—he asked me, could I suggest a country hotel? Loch Craggan, I said.'

He struggled to escape her grip.

'I'll help you to avoid him. It's the least I can do. You can stay in one of the back rooms. I'll fetch your bag.'

He ceased struggling. He slumped, speechless.

'Though actually, it wouldn't matter if you did meet him, would it? Because he doesn't know,' she faltered, 'you know, about you.'

Dear God, she didn't know the half of it. She didn't know about the letters. And the photograph.

She read his face. 'Oh dear. But please, don't worry. And if Peter starts stirring things, I'll stop him before he—'

'It's all right,' Henry managed to say.

For yes, thinking sensibly, what harm could McCoy do? He took a new hold on reality, remembering the resolution he'd reached with the fellow's ghost last night. He must refuse to be embarrassed. He ran soothing lines through his head. Great books, M M. And sorry about the mix up, but let's say no more, eh? Let's leave it there.

Beyond Fiona's anxious face the room was chaos. Even the old man seemed upset. Elena leapt across Henry's vision, brandishing a cushion.

Of course! Elena! How could he even think of abandoning her when Angus Urquhart was slipping from her grasp?

Elena

'No! Stay! Please, I am not finished!'

'No more am I.' Urquhart's voice had shrunk to a whisper.

Elena stared at him—had he realised who she was? But his eyes were on Peter, who was shouting, 'Michael McCoy! Fucking wonderful!'

'No! Peter! Please!' She implored him with her eyes, to let her finish what was begun.

He stared at her. He did not understand. He did not know. He knew only his contempt for his brother.

The room was emptying fast. Janet Urquhart was gone, followed by the chef, two children and a dog.

'No!' They must stay. They must hear. There was a

cushion in her hands. She threw it at Urquhart, but he paid no attention. She picked up another.

Janet Urquhart was back. 'It's past your bedtime, Georgie.'

'Nae, Janet,' said Angus. 'Stay awhile. For there's more to say—is that not so, Fiona?'

Why ask Fiona? Elena began to shout, 'Yes, there is much, much more to say!'

Fiona turned to stare at her—everyone was staring—but she did not care. It was what she wanted. This was—it had to be—her moment of revenge.

Fiona spoke. 'Father. Please. Now isn't the best time.'

'There is no best time,' he said. 'Time chooses us. Yes, Janet, stay. For there's a thing ye all must know.'

Peter

'Woof!'

And fuck it, whole clan back, more fuss and chatter when all he wanted was to be alone, speaking of poetry with this battle-scarred warrior time-lord, framed by firelight, whose wild eyes still searched for his. Away, then back, away.

Henry's idiocy with the poofter writer milked apparently, barely registering on the Richter scale. Mad Señorita erupting, clutching at cushions and squawking as though about to lay an egg, face flushed and blouse adrift from skirt. 'Yes, Janet. Angus. Please. Stay with me in the past. Before the war, you are in Spain, *my* country's war. We must speak of the Sierra Nevada. The February cold, the fall of Malaga.'

Calum spinning on his heel to look at her. What was

this? The warrior dismayed?

Hang about. Hot-lipped Señorita, cold Sierra?

Far far colder, that is how it was.

Wham! Getting warmer! Calum's eyes wide for Spanish babe, his poetry laid bare. *Here* was the key to the Gaelic, the clue to its meaning. Voice lost in nineteen thirty-eight—the answer to the riddle lay in Spain!

'I know the truth!'

All eyes on him, Calum's too, rusty old warlord poet, etching lines in dust with broken sword, recalling lust and loss and—

'*What?* Thou knowst what, Peter?'

His eyes blue terror! And all for poet Peter, shouldering an old man's burden, knowing the leaden weight of it, the tragedy of half a century of writer's block.

'Your *poem*. I see what it's about. Your love lost! Your honour lost! *Calum Calum* lost! In *Spain!*'

Consternation in the ranks, ripple of Urquharts' heads swivelling twixt him and proud bard trembling on hearth before subsiding logs, his eyes blue water. Flurry of sparks up chimney, throwing six decades' silence to the stars. Opening mouth to speak his golden words.

Henry

The old man looked suddenly frail. He was reaching for the mantelpiece to steady himself. Was he about to confess? Henry heard Elena whisper, 'Yes.' But Urquhart didn't spare her a glance.

'Aye, tis true, thou hast it right. But—'

'Grandfather?'

'What, Mary?'

'I'll tell you bloody what, Father.' Red-crew-cut Gavin had muscled his way forward. 'You made us promise never to let on you were Calum. And now you're admitting it to anyone, as if it's nothing.'

'Hush. Please. Listen.' Fiona was trying to quiet Gavin, but he took no notice.

'Not if someone guessed or pressed us, you said. Not even when you'd gone, you made us swear it.'

Red-faced William was up and shouting too. 'Gavin's right. Calum was dead in you, you said. Dead and buried, not to be dug up. We did your bidding though we didn't understand. What the hell are you doing, with your glib "Aye, tis true" to three complete bloody strangers?'

'Calm thyself, William. Let me speak,' the old man was trembling violently, 'for I've good enough reason to change ma mind.' His voice was raw, forcing an uneasy hush on the room. His eyes were fixed on Peter. 'I thought to be silent yet, or somehow to tell this gently. But I cannae see how, for it must be named the way it is: nae more, nae less.'

His voice shrank to a husk. 'The reason is that Peter is ma son.'

Chapter Twenty-six

Peter

What?

What did Calum say?

He was saying it again. To him alone, as though no one else were here. 'I sired thee, Peter. Thou art ma son.'

Poetry. He meant the poetry. 'You mean the poetry?'

'Nae, lad. I mean thy mother. Maggie. Thirty year ago.'

Wham! Shock waves of understanding. All at once, so many things. Pa's frozen shoulder. Ma's Gaelic lullabies. Henry's loot.

Calum's eyes casting him adrift. Turning to William. 'Let me explain to thee. To all of ye. Thirty year ago I met this lass.'

Wham! It was Ma in the poem! The poem was about Ma!

A roomful of eyes bored into him. His mouth hung open. Shut it, no words to say.

'Hold on, Father.' Fiona leaping up. 'Go slowly. They're stunned. They need time—'

Wham! God! No! Fiona, his *sister?* Fuck it, fuck it, no! But yes, he'd known it, seen it from the start. Those haunting eyes were his own!

The brothers were yelling. 'You knew about this, Fiona?'

Wham! His brothers! Four of them! Because Calum... Calum, his father...

'You're telling us this nasty bit of work is family?'

'What does he want? What the hell's he doing here?'

'Thirty years ago? Did Mother know?'

'Oh Father, you incorrigible rogue!'

'Hush the lot of ye. Fiona has it right. Ye need time, and so do I, with ma new son, alone.'

Calum's eyes were back. Watered blue, shining with tears. With feeling. And he too, awash with feeling but no words. Feeling demanding to be named. What name? His father, Calum Calum. Good or bad, this feeling?

Good. Definitely good. His whole being flooded with the goodness of it. Oh vastly, vastly good! Ma, Pa, Henry, the rottenness explained.

And more. Much more. His thesis, his poetry, his Muse, his odyssey, his houseboat rising and falling on the stinking tide, the whole universe made sense!

What to do? Cry 'Dad' and run towards him? Rooted to spot, brain stalled, ears deaf, eyes locked on Calum's, tongue swollen with nothing to say.

Calum Calum and he. Calum and Son. Calum and Peter Jennings Urquhart Calum.

They had to be alone.

Elena

'*Ay!*'

She screamed, but no one heard her.

'My village!' She hurled the cushion at Urquhart. 'The fall of Malaga!'

She hurled herself after it, but big Owen caught her. 'Not now,' he said.

She was nothing. She was no one. She struggled to escape Owen. He pushed her into a chair. 'Not now!'

'*Es malo! Es bastardo!*' She shrieked into the growing noise of Urquharts, into a room furious with Urquharts.

Urquhart had outgunned her. Peter was his son! She had kissed Urquhart's son! She screamed again.

'Come on to bed, Georgie. And the rest of you.' Janet Urquhart was herding children towards the door. 'Yes, Mary, you as well. You'll hear about it tomorrow.' She turned before leaving. 'For shame, Angus. Springing such things on children with no warning.'

Elena heard herself howl like an animal.

Henry sat trembling on the sofa opposite. Henry was not an Urquhart.

'Henry,' she pleaded. 'Henry.'

His face was white, his eyes were closed. He could not help her.

Mikhail. Suddenly she wanted only Mikhail. She would ring the whole of Brussels until she found him. She struggled from the chair and ran from the room, pushing past Janet and the children in the passage, escaping the wood-smoke, finding again the hall that smelled of Spain, oh God, driven by the need to hear her lover's voice, as rough and gentle as a cat's lick.

Elena. The memory of the way he spoke her name.

'Mikhail,' she called. 'Mikhail. Mikhail.' She was running up the stairs.

Elena. Yes, I know. I understand.

Here was the door. She found the key, dropped it, found it again, his remembered words running in her head. *Always I will understand. But why can you not forget this pain?*

The key was in the lock. He was right, she had to tell him he was right. Her memories, her anger, they brought her nothing. Carlos's shame, Marisa's death, a funeral procession, her mother's opened grave. Then nothing but Urquhart, Urquhart, Urquhart. What was she doing in this place?

She burst into the room of pink roses. Her bag was on the bed. She dug inside it for her mobile. She could not find it. She tipped the contents out. It was not there.

Her case was on the floor. She opened it. Searched for the phone. Threw out the clothes. Searched again. It was not there.

Henry

Shock. Too many shocks.

It was obvious, why hadn't he seen it before? His brother's eyes and Urquhart's eyes were so alike. And Fiona's eyes. Everywhere he looked, he was seeing the same eyes. He must get away from them. 'Fiona. Please. You said you would find me a room.'

'Yes, Henry. A moment.'

He couldn't bear it. He had to be alone. He needed to look at himself in a mirror and find out who he was. This room was so hot, and there was so much shouting.

'Why have you sprung this on us, Father? How many more bastard worms are there burrowing in the woodwork?'

'Yes, and what's your game, Peter Jennings?'

These two loudmouths were horribly like his brother.

'William! Gavin!' Fiona spoke sharply. 'Do as father says. Leave them alone, just for half an hour.'

'You bloody knew, Fiona, and you didn't say.'

'I couldn't, William. He swore me to silence.'

'Huh!'

But the brothers were leaving. Big Owen first, then William and Gavin, scowling and grumbling, pushed out bodily by Fiona, followed by James, the grinning chef.

Peter's half-brothers.

'Wait here, Henry. I'll fetch your bag. I won't be a minute.'

Peter's half-sister.

She was gone. Leaving him alone with an old man and a half-ex brother, two dogs and a dying fire.

He might as well not exist. Peter and Urquhart hung in a trance together, waiting for him to leave. When he left, they would begin to speak.

Fiona was back with his bag. 'This way,' she said.

He rose and followed her dumbly, through a door beside the fireplace and up the servants' stairs. Bloody suitable.

'Will this do? Are you sure?' She had unlocked a small bedroom that looked out on dark mountainside.

He nodded. 'Could I have some brandy?'

'Of course. I'll send Gordon with some. He won't be five minutes. And then...'

He was staring through the window at the mountain. Staring through his reflection at rock and darkness.

'Henry...'

'What?'

He turned to look at her. She was scribbling a number on a scrap of paper. 'I'll be with my brothers. I don't know where exactly, but you can page me.' She put the scrap of paper on the bedside table. 'When you want to talk, I'll come. I'll tell you everything I know.'

She was at the door. She smiled, but he could not. She

was gone. He needed the brandy to arrive.

I'll tell you everything I know.

He knew already. His mind, crawling out from under its stone, was hit by an agonising weight of knowledge.

It was Urquhart, not Peter, who stole his mother's love.

Chapter Twenty-seven

Peter

'Are you all right, lad?'

Still no words. Knees weak. Totter to nearest sofa and drop down. This was the feeling: desire to drop, almost to sleep. How could that be?

Calum, his father. A great man, his father. So much to know, to ask, to tell.

Not so. All done. All answered in two words. *My son.*

'Peter. Dinnae be angry with me.' An old man, leaning from his chair, reaching a nervous hand. Too far away to touch.

'I'm not. Truly I'm not. Not angry with you.'

That was the feeling. That was its name. Not angry.

'With thy mother then? With poor Maggie?'

Shaking head, numb with this absence of rage. 'Nor with her either.'

An old man leaving his chair. Edging closer. 'With who then? With Fiona?'

'No.'

No anger. What to take its place? An old man in a kilt? He took the old man's hand between his two. Turned it palm up, palm down. His father's hand, the finger-ends hard-bitten like his own. 'What shall I call you?'

The old man shook his head. He gripped his father's hand. The answer spoke itself.

'Calum. I can only call you Calum.'

Elena

She rocked and wept, crushing the receiver of the bedside telephone to her ear, hearing the ringing, far away. She imagined the clamour of it in the empty office, closed for the weekend. She pictured Mikhail's desk: his dictionaries, his mug for coffee, the calendar with scenes of Moscow, the telephone calling and calling into silence.

'Please, Mikhail. Please speak to me.'

His desk was orderly. Pencil, pen, highlighter, notepad, keyboard, monitor. Nothing more. Or maybe, was it so, a small heap of papers waiting? Post-it notes, requests and messages? One of them headed 'Tuesday'? Elena rang. Please call her.

She sobbed and rocked, in time to the distant telephone. *Madre de Dios!* Where is he? Is he ill? Please no.

Click. 'Hello?'

She leapt with hope, off the bed onto her feet. 'Hello? Mikhail?'

'Mikhail is no more here. No one here today. Is veekend. But I okay perhaps? I help you vot you need?' The halting voice dissolved her with longing. It was not Mikhail's voice, but so much the same.

'I need to speak to him urgently. Please, do you know where he is?'

'Sorry. He qvit job is all I know.'

'Quit?'

'Yah, he go. Leave Brussels. Vait, I get number.'

She could hear the man whistle as he looked for it. She clutched the phone, praying, 'Please, Mikhail. You must not do this.'

'Hello. You there?'

'Yes.'

'I have number.'

She grabbed a pen from the mess of luggage on the bed, and a piece of paper. The photocopy of Angus Urquhart, smiling in his kilt.

'Number is...'

She started to write. She stopped. 'No. Please. This is his mobile. I need his *new* number.'

'This all I have. Sorry I no more help. Okay?'

'Okay,' she whispered. 'Thank you.'

She hung up. She stared at Angus Urquhart's photocopied smile. Not okay. Never again okay. With Mikhail in Brussels she had been almost happy. 'Think of the future,' he said, making her smile. But always she ruined the future, staining it with the past.

Slowly she began to sob. Hard sobs that hurt her throat and brought no peace.

Henry

The brandy had arrived, but he'd been drinking too much, he decided abruptly. He broke the seal, sniffed at the open neck of the bottle, then resolutely screwed the cap on. Reality remained the watchword. It was pouring on his head by the stinking bucket-load, but he was damned if he would hide from it in drink.

Reality. He concentrated hard on his mother, his childhood mother, seduced away by that abominable Scot. Her elderly ghost was here, skulking shamefacedly in the corner, trying to distract him from the truth. How much had his father known?

No need to upset yourself, Henry dear. He simply meant to appoint you head of the family.

Lying to the last! Violent anger seized him. He glared at her phantom presence, daring it to make excuses. How could she have stood by smiling for three whole years after Father died, watching him suffer such guilt? Watching him sweat blood to make amends to her and Peter. Toiling through the lonely life that *she* had programmed him to live. Could she not, just once, however privately for his ears only, have confided the true meaning of his father's will? It's yours, Henry, because you are his child as Peter never was. It's yours, every penny of it, because I played away.

Decades of paternal reticence were screaming to be re-examined. How much was temperament, how much the silence of the wounded beast?

Damn her. His anger grew. Three years she'd had. Nothing to lose but face. How dared she go to her grave without telling, leaving him nothing but memories stewed in lies?

And Peter! What a wrong to deal his brother! *There was no love lost between you and Pa.* As if that was Peter's fault! Pa's black-sheep, Gaelic-literature-studying, wastrel poet son! Had Peter ever been offered any love to lose, and could Pa be blamed for not offering it? He'd been despised—no, loathed—for doing what he was good at, what his genes programmed him to be good at, and never once told why. What did one of those Urquharts call him? A nasty bit of work? Was even that his fault? *My Ma sang Gaelic lullabies.* The poor sod never stood a chance.

But at least, unlike him, his brother would know the

truth. A living, breathing, Gaelic poet father would tell it to him. A father with skeletons rattling in his cupboard, yes, like the disintegrating biscuits in his rusty tin, but what did skeletons matter—who cared if Elena opened the cupboard door? All fathers were flawed, or worse. To know his own father, warts and all, what wouldn't he give to have what Peter had?

His mother's ghost stood silent, fresh out of lies.

'Damn you. Damn you, Mother.'

Help. He needed help.

I'll tell you everything I know.

But Fiona wasn't there when it happened, she would have been, what? Six? Only Urquhart knew the facts. Dates, places, his mother's excuses. Taciturn husband, namby-pamby child. More lies, but new lies, holding seeds of truth. Didn't lovers sometimes speak the truth?

Yes, he must hear Urquhart's fairytale of brief encounter. Later, when he could listen without screaming. *Thirty year ago I met this lass.* 'Lass' be damned! An Englishwoman, pushing forty, that was his mother thirty years ago. A frustrated romantic, ripe for seduction. Damn the pair of them!

Help. He needed help.

It would have to be Fiona. He sat on the bed, picked up the phone and the scrap of paper she'd left beside it, and tapped in the number.

Chapter Twenty-eight

Henry

She was with him in two minutes, small and businesslike in her no-nonsense jeans and sweater, bearing a plate of salmon sandwiches. From her wrist she unhooked a carrier bag that clinked. 'I don't expect we'll be having a family meal, what with one thing and another.' She sounded furious, though not with him.

'No.' He managed a smile. 'Thank you. You're very thoughtful.'

He was ravenous he realised as he wolfed the food. He'd had only a chocolate digestive and a scone since the steak he'd been too traumatised to touch.

He was still sitting on the bed. Fiona briskly closed the curtains, shutting out the darkness and the mountain, then dragged a chair across the room. She yanked a bottle of malt whisky and a tumbler from the carrier bag. 'This is my tipple. Though you're not drinking, I see.'

Her anger was making him want to change his mind. He'd put the brandy on the dressing-table, out of reach. 'No. Yes. I thought I would, but then I decided against. It seems important to face this sober.'

She frowned at the whisky, then threw it on the bed. 'Okay. I'll join you.' She produced mineral water. 'Though I must say it's tempting to hit the bottle. William's carrying on as if this is entirely my fault. Maybe he's right. I should have let things be.'

'No!' said Henry.

She looked at him.

'No,' he repeated more quietly. 'You should not have let things be.'

His words seemed to calm her. She poured the water and smiled at him. 'Flat, not fizzy. Cheers.'

They clinked and swallowed. She sat at last, knee to knee with him, blue denim to green moleskin.

'So,' he began, then paused to clear the emotion from his throat. 'So. He confided in you, your father, about Peter?'

'Yes. He did.'

'And asked you not to tell anyone?'

'Yes. Not even Owen.' Her eyes, grey not blue, were unsettlingly like Peter's. 'He was in a dreadful state. It was Hogmanay. He'd been low since before Christmas, but refusing to speak about it. Shaking his head, shutting himself away up the mountain, unwilling to come down. He had us afraid for him. I climbed up that night, and I was glad I did, for I'd never seen him so bad. Maudlin drunk, despairing, weeping over his new poem. And I was in a state myself, about,' she shook her head, 'about something. I was needing to talk. It was why I'd come. So I joined him in the drink.'

She lowered her eyes and stared into her glass. 'And we spoke about such things, you know? Shared them. He was distraught at first, with talk of putting an end to himself. He'd been too long alive, he told me. He'd done terrible things, worse than I knew. What things, I asked. I wouldn't think of judging him. And then it spilled out. He was telling me about your mother, how she had his child, how much he loved her.' She broke off and looked past

Henry at the wall.

'I loved her too,' he whispered.

She was speaking again. 'But then he was vowing me to silence. "Don't tell," he made me promise.'

'He didn't want you to contact Peter?'

Her disturbing gaze came back. 'I don't think it occurred to him. He'd given me nothing, not even a name. But when he said this son of his wrote poetry, had studied *his* poems, well, I had a hunch. I remembered the thesis on his shelf. I don't know how he'd come by it. Maybe your mother gave it to him. Most likely he'd forgotten that I'd read it. Anyway, there it was still. It's unfinished—really a very sketchy piece of work. But he'd told me once how much he liked it, because... well, what he'd said was... in the way it was written, it seemed to know... to know he hadn't died, only stopped writing. But now I realised, no, there's more to why he likes and keeps this thesis.'

She sighed and took a sip of water. 'I rang the university, spinning a line about our library archive. And then it was easy. The dates fitted. The facts fitted. I had no doubt this was my father's secret son. A boat in Surbiton, they told me, called 'The Styx'!' She grinned. 'I couldn't leave it there, could I? I had to know, I had to meet him. After all, he is,' she paused, 'my brother.'

'Yes.' Henry absorbed the bizarre fact all over again. It could prove to be a relief, he thought, to share this dubious privilege.

'My father had given me a fair copy of the poem. It doesn't identify your mother, not at all. So I don't know, I thought I'd send it—see what Peter made of it. As a Gaelic scholar. It was a way in, do you understand?'

He nodded.

'It felt unreal. I didn't want to tell lies, but I needed to meet him before I knew how much of the truth to give him. So I wrote an enigmatic note, trying to tempt him to Scotland. I didn't think it would work. I never dreamed he would identify the poet—the world is convinced that Calum's dead. But I thought, maybe he'd ring—or, more likely, after a while I'd go to Surbiton myself, knock on the door—does his boat have a door?—and take it from there.'

'It has a door,' said Henry.

'Even if he came, I didn't think I'd tell him. I didn't expect to bring him this far, to Loch Craggan. But then, last night, when I saw how passionate he was about the poem and how... how...' She waved a hand.

'How what?'

'How jangled he is. Do you know what I mean?'

'Yes.'

'Well, I thought it isn't fair, this secret. He needs to know. It isn't fair that he doesn't know.'

Exactly.

'Exactly,' Henry said. 'It isn't fair.'

'So I thought, if I were to bring him and Father face to face...'

'That things would happen?'

'Yes. But then Elena was pestering, could she come too? I tried to say no. I knew she would distract my father and complicate everything. But she was so pressing, she wouldn't take no for an answer. Then, dear me, this morning, *you* appeared. You must have thought me very rude, staring at you with my mouth open. While I was thinking, oh my God, Peter's *brother?*'

'This madman—'

'No.' She put her hand on his. 'Not mad. I never thought you mad.'

'Pretty damned eccentric.'

'Not even that. No, really. What I thought was... No, forgive me.'

'Please. I won't be offended.'

'Well, "jangled" is maybe a word that fits you too. Or something like it. Not the same way Peter is, not at all, but... I'm sorry, how presumptuous of me.'

'It's all right. I know exactly what you mean.'

'And I'd ratted on you. Told Peter about you.'

'That hardly matters—'

'But what a tangle I was in. I'd followed a thread, playing a game, thinking I could meet this unknown brother and see what I made of him. I thought I was doing no one any harm. And then it was happening, lots of harm, faster than I could keep up, and—God, that's another thing. Poor Peter, he's been trying to *kiss* me. What a mess I've made!' She sat back in her chair, hand over mouth.

Henry lurched forward. '*You* didn't make the mess. Your father made it. My mother made it. Not by doing what they did, but by not telling. Not telling is what's unfair. *You* have put it right.'

'It is better, isn't it?' She didn't sound too sure. 'To know rather than not to know?'

'Yes.' He wasn't too sure either.

'It hurts,' she said. 'It's difficult.'

But yes, he was sure! 'It *is* better,' he insisted. 'To know who you are. To know where you've come from.' God, he was livid with his mother.

Fiona stared into her empty tumbler. It wasn't only her

eyes. Her mouth too. How uncannily she resembled Peter, now he knew. He gathered himself, fighting the urge to reach for the brandy. 'You said you would tell me everything.'

She looked up. With Peter's eyes.

His chest clenched with rage and pain. 'Please tell me all you know that happened between your father and my mother. It hurts more than you would guess or imagine. It's hugely difficult for me, but I need to hear it.'

Peter

'The poem, this poem you wrote last year. It's about my mother, isn't it?'

Long silence. Collapse of ashes in grate. Old man's gaze blue water, far away. His father.

'I met her thirty years ago. In nineteen-seventy.' Calum, his *father*, finding words. Gathering energy with each one. Starting to smile. 'She was debating in the bar with two other English lassies after the show. I listened a while before I spoke. Then, "Maggie has it right," I said. "The first was rubbish. The second was better."'

Struggle to hear through drumbeat in head. His father, father, father. 'The second what?'

'The second poet.'

Fight to understand. 'And this was where?'

'The Festival.'

'The Festival?' Light dawning. 'Edinburgh?'

'Aye, I go each year, for the new voices.'

'You do?' Ah heaven, could it be? 'Do you go still?'

'Aye lad, thou'st guessed it right.' Eyes full of tears. His father's eyes. 'I heard thee there in ninety-eight. Nae bad at all. I was right proud of thee.'

Nae bad at all. Not rubbish then. Tears spilling from his own eyes—let them spill. Too much to take in—fantasy made flesh. Urquhart, Calum, kaleidoscopic strange old man, somewhere in the Edinburgh crowd, applauding his son's poetry. Nae bad at all. His father, father, father.

Old man sighing. 'But oh, thou shouldst have seen thy mother then.'

What? But yes, of course, his mother. Calum and his mother, making him! Rewind to nineteen-seventy.

'They'd come up from England, these three lassies, seeking adventure, though they didnae care to admit it in case it didnae appear.'

Listen. Listen to Calum. His father, father, father.

'Maggie was thirty-nine, but she had a look on her like a new bird that is nae sure how to fly. Wild-eyed with unused freedom, envying the youngsters their miniskirts, thinking she might wear one. She had bonny enough pins, thy mother.' His old voice full of yearning.

'And you were her adventure?'

'Aye, that same night.' Sighing. Sorrowful.

'So, that's how it was? I was conceived in Edinburgh?'

Nodding. 'Aye, thou mayst well have been, lad, though I followed Maggie south.'

'You did?'

'I was fifty-four years old. With five bairns. The littlest just five years old.'

'Fiona.'

'Aye.' Grunting with grief. 'Ma bonny wee lass. And four braw lads. But things were nae too guid with ma wife just then.'

'And so you followed Ma.'

'Aye. I didnae mean to. I battled with ma-self. But she had a look on her that tugged ma heart. It put me in mind,' old fingers tightening on his, 'in mind of ma youth, lad. Of times I'd thought were lost. I couldnae help myself. And so I begged sweet Maggie, "Come away with me."'

His father begging his mother. Come away from Pa. 'But she wouldn't come?'

'Wouldnae, couldnae. She was afeard. I told her, "Maggie, leave him. There's nothing here for thee." I waited nearby a while.'

Vision of Calum pacing avenues of Wimbledon, head full of Ma, kiltful of lust for her, kipping in foxhole or up tree on Common, fingering pistol, praying for jeep on silken parachutes.

'Did he know about you?'

'Och aye, she told him. She wanted him to throw her out, I think. I prayed for him to throw her out, but he wouldnae.'

New vision of Ma and Pa, facing off across the clock-ticking hall, Pa in his Marks & Sparks cardigan, and Calum in the wings.

'Where did you stay?'

'A room in Clapham. Maggie made white curtains for ma window. She bought a bedspread woven in India. She wore her miniskirts. I read her ma poetry. She learned it by heart.'

His Gaelic lullabies! *That damned Scots drivel.* 'How long did you stay?'

'Six weeks perhaps. It got to be winter, too cold for miniskirts. Ma bairns were missing me. Ma wife was forgiving me. And poor wee Maggie said, "Go home."'

Woman lost in unrelenting cold. 'And so you went?'

'Aye.' Old man staring into ashes. 'What else was I to do?'

'But...'

'But what, lad?'

His father, Calum, abandoning him to Pa. 'What about me? Didn't you know about me?'

'I told her, "Maggie, thou'lt be pregnant," but she didnae care. "Let the dice fall," she said. Maybe she knew already. Her wee boy was away at school. She wanted another bairn, I think.'

Condemning him to Pa. Leap up and pace the room. Spin to face him. 'But didn't you want me?'

Nodding. Anxious. 'Aye, lad. I hungered after both of ye. We wrote letters. Through the post office. Box number thirty-two.'

'She told you when I was born?'

'Aye, lad, she did. And sent a photograph each year on thy birthday.' Full, blue beam of paternal pride.

Huge swell of rage. 'But that was it? That was all? You never once thought how much I might have needed you?'

'Nae lad, dinnae be vexed. Of course I thought it, but what could I do when Maggie told me nae. And once I did see thee.' A tremble in his voice. 'When thou wast small and ma wife went into the hospital for her hysterectomy. I wrote to Maggie, wanting her to come. And so she did. She came, she brought thee here.'

'Here? I was here?'

'Aye, thou wast but four years old. Same as wee Georgie now. The pair of ye near broke ma heart.'

Found and lost again, the poem said. Blue eyes astray past Peter's shoulder to remembered image of Ma.

Wham! Déjà vu in hall explained. Dark stairway, carved oak chair, those same eyes lifting from his to his mother's, awash with tears. All these years he'd known his father. Always known him.

'And that was it? You never met again?'

'Aye, we did, but it was hard to do. There was nae joy in it. The last was a few years ago, after thy father died. We met in Edinburgh again. I was near on eighty, she was sixty-four. It was done with. But the old bugger had left the pair of ye nothing, and thou wouldst take nothing from thy brother, and should she tell thee who thou wast? She couldnae decide.'

'And you said no?' Rage exploding. 'How could you do it? Didn't you want me ever to know the truth?'

Old man clutching his hands and pleading. 'Aye, lad. I'm sorry, lad. Twas for the best I thought, but I see I was a coward. This is best. I am your father. This is best.'

Elena

Trust me, Carlos. Urquhart.

She slid the postcard into the pocket of her shirt. Then she leant over the banister and listened to the noises of the house below. The laughter of the American guests floated through the stone archway and up the stairs, mixing with the evening aromas of wood-smoke, whisky and roasting meat, which masked the shuttered smell of Spain. The laughter of strangers was painful, but also calming. Always the world continued, indifferent to suffering and so making it less.

Others were suffering also. Somewhere in the house, William, the angry brother, was shouting. She could hear no words, only crescendos of indignation. She understood. He had a new brother. He had brothers enough—he wanted no more. Suffering came in different forms.

Her cheeks stretched tight where the tears had dried on them. She touched them with her fingers, almost expecting to find a mask.

A door was opening nearby. She straightened and turned. A hotel guest was stepping into the corridor and locking his room. She pulled her key from her pocket and started towards him. He wore a suit and a dark-pink bow tie. His bald head reflected the ceiling lights. Ah yes, she recognised him—the man from the library who wrote as a woman, the cause of Henry's suffering.

He smiled at her. 'Good evening.'

She nodded as he passed. Michael McCoy, that was his name.

Poor Henry. His lover was imaginary, his wife gone away, his mother dead. And now his brother was stolen by these Urquharts, who swallowed everything like a rolling ball of ice.

Hearing the man's footsteps begin to descend the stairs, Elena leant again to watch him go, his hand lightly following the rail. In the hall, Hannah snorted and came to greet him. He paused to speak to her, 'Hello there. Good dog,' then turned right beneath the stone archway into a murmur of American greetings, polite remarks about the scenery and the weather. The waiter sailed across the hall, carrying stomach and nose as high as his tray of drinks. The world proceeded calmly as though nothing ever were or would be wrong.

'Hannah,' Elena whispered from her landing.

The dog lifted its head and saw her, but did not bark or

wag its tail. Why would even a dog care for her?

A door slammed below, and more footsteps echoed, accompanied by the sound of whistling and clicked fingers. Another bald head, shaven not shiny, crossed the hall. James, the brother with the spikes. He reached the stone archway and swept the air with his white chef's sleeve. 'Mr McCoy. I'm charmed. You will dine here tonight, I hope? With what delicacies may I tempt you?'

The same door slammed again. William's shout erupted in one of the passages below. 'They've had their bloody half an hour, and more. It's our turn. And the old bastard had better not mess us about!'

The old bastard. Yes. The moment had come to confront him. This time he would not escape. Elena stretched her back and smoothed her hair. She took the postcard from the pocket of her shirt. She drew a deep, steady breath and started down the stairs.

Chapter Twenty-nine

Peter

Dambust of Urquharts through door. Will the builder, shouting odds. 'Come on now, break it up!' Muppets multiplying. God help him, his relations! 'Get an eyeful of this, Gavin. Straight in and bonded like shit to a blanket.'

Drop Calum's hand. Rise grinning. Breast the flood like Kermit the frog. Good grief, Will and Gavin, pond-life, welcoming him to the pond. 'Hi, guys.'

Wham! Chest-thump from Gavin. Arse hitting cushions. 'What's your game, Peter Jennings? What d'you want from us?'

Questions bursting in brain like stinking, green bubbles. '*Want* from you?' Huge rebound of rage propelling him from lily pad, fists and feet like pistons. Gavin's nose, William's stomach, Gavin's thigh, William's shin. 'Fuck you, you pair of crabby, Scots, pissing, bastards.'

Brothers grim. Gasping, bloody, coming at him.

'Cool it. *Cool* it!' Owen's giant hands and shoulder. 'Enough. Stop right there! I'll only have to patch you all up.'

'Aye. Calm down, the lot of ye.' Calum laughing.

Owen frowning. 'And you're no better, Father. Pleased like a woman to be scrapped over, are you? Making a joke of your bad behaviour?'

Calum's face falling. 'Nae, Owen.'

But Owen persisting, 'So tell me then, Father, even if no one else cares to know. What new trial did you put our poor mother through?'

Henry

A commotion had broken out under the floorboards. Raised voices, loud oaths and yelps of pain.

'For goodness sake!' Fiona dumped her glass and ran to the door.

Henry followed her. The corridor was uncarpeted and bare. Fiona had turned left and disappeared. A few yards along, Henry found the staircase in the wall. A quick spiral of steps and he was through the fireplace door again, into the family sitting-room.

Everyone was on their feet, glaring and growling. Gavin's nose was bleeding. The old man was pleading with his gigantic son. 'She didnae know, Owen. She didnae care to know. I was away but two months—perhaps thou remembers, thou wast twelve years old? I came back. She took me back. She said nae more about it.'

'You think you can do anything, don't you, Father?' William's face was purple, his finger jabbing dangerously. 'You think, anything you want, oh yes, wade in and take it. Let everyone else pick up the pieces.'

'Yes.' Gavin took up the chorus. 'War hero. Long lost poet. You're so bloody marvellous, you think you're God.'

Fiona was tugging at their sleeves. 'Stop it, the pair of you.'

They took no notice. The old man shook his head and retreated towards a chair. William and Gavin closed on him, shouting. These younger brothers were bullies, Henry decided, like Peter but lacking his finesse. The buggers were still bellyaching. God, this place got more and more like school.

Elena had arrived, followed by an excited Hannah and the weirdo chef. Wonderful—a spiked skinhead was all this playground needed. Hannah was barking. The bullies were shouting. Henry could barely string two thoughts together. But the chef seemed uninterested in the fight. Instead he was staring at Elena. He looked alarmed, almost afraid of her. And yes, one glance showed why. Elena's demeanour was unnerving, fierce as a headmistress about to read the riot act. Henry felt a rush of desire.

'Listen.' Her voice rang out above the uproar like the school bell. *'Listen to me.'*

Elena. Of course, Elena. Elena had something original to say.

Henry had had quite enough of all this noise. He stepped forward and filled his lungs. 'BELT UP THE LOT OF YOU. LET ELENA SPEAK.'

They turned to stare at him like silly sheep.

'Not me,' he said. 'Elena.' He pointed to where she stood. 'Elena, they're all yours.'

Elena

The brother with spikes had been skipping across the hall when she reached the bottom step, drawn by the sounds of battle. But when he turned to look at her, his smile vanished. He held out a hand as though to stop her falling. 'Dear me, what's up? Don't say you're ill again?'

James. He had forgotten her name. He did not care if she was ill or well. She refused his hand. She held tightly to the postcard. 'I am not ill, James. I have things to say, worse than you know. I wait all my life to say them. Follow, you will hear.'

She crossed the hall. Hannah trotted after her, and James also. It was time. They must listen. She had important words to speak. Anyone who looked at her must see this. The passage was dark and narrow like the village well, but at the end of it were light and noise. She had no fear, or shame, or pain. Her rage was clean, and speaking would make her free.

The door stood open. The room was furious with Urquharts, shouting and snarling. Henry was there. Henry saw her power and raised his arm in welcome.

'Listen!' she said.

Some heard and turned. The two angry brothers continued to shout.

She extended a hand, then withdrew it. She did not like to touch Urquharts. '*Listen to me.*'

William spun round, scarlet-faced.

'It is my turn,' she told him. 'My turn to tell the truth.'

'Well, excuse *me*,' he began.

'BELT UP THE LOT OF YOU! LET ELENA SPEAK!' Suddenly the room was silent. Henry had silenced them. 'Not me. Elena.' Their eyes followed his finger. 'Elena, they're all yours.'

They stared at her. Spiked James and angry William. Gigantic Owen and wife Janet. Red-haired, scowling Gavin and girlfriend Kim. False Fiona. Peter, the mirror. And here, at the centre of the room, *el malo*.

She did not plan her words. They sprang like fire in dry wood. 'You are a traitor, Angus Urquhart. A murderer. You leave the men of *my* village in Spain to die. The old men, the young men, the boy-children. Eighty-nine dead, and one more is ninety. France is nothing. France does not make this right.'

He stared, mouth open, blue eyes terrified. She went a step closer. 'Look. Read this.' She thrust the postcard in his face. She spoke the words on it, mockingly. 'Trust me, Carlos. Urquhart.'

'Who are ye?' he whispered.

'I am Elena Martínez.' The words lifted her like wings. 'I am Carlos's granddaughter.'

Chapter Thirty

Henry

My God, she was something.

William had begun to snarl. 'What the heck are you on about?'

Then Gavin, 'We don't have time for this.'

Henry stepped forward, ready to call silence again. But Elena didn't need his help. Her voice was calm, almost hypnotic. Henry was mesmerised. He adored her.

'Carlos, Angus. Tell me you remember Carlos? *Su buen amigo Carlos Martínez y sus niñas, Juanita y Marisa?*'

'*Si*,' the old man gasped. '*Me acordo.*'

'Juanita was my mother.' She went closer. Urquhart shrank in his chair. 'Juanita is seven years old, Angus. Marisa is five. Juanita holds Marisa's hand. She hides with Marisa *en la puerta de la casa*. She watches as her uncles, her cousins,' Elena's eyes closed, then opened again, 'as Franco's bullets rip their flesh.'

She seemed so defenceless, delivering her story to this circle of strangers, her throat rasping with tears. Henry wanted to go to her, to put his arms around her.

'Miguel is Juanita's friend, Angus. He is seven years old. He is running to Juanita. But no, he is flying to her, like an angel with no face. His face is falling on the stones like rain. And now he is at her feet. Miguel's hand touch my mother's foot. It is Miguel's hand, exactly as before. There is earth under the fingernails. But his face is gone, his head is gone. Miguel is nowhere, like the flame of a snuffed candle.'

These were Juanita's words, Henry realised, not Elena's—the words of the seven-year-old who had witnessed this horror. The old man was moaning and twisting, trying to escape. But however he squirmed, the tattered postcard followed him, and Elena's voice. 'The blood make puddles on the stones of the square. The sky is blue, Angus, *blue*. Will you wink and smile at this? Red blood, white stones, blue sky?'

The old man shook his head.

'The smells, the sounds, can you imagine them? No? Then I tell you. There is the stink of smoke, and fear, and blood. Women are screaming, men are groaning. The guns are loud, so loud they hurt your ears. *Los estampidos*—the explosions—they come, again and again—they are silencing the groans and turning the screams to howls. And then the explosions end, and there is only silence. This silence is as wide as the horizon, as high as the blue sky. There is no sound at all. Even the women make no more noise, listening to the silence of their men.'

Glancing around, Henry saw motionless faces. Elena—no, Juanita—had transported them.

'The explosions are from Franco's guns, Angus, only *Franco's* guns. My village has no guns, not one. There are no men, no boys. Only puddles of blood under the cold blue sky.'

Urquhart's face was pouring sweat. Henry could smell his fear, a shadow of the imagined stench of massacre. Elena with her terrible postcard reared at him, like a cobra dripping venom.

Urquhart opened his eyes and blinked at her. 'Franco

shot Carlos? Is that what ye're telling me?'

'No, Angus.' She uncoiled herself. Pressed closer. 'Carlos is not here, Angus. He is away in the mountains. He is searching for you, his good friend who brings guns.'

The old man covered his eyes again. Henry felt for him.

'He does not find you, Angus. He find children dumb with terror. Women who wail and curse and batter him with bloody fists. Eighty-nine corpses. He dip his hands in their spilled blood. He pour it on his head.' She lifted cupped palms over Urquhart's white fan of hair. 'There is a well, Angus. In this *my* village there is a well. Shall we laugh at this well? No? You not wish to laugh? It is there still. Three months ago I lean and look into it. It is deep and dark. The water is too far to see. Even the echoes die. Carlos, my grandfather, he leave his shoes at the door of the house. He is walking barefoot through the blood, towards the well. His feet make prints, the heels, the toes. Juanita, my mother, she is running after him. She is afraid, she want her father's arms. But he forget his children. He is standing at the well. He is securing the rope and fastening it round his neck. He is folding his arms, tight across his chest. He is stepping onto the wall. Into the well.' Elena stood so close, her lips almost touched Urquhart's fingers. 'This is how it is done,' she hissed, 'the murder of a friend.'

William moved—Henry was too late to stop him. He had taken rough hold of Elena and was dragging her away from Urquhart. The postcard fell to the floor. 'Watch yourself, lady,' he said. 'That's not murder.'

'Let her go!' Henry balled his fists.

'Aye, William. Do as he says. Let go.' Urquhart had

lowered his hands from his face. He leant to retrieve the postcard from the carpet. He read it, turned it, read it again. Then he made a strange sound—half cough, half sob—and stared wildly around, as though seeing the bodies of the dead. 'A traitor, aye,' he said at last. 'A murderer, aye, I am. These things and more. Tis every word of it the truth.'

Henry shivered as the old man stretched to touch Elena's cheek. 'I see it now. Thou art so very like.'

Elena

Now would come his supplications. Yes, here they began, creeping like rats from his evil mouth. His eyes pleaded, his bony fingers reached for her. She threw off William's hands and backed away, lifting her own hands, sticky with Miguel's blood, where *el malo* could not touch them.

But the old man was following her, pushing past those who tried to prevent him. His tears had dried, his eyes burned bright, she could not look away.

'It was revenge, Elena,' he was saying. 'It was revenge I was taking. But it was nae use. Believe me, revenge is nae use at all.'

She would not listen. She would not hear. Revenge would make her free.

'Not bringing guns in someone else's war?' William shouted stupid excuses. 'That's not murder. How is it murder?' She swung to face him, mouth wide with fury.

But Angus Urquhart was answering for her. 'I took money, William. I promised guns. I smiled and wrote this lying postcard. Look at it. *Trust me, Carlos. Urquhart.* Picture of Nessie. A grand wee joke, dost thou think?' He cackled like a soul in hell. He followed each step she retreated. "'*Adios, mi amigo,*" I said to Carlos. "To God, my friend." While in ma heart I wished him to the devil. I had guns to bring, but I ne'er intended to bring them, not to this village. I wanted ma revenge.'

Almost his look was proud, as though she would applaud him. She stared in horror. He saw her horror. 'But Miguel, Elena,' his eyes implored her, 'it was a terrible war, but I didnae ken that they would kill the bairns.'

'But why? Why do it, Calum?' Peter it was who asked. Peter, her mirror. 'Revenge on whom? For what?'

The old man did not look at Peter—instead he pressed closer still to her. Her back was against the panelled wall. His eyes searched hers, his bloodless lips in the white beard moved to speak again.

'No!' She shook her head. She almost screamed.

El malo took her hands. 'Murder for murder.' His words cut into her head. 'Thou art so like, ma heart breaks even now.'

She stared at him. He did not mean her mother.

'Teresa. They killed ma love. Teresa.'

Peter

The Sun's rim dips; the stars rush out:
    At one stride comes the dark.

Calum, his father, skinny hand and glittering eye, holding Señorita like the Ancient Mariner. 'They murdered her for loving me.'

Of course! Spain! True meaning of the poem! He'd known the truth, held it then lost it, side-tracked by vision of Ma and Calum eagerly begetting him. But no, it would not do. *Far far colder, that is how it was.* Clapham not cold enough by far. Ma's heat not hot enough and several bra-sizes too small.

'Teresa.' Calum whispering the name. *Teresa.* His Eve, his Aphrodite. Some shadow of her found and lost in Ma. And found now, found again in glorious, angry Señorita. The old man's fingers hovered over cheeks, lips, shoulders. Elena was a risen ghost. Peter had tasted where his father had feasted.

'Teresa.' The name was poetry, offered up as prayer. 'I loved Teresa. She loved me. Thy grandfather, thy uncles—they knew, but they didnae say they knew. They killed her, but they didnae tell me they had killed her. She fell from the mountain path. They wept, and I believed them. I wept too and watched them bury her.' Calum clutching Señorita's sleeve, spilling grief. 'But then, her mother, Teresa's own poor mother, confessed the truth to me. Whispered how Carlos wasnae ma friend. Told me how Carlos, his brothers, his neighbours, all the men together, carried her sweet Teresa up the mountain and threw her down, screaming out ma name. And they would kill me too, her mother said, the minute they had ma guns.'

Señorita shrieking, 'No!' Ducking through Calum's arms, landing in Henry's, who dived like portly Superman for Lois Lane.

Room full of dumb Muppets. Was no one keeping up here? Would no one state the obvious? 'But Calum, you still haven't told them why. *Why* did Carlos kill Teresa?'

His father turning, blue eyes vacant, fixed on sobbing Señorita rocked in Clark Kent's arms. Opening his poet's mouth again. 'For the worst of all reasons in the world. Because she was his wife.'

Chapter Thirty-one

Elena

'It's all right. It will be all right.'

Henry's arms were tightening round her. He pulled her to a sofa. She went with him. There was nowhere else to go.

Nothing had changed. She had told the truth, yet still she had no peace.

'Do ye understand me, Elena?' Urquhart had followed her. His hand pawed her arm. She could not lift her eyes to see his face. She saw instead his knees, bent sharp and white on the blood-red carpet below the pleats of his kilt. Urquhart kneeling at her feet. Her grandmother's lover. 'Tell me ye understand.'

A selfish old man demanding her forgiveness. A man who robbed a husband of his wife, two children of their mother, murdered a whole village, expecting her forgiveness! A great cry burst from her.

'Leave her alone,' said Henry. He was pulling her closer and pushing the old man away. She could smell the sweat in the soft fabric of his shirt.

'Nae, Elena,' Urquhart pleaded.

You think you can do anything. You think you are God. These insults she had heard from the mouths of his angry sons. Sons who had known their father all their lives and did not forgive him.

'Tell me ye understand why I brought nae guns.'

It was shame that kept her eyes downcast. Understanding this, she was suddenly free of shame. Into her mouth sprang the word that would defeat her enemy. She broke from Henry's arms to scream in the old man's face. 'It is *romance*. Your heroic deeds, your poetry, the tragic story of your life. It is nothing but *romance!*'

She saw his eyes widen with self-knowledge. He had no answer for her. She watched him blink and begin to crumble.

The Urquharts were muttering and protesting, but—

'Bravo, Elena,' Henry said fiercely. 'To hell with romance. You tell it how it is.'

She took a breath. Hannah came nosing into her lap, but otherwise the room was motionless, waiting for her words.

At her feet an old man was weeping. In her lap lay the uncomprehending head of a dog. At her side was Henry Jennings. She was in the Scottish Highlands, far from...

Far from where? From home? All her life she had been far from home.

Tell it how it is? It was difficult, but yes, there *was* more to tell. Her own story. Her own pain.

'My mother and my aunt,' she said quietly. 'Seven and five years old, they see these terrible things. And then they are alone. The women hate them. The priests, returning, hate them. The hatred is for you, Angus. And yes,' at last she understood, 'for Teresa and Carlos also. But you are gone. Teresa and Carlos are dead. Teresa's mother also soon is dead. There is no one left to hate through the years of hunger and the longer years of throwing blame. No one but two little girls. And then me. Another little girl.'

She understood completely. She spoke with passion to

these staring Urquharts. She needed them to understand with her. 'For that is our sin, also, to be girls. If we are boys, we are dead, like the sons and brothers of these women. But we are alive. This is our shame, which we cannot escape or confess. Which we cannot be forgiven. But it is not our shame. It is not my shame, Angus. It belong to Carlos and Teresa. It belong to *you*.'

'I know.' Urquhart lifted his agonised face. 'D'ye not think I know? I lost the woman I loved. I betrayed ma friends. I gave the war to Franco! And then I found I'd lost the power to write! I tried to throw away ma life in France to bring the poetry back, but God refused ma life and still the poetry wouldnae come.'

He gave a great, gasping sob. She stared at him. He gave the war to Franco? God refused to take his life? Did his vanity have no limit?

'Honour, honour, honour lost. Lost and never found. Searched for in the bowels of hell. Glimpsed—I have it still—and lost again.' Peter was reciting. Was this Edgar Allen Poe?

'Ah, Peter, lad.'

Hands were lifting the old man from the floor, were patting and comforting him. Tears were running through the wrinkles in his cheeks and into his beard. Elena watched them, feeling nothing.

Henry was stroking her hair. 'It's all right, all done, Elena. You will feel better.'

But she felt nothing. This was how it was.

Henry

He was touching her ear! He was touching her hair! His

242

shirt was splashed with her tears!

Hannah settled herself more heavily on his feet. Elena sighed and closed her eyes.

The Spanish civil war. Revenge and counter-revenge. The room was boiling with it, but what did any of it matter? He was floating in a bubble of bliss with a real woman and an equable dog.

'This is brilliant stuff and I hate to say it, but I have to get back to the kitchen,' said James. The metal in his face glinted as he winked at Henry. He swept the floor in a low bow and exited.

Elena's hair had a lemony smell. Henry gazed happily around the room.

Big Owen and efficient Janet were guiding the old man to another sofa. Janet was dabbing at his face with a handkerchief, while Owen spoke in calming tones.

William and Gavin were in a huddle near the fireplace, glowering first at Urquhart, then at Elena, then at Peter, uncertain on whom to vent their bad temper.

Peter seemed dumbstruck. Thin and shabby in his black poet's uniform, he crouched in an armchair, hugging his knees with his nibbled fingers. He gazed at his curate's egg of a father.

In the centre of the room, Fiona stood motionless, hands by her sides. Her cheeks were wet too, Henry noticed—he should help her somehow. But no, Gavin's girlfriend, Kim, was doing the job. The two women embraced in a long, wordless hug.

Peter's family, he was seeing. His own family too in a sort of a way. His brother's father's family. His mother's lover's family. He tried to comprehend the net of relationships into which he had stumbled.

Elena's man. That was what he wanted to be. Her hair tickled his nose. She opened her eyes and looked at him. 'I think I must go to my room, Henry. I must be alone.'

'Yes, of course.' He couldn't bear to part with her. He heaved the dog off his feet and helped her to stand. 'Of course you must.'

He would escort her, see her safely there. He might encounter Michael McCoy on the way, but it didn't matter, not in the slightest—he would risk embarrassment for Elena. He would risk more than embarrassment for Elena. Only Elena mattered now.

Peter

Honour lost.

He hugged his knees.

The power of writing lost.

He stared at Calum.

Calum, his father. His *father*. Found.

His father weeping. Lost.

Revenge nae use at all. Nothing salvaged but *'romance'*.

Pitiless Venus, reborn from the foam of time. Her lover, Mars, slain by a word. *Romance.*

All wrecked and swept away. His poems, his father's poems, worthless romance. No point in poetry.

Crazy flotsam of characters. Venus with Charon and Cerberus, floating by on the ebbtide. Hercules harbouring Mars on sofa. Castor and Pollox dampened, muttering by dead fire.

Love, lust, murder, rage, revenge, the deeds of war, the fires of Calum's soul. All doused by dishonour, drowning in romance.

No, not so!

Far far colder, that is how it was.

Poetry mattered!

The famous poet is here with me today.

Leap from chair.

Ma last and greatest.

Yes! The poem! Beautiful in its despair and honesty. No, more than honesty, in its transcendent truth!

Where was it? He must read it at once, from start to finish, knowing all. Spain and France and Clapham. Teresa, French petticoats and Ma. Yes, no time to lose. Whole world at stake.

Fuck! Where was his rucksack? Quick! Rewind!

Here? No. Up mountain? No. In the aquarium out front? Yes! Shit! Scramble for door, elbow past Venus and Clark Kent. Oh fuck, fuck, fuck, it had to still be there!

Chapter Thirty-two

Peter

Honour, honour, honour lost. Calum's words drumming in his head. Brain blank with fear of loss, feet a-skid along passage into—

Wham, *déjà vu!* In Surround-sound, Technicolor Smell-o-Vision. Four-year-old alter ego with backdrop of iron-studded door, in creaking, woodworm-scented hall. Georgie in jimjams with puzzled blue eyes. 'Are you my uncle?'

No time for this. But no, it mattered! Knock history from its groove! 'Yes. Too right. I am.' Sweep child off doormat, clasp him to chest. Heavy little legs agrip round waist. Twenty-five years ago, if Calum had done this, the world would have shifted.

Lost and never found. No! On and under stone arch, child clinging like monkey. Tripping on rugs, brain vaulting ahead. Deserted aquarium, glass wall black sheet of night. Race round sofa end, willing rucksack to be there. 'Oh no! Oh please!'

Searched for in the bowels of hell. Spin, lurch, bend. It must be here. Black canvas bag. A simple enough request of the universe. It existed, *here* on this sofa. Elena's bags, his rucksack. Did she take it? No! It was *here*, he left it *here!* Child's head bumping against chin. 'Oh fuck, fuck, fucking hell, I've lost it, Georgie!'

'May I be of assistance, sir?' Obese waiter with slimy smile.

Pleading, out of breath. 'My bag. Black. A rucksack. It was just—'

'Yes, sir.' Voice of high disdain. 'I believe I have the item. Be so kind as to wait here. I will bring it to you.'

Collapse on sofa, chest tight with joy, arms tight with child. 'Oh thank you, thank you, God!'

Open eyes. Meet child close-up. Child whispering. 'I like rude words.'

Sudden thought. 'Do you like poems?'

'Yes. Is your name Peter?'

'Yes. Truly, you like poems?'

'Yes. And you're my Uncle Peter?'

'Yes. Which poems are best?'

'Winnie the Pooh. My uncles give me presents. Will you give me presents?'

Winnie the fucking Pooh? 'Yes, I suppose, if you remind me.'

Unctuous waiter back, nose wrinkled, bearing miracle of scuffed black canvas.

'Ta, mate.' Wrench cord loose, and reach in—yes! wham! yes!—find miracle of Jiffybag stuffed with worn A4.

I have it still. He had it still! Calum! Calum's genius.

'Will you be requiring anything from the bar, sir?'

Bounce child, nod vigorously. A toast to genius past and future, and to A A Milne.

'What've you got?'

'The local malt is considered fine.'

'Right, mate. Wheel it in.' Shift child to cushion. Pull

out poem. Smooth pages. Count them. Fiona still had the last.

'Georgie! What are you doing out of bed?'

Speak of the devil, angelic Fi—his sister, hold that thought—luminous in stone arch. Her eyes—his own eyes—pink from weeping.

'It's okay, Fi. He's fine. We're getting acquainted.'

'He's my Uncle Peter.'

'Yes.' Advancing her petite self from archway across baronial rugs. 'That's who he is.'

Waiter in swift, sly overtake, silver tray afloat on fingertips, oily malt swaying in cut glass tumbler, smart aleck eyes aflicker over denims. 'That will be three pounds fifty, sir. Or do you prefer I charge it to your room?'

Open mouth to trash the bastard, but Fiona was there first. 'Gordon, I'm so sorry. Has no one explained? This is Peter Jennings, my half-brother from London, one of three family guests we have today.'

'Hi, Gord.' Seize squeamish hand.

'I beg your pardon, sir.' Fleeing the scene.

Respect, a poet father, everything: the whole lot, FU's doing. *Peter, I promise, be patient, the reward will surprise you.*

'Fiona?'

'Peter?'

Leaning close, over Georgie's head. 'The poem. It's great.'

'I know.' Her eyes shining wet. 'Whatever my father is, whatever he's done—'

'Yes!' Make her believe it. 'Truly great. I must read it again. There's no doubt, Fi, the story's there. But more than any story, the human soul laid bare.'

His own eyes filling with tears. Blink them away.

'So now, the last page, Fiona. May I?'

'Of course. I'll fetch it.' Showering blessings on his head. His fairy godmother.

'Thank you. I'll take good care of it, I promise.'

Smiling through her tears. 'It's not the only copy. I'm sorry I made you think so. But all the same, he wrote it, so it's—'

'Precious, you said.'

'Yes. He copied it for me.'

Deep breath, expecting to be angry. He should be angry. Twice he'd thought he'd lost the only one.

Not angry. Absence of anger. Another gift from Fi.

'I'll bring it straightaway. Come on, Georgie. Time for bed.' Such lovely, sad, grey eyes.

'O-o-oh.' Georgie whingeing like a good un. 'Please let me stay. This is my Uncle Peter.'

Lean forward, touch her hand. 'Hey, little Fi.'

'Hey what, impossible P?'

'Hey, thanks for everything, big sis.'

Henry

'This is my room.'

The door was open, the space beyond was floral pink. Henry made himself let go of Elena's arm, but she seemed stuck, unable to cross the threshold. The dog stalled too, wagging her tail nonsensically. On or back, it was the same to Hannah.

Henry remembered last night outside the guesthouse under the frozen stars, how Elena had shivered as she began to take off his Barbour, how she'd relented and invited him in. *To be more warm before you go.*

He took courage from the memory and spoke. 'Are you quite sure you want to be alone?'

Her face was calm. A tear swelled and spilled as though it belonged to someone else, as though it had no meaning.

He understood. He knew what it was to weep like this. After Ingrid left, after his mother died, he had wept like this.

'Because you aren't alone,' he told Elena lamely. 'Things will, you know, seem better.'

She nodded, and then shook her head. 'I am alone completely. I am always alone.'

What better moment would there be than this, what clearer cue? He banished nervousness and second thoughts. 'Not if you don't want to be.'

Her eyes lifted to meet his, startled yet shining. She understood. 'Henry.'

She might say yes. He couldn't bear to hear her say no. Nonsense began blurting from his mouth.

'I know I lied to you, but I'm not, you know...'

'Yes, Henry. I know.'

'Elena, it's... won't you...' He could find no sensible words. Reckless words offered themselves, words he couldn't possibly speak. Her eyes shone as dark and deep as last night, trusting, grateful, full of—dare he believe it? Dare he even think it? 'Elena, you must...' No. That was wrong. 'I don't mean... I realise...'

She took his hand. 'Henry. Please. Come.' She put a finger on his lips. She led him and the dog inside and closed the door. 'Cognac,' she said. 'We both need cognac.'

The room throbbed with pink. Hannah reconnoitred

the furniture. Elena headed for the minibar, opened it and peered inside, then hung her head. 'No cognac. Only whisky. And cold. It should not be cold.'

Her voice was flat, she wasn't meeting his eyes. He tried to cling to hope, but it was useless. She meant to pour him strong drink and to tell him in the gentlest way—if he were the last poor bugger on earth, she wouldn't in a million years.

'You want me to go. You want to be alone.' Please say it wasn't so.

'It is not so, Henry,' she whispered.

She knelt by the mini-bar, staring dismally at the roses on the carpet, tracing their petals with a finger. The dog slumped flat by the bed and heaved a mighty canine sigh.

How selfish he was being. Her grandmother had been murdered. Her grandfather was a murderer. Urquhart had outmanoeuvred her at every turn, producing Peter like a moth-eaten rabbit from a hat, then capping her, outrage for outrage, until she had nothing left to throw at him. And now, to cap it all, poor Elena, she had to deal with an unwanted suitor. God, this reality business was hard to do.

Though it made speech easier. 'Look Elena, I'm sorry. Please forget it. Gone as if I never spoke. Don't know what came over me. Brandy's an excellent plan. There's a nice warm bottle of it in my room. I'll be straight back.'

Hannah struggled to her feet and lumbered after him.

Elena

The door closed. She stared at the carpet. The roses mocked her.

It was done. She had shamed Urquhart. With one

251

word she had killed the arrogance in his eyes.

Romance.

The word was a bee's sting—it had killed her also. Its poison had spread from her mouth to her brain. There was no antidote. Her shame and rage, her exile from her native land, all romance. Her life was melodrama, her revenge was spite.

She had gained nothing. She had lost Mikhail. Her throat tightened with grief.

And now, Henry—this gentle Englishman in a soft checked shirt that smelled of anxiety—he offered her romance.

This room, with all its roses, screamed romance.

Henry's eyes had been wide with hope, watching her mouth, wanting so little from it, only the small word 'yes'.

A sheepskin coat was on the bed. New boots stood beside it. Almost happy she had been this morning, choosing these things with Henry from a shop bright with sunshine, while children played music for dancing.

Henry was alone. She was alone. Shall we go on *together*, that was his question.

She had no place in the world. *I* am your place in the world, that was his answer.

She rose from her knees and went to the window. She could see nothing, only Land-Rovers and Fiona's little Citroën in the light from the salon below. The lake, the mountain path, the road to Inverness, all were swallowed by the night.

Things will, you know, seem better.

She could see nothing. She felt nothing. This was how it was.

Chapter Thirty-three

Henry

The only route he knew to his room and to the abandoned bottle of brandy was down, along and up again through the back parlour. There was no one about as he and Hannah negotiated the creaking spiral staircase to the hall. Presumably Michael McCoy and the Americans were busy admiring their reflections and tucking into their steaks in that appalling tartan Underground station. Because actually, speaking frankly, Mr William bully-boy Urquhart, builder, decorator, and 'entrepreneur', no, he did not like the house one bit.

Most of all he detested this hall, the gloomy, evil-smelling hub of the web. With Hannah close at his heels, he sped across it into the oppressive passage beyond. So far, so unobserved. He'd had a bellyful of other people. He'd be up the fireplace stairs, have the bottle safe and be winging it back to Elena in no time.

Elena. Elena. She hadn't wanted him to go away. She hadn't told him to get lost. He was crazy, fantasising again. But no, how did any normal chap go about landing a woman? You had to imagine what could be and chance your luck, didn't you? You had to say, 'Will you?' You had to risk the answer no.

He pushed open the parlour door. With its old-fashioned panelling, assorted sofas and dead fireplace, the room had the deserted air of a stage without actors. But then, damn it all, James's disembodied head twisted to grin at him above a chair-back, and Hannah bounded forward, delivering her usual sneezes.

'Hello there. Were you wanting to join us?' The spikes in James's lips gleamed.

'Hello. No, thanks.'

Henry managed a smile. There were worse encounters to be feared. This fellow was completely off his hostess trolley, yet the craziness seemed honest, not put on. But there was no space in Henry's brain for merry chitchat. He gathered momentum towards the fireplace.

'Just passing through. Fetching brandy. Elena feels the need.'

'I'll bet she does, poor kid. Hannah! *Sit!*'

Henry had the door in the wall open and his foot on the stair. He swung to smile again.

'Oh. Good heavens. I'm sorry. I...'

Kneeling at James's feet was Michael McCoy, offering Marjorie Macpherson's smile. 'It's good to see you, Henry. I hope things are working out for you.'

Henry's feet were backing him up the stairs. He could no longer see the two beaming faces, only knees, trousers, Hannah's thrashing tail, and the twitching head of the Loch Craggan monster.

He turned and scurried to his room, where he poured and downed a triple slug. He was shaking with he didn't quite know what emotion: shock, relief, a piquant, foolish stab of loss. Only one thing was for sure, he would have to find another way back.

Elena

She was ready when his knock came. She knew what she would say. But he seemed changed also when she opened the door. More strong perhaps, more tall and confident, less fearful of her answer, yes or no. He smelled of cognac, but that was not the reason, or not all of it.

'Where is Hannah? Has something happened, Henry?'

'Yes,' he said. 'Something has.' He filled her glass. 'Or perhaps not quite yet. They had a way to go.'

She did not understand him. She inhaled the cognac fumes and took a gulp. It made her shudder. 'What do you mean?'

He poured one for himself, then stared past her, through the window, speaking as if to the mountain. 'Michael McCoy and James Urquhart. I found them at it in the back sitting-room.'

'The writer... and the chef?' She struggled to comprehend.

Henry's gaze dropped from the window to examine his cognac. 'Yes. You know. At it. Having sex.' He drank it in one swallow, then lifted his eyes to meet hers. 'They weren't bothered by my passing through. Hospitable, one might say. But I explained I had a prior engagement, and they let me go, no fuss.'

She did not know what to say.

He pulled a face. 'I'm sorry. Perhaps this offends you?'

'No. No, not at all. I... It confuses me.'

'To say the least. But then again,' he paused, 'it settles so much.'

Elena giggled. The giggle surprised her. 'But I should not laugh.'

'Yes, you should, I think,' he said gravely. 'And so should I.' He poured himself more cognac and turned to face her. 'So. What d'you know?' He raised his glass.

'What do I know?'

'Sorry. It's an Englishism. It means "funny old world."'

She clinked his glass. 'What do I know?'

He was grinning suddenly. 'No,' he said. 'It's "What d'*you* know."'

She tried again. 'What do you know?'

He began to laugh. He took a giant swallow of cognac. 'Nar-thing,' he said in a strangely altered voice. 'I know nar-thing. I'm from Barcelona.'

Peter

'Night-night, Uncle Peter.'

Fiona off to fetch last page, Georgie on hip. Great arse his sister had, regrettably. But hang on, multiple choice, sister with great arse, sister with sad arse, not so tricky, and there were shoals more fish in the aquarium. Elena, do *not* forget Elena. Teresa resurrected in seminal snog. And here swam another. Doable Kim, property of brother Gavin, drifting under arch towards him. Great hair, great legs. 'Hi, Kim.'

'Hi, Peter.' Landing beside him, abounce in her pink boob-tube, face flushed and eager. 'Boy, wasn't that something else? More excitement than we're used to round here. Houseful of casualties. Are you dead or only wounded?'

'I'm fine, thanks. More than fine, I'm blown away. High as a space station, not sure which way is up.'

'Because Angus is your father?'

'Yes! Would you believe it!' Lift pages and kiss them.

'What's that?'

'An incredible new poem of his. An epic lament for his life. Spain, France, my Ma, the lot.'

'Gosh, really? May I see?' Hair ablaze, back-lit by lamp. Folding long legs beside him. Shiny stockings.

'It's in Gaelic. I'm translating.'

'How exciting. I could help.'

'Do you know Gaelic?'

'No, but I'm an ace at synonyms.' Her smile was wicked.

Lean in closer. 'Won't Gavin chew my balls off?'

'More than he wants to already, you mean?'

Here came Fi with Calum's last page. Quick, unpack dictionary from rucksack, get stuck in.

'Can *you* read Gaelic, Fiona?'

Good question, Kim, and, 'Yes,' she said, 'I can.'

Unbelievable. His *sister*, Fiona. Leaning over sofa-back, hand on his shoulder, scanning final stanzas.

His father, Calum Calum's blue Quink trail. Brain not in gear, swallow pride. 'I don't get it. Who's he talking to here?'

'Himself.'

'It can't be, it's two people.'

'Himself as poet *and* as man. Look. *Mar bhàrd agus mar dhuine.*' Perfect pitch, her accent musical.

Kim's thigh pressing. Savour female heat of it. 'So what's he telling himself?'

Fiona answering. '*Se bàird a tha annaibh le chéile.* You are poets both of you.'

'Of course! As poet *and* as man!'

His sister's weight on his neck, her breath in his ear, his

sister's finger tracing Calum's thread of blue. '*Bha fìor dheagh bhàrdachd anns na h-òrain sin.* There was fine poetry in those songs.'

'Yes!'

'*Is anns na sgeulachdan cuideachd.* And in the stories too.'

'Meaning his *life* is poetry!' Rush of adrenaline. Race to decode last verse in bliss of sibling rivalry.

Fiona too fast for him, one beat ahead, reeling the meaning out. 'Each kiss now cold. From cold, through cold, to cold.'

Skim eye ahead to last line. *Mar sin leibh.* Too easy, but better than nothing. Point to the words. Hold steady. Fiona unspooling line before. 'All done, all gone. No more to do or write. No more to know.'

Jump in. Declaim. 'Farewell!' Meet Kim's bright eyes, triumphant. Turn to Fi. 'What is it, Fi? What's wrong?'

Her face transfixed, alarmed, staring at poem. *Mar sin leibh.* Angus Urquhart 1999. Unsteady signature.

'Where is he?' Fiona upright, staring through archway, starting to run. 'Father! Who's with father? Father, where are you?' Feet clattering on flags, voice ringing echoes. 'Can anyone hear me? Does anyone know where Angus is?'

Chapter Thirty-four

Elena

Henry had stopped laughing and swallowing cognac. His face was serious again and close to hers. The time had come to answer him.

She put down her empty glass and took a breath. Then she faced him squarely and touched his hand. 'You are kind and good, Henry. The question you ask me before. I am flattered, truly, but I must say no.'

He retreated from her touch. The light left his face. 'Of course you must,' he said. 'It's quite all right.' Already he had found the door and was turning the handle to escape. His wretchedness was hard to watch. His hurt was hurting her.

'Henry, I do not mean to distress you. Permit me please to explain?'

He let go of the handle and stood, with eyes downcast, like a kicked dog waiting for the door to open.

She had prepared her words. She thought they would be easy to say. But they seemed impossible, and wrong. 'I should have said. In Brussels I have... I had... a friend.'

'Of course,' he repeated. He glared at the pink roses. 'Of course you have. Attractive woman like you, presumptuous of me.'

'No, Henry. Not presumptuous, not at all. I had a friend, but it is finished. He is gone away.' To say the words aloud made them true. Gone away. She felt the tears rising and swallowed them. To cry would be unfair to Henry. 'But he, my friend... Please understand, it is too soon.'

Henry made a tortured sound. She was explaining this so clumsily.

'I am truly sorry, Henry. It is not you. I am to blame. There is much wrong in me.'

He blinked and lifted his eyes. 'There is nothing wrong with you, Elena.'

His kindness swelled her tears. She almost yielded to them. But no, she would remain strong, for Henry's sake. 'There is much wrong.' She found that to confess this increased her strength. 'I am injured by my past life, as... as you are also, Henry. So you are not right for me, I am not right for you.'

Mikhail was uninjured. She had not understood this before, and now it was too late. She swallowed the sharp lump of grief. She went to the window and stared into the pool of light below. Gone away. She struggled to comprehend. She must return alone to Brussels. She must find her way without Mikhail.

Henry had followed her to the window. He stood by her side, staring into the night. 'I'm changing,' he said. 'I think I'm recovering. It's early to say. Not completely of course, I won't ever recover completely. But maybe, perhaps, do you think, rather than be alone, we might be stronger, you know, together?'

She looked at him. He looked at her. He was right. She had not answered him with truth. 'But I do not think I can love you, Henry.'

He closed his eyes and opened them again. 'You're sure?

She barely nodded. He turned his face to the window. She moved so her shoulder touched his. He did not move away—he leant against her. They stood a moment, feeling the contact. He cleared his throat. 'So what will you do?' His voice was sad. He did not hate her.

What would she do? But of course, the decision was made. 'I will go to live in Spain.'

'Father! Father!' Fiona was calling in the corridor. 'Father, where are you?'

'What's the matter?' Henry ran to open the door.

'I can't find him anywhere.' Fiona's eyes were searching the corridor as she panted words. 'He was with Owen, with Janet. But then, the guests... he told them he was fine. He told them he would be with me... with Peter.'

Peter

Up, up, haring up the creaking spiral, seeking Calum, house below echoing with voices. 'Father!' 'Angus!' 'Mr Urquhart!' Only he in search of Calum. Hugging rucksack to chest. Poem safe, but Calum lost—no, let it not be!

High landing, abandoned passage off. Line of low doors, each locked or opening into cell of nothing. No heat, no furniture, no Calum. Race to stairwell, climb and climb again. No use, he knew where Calum was.

Rewind. Replay. Mars slain by a word at Venus's feet. Only he heard that word's killing power. Only he saw Mars stagger and begin to die. How had he abandoned him?

Drive himself upward, heart bursting, knees aching, spiral narrowing to turret door and elements beyond. Push, hard, shoulder to oak, patter of rust shards from complaining hinges, burst through into whirling Highland space.

Lightning flickering across the sky. And there he was, the old man on the mountain! Mars shrunk to Lilliputian, scaling Gulliver's side. Petulant growl rumbling down valley, shaking the black waters of the loch. Yell back. '*Calum!* CALUM!!!'

Useless. Words hitting wall of Gulliver's condensed breath and dropping like Elena's phone to the gravel.

Turn. Run. Back to wooden corkscrew. Down, round, hurdling steps, stumbling, dizzy, yelling again, 'He's on the mountain. He's climbing the mountain. We must go after him.'

Henry

Peter collapsed against the banister rail, his face streaming with sweat. Fiona cried out, 'Oh my God! Father! Please!' and started down the last two flights.

Henry threw Elena a look. She nodded. He went after Fiona. He caught up with her in the hall. She was fighting her way into a yellow windcheater. He fumbled to help her, comprehending dimly that he was drunk.

'The flashlight. Where have they put it? I need the flashlight.'

But not incapable. He checked his breast pocket. 'I have my torch.' He seized a windcheater for himself and managed to get it on.

Urquharts were emerging from the woodwork, though none of them seemed to share Fiona's alarm. Come to think of it, why *was* she panicking? Kim arranged herself languidly in the stone archway. James peered with a sleepy smile from the first floor landing. Two children had joined Elena on the one above. William and Gavin stuck their heads around a door, sneering, 'What's the fuss?'

'Father's on the mountain!'

'So what?' 'What's new?'

'He's in no state to be alone. I'm going after.'

More people were arriving. Peter, still out of breath, plus Owen, Janet and Gordon the waiter. The mayhem was growing. Hannah and Mabel had started up barking and, bugger it, here came the Americans. 'What's doing here? Can we help?'

'No!' Fiona screamed at them. She heaved the front door open and ran out.

Henry tried to focus. Someone had turned on the hall light. People seemed afflicted with slow motion as though drenched in honey. If he hesitated the honey would engulf him. It was nice and warm here. The old man was probably just toddling off to bed, which was where Henry yearned to be too, horizontal, eyes shut, in a vortex of brandy. But no, damn it, he couldn't let Fiona go alone.

A tidal wave of drunkenness swamped him as the cold air hit. He made himself survive it. He could barely see her—she had already crossed the pool of light from the glass wall. The scrunch of her feet on the gravel told him she was running. He blundered after her.

'Henry?'

'Yes?'

'Your torch?'

'It's here.' It was out of his pocket. Click, and there was light. A slender beam reaching through the rain, finding the start of the path. And Fiona was off again, calling, 'Father! Wait for me! I'm coming!'

Behind them, the honey was spilling onto the porch. Voices were calling, the words too faint to hear. Hannah's barks were growing louder, beginning to catch them up. More people were following perhaps, but there was no time to wait for them.

Chapter Thirty-five

Henry

The brandy glow had evaporated—he was sobering up fast. The wind clawed through the thin waterproof. His jacket was no match for this cold. He tried not to think about his cap, gloves and Barbour, lying useless in the bedroom far below. A couple of minutes was all it would have taken to fetch them.

The night was pitch-black and thick with mist, which numbed his face. The beam of the toy torch, dissipated by tiny droplets, scarcely illuminated their feet. It was impossible to go fast, hard to know where next to tread. They should have taken the time to find the flashlight. Hannah wasn't helping, bumping against their legs, a guide dog with no eyes.

'Oh Hannah, stop it! Please!' Fiona seemed on the verge of hysteria.

Henry tried to calm her. 'Your father, he can't go fast either. He has no light.'

She moaned. 'He needs no light. He knows the way blindfold.' Hurrying along in the dark beside him, she began to sob. 'It's all my fault—I should have realised. What upset him so—why he wrote the poem. It wasn't your mother, it was Spain.'

'What do you mean?'

'The book group, December, they talked about *Homage to Catalonia*, and he was there. They wanted his recollections. You've seen how stirred up he gets. As if he were back there, living it again.'

'The bloody book group has a lot to answer for.'

'Oh no, please no!'

'What? What's the matter?'

'Too long alive,' she wailed. 'That's what he said at Hogmanay. "I've been too long alive."'

She started to run. Henry battled to keep up, to keep her in sight with the absurd toy torch. 'We'll find him,' he panted. 'I'm sure we will.'

Lightning flickered around them. For an uncanny instant he could see where the path encountered sheer mountainside ahead. There was no sign of Urquhart. 'The steps—they'll be easier.'

God, he was cold. And here came the thunder, threatening, then fading in a snarl. Hannah whimpered and barked. 'It's all right, girl.' He patted her damp flank.

He found Fiona's hand and put the torch in it. 'I'll go first. You follow with this. I'll feel my way. I'll keep saying "I'm here" in case you lose me.'

He stretched through the darkness and found wet stone. He began to clamber. Right hand, left foot. Left hand, right foot. The steps were high and slippery, and his fingers were freezing already. 'I'm here,' he yelled. 'I'm here.'

Right, left. Left, right. Furious with Urquhart. Rotten old devil, still set on upstaging Elena. 'Elena. Elena,' he mumbled into the fog. Right, left. Left, right. He remembered her descending these steps ahead of him. Her bouncing hair that smelled of lemons. Her sumptuous, sexy voice. *I do not think I can love you, Henry.* Oh God. He must put her out of his mind. Right, left.

Left, right. As fast as he could manage. 'I'm here. Take care, Fiona. Are you all right?'

'Yes. Thank you.'

How many more steps? And then what? A flattish bit, he recalled, cut into the side of the mountain, with a precipitous drop to the right. They would have to hold hands, hold the dog's collar and go slowly, before the steep climb up around the huge rock to the hanging valley and a blind grope along to the croft.

He was crazy. Why was he doing this? *You are kind and good, Henry.* Right, left. Left, right. He wanted to howl, at the cold in his hands and the desolation waiting to seize him. 'I'm here,' he gasped.

'I'm right behind you.' She too was out of breath. 'Thank you, Henry. Thank you for helping me.'

Elena

'Let go of me! Fuck off!'

'Calm yourself. We're not leaving without the flashlight.'

Elena stood alone on the landing, watching Gavin and Peter wrestle in the hall, two floors below.

'Stand back! I'm telling you! I'm a mountain guide!'

'You're a cretin! There's no time for this! Hands off!'

Urquhart had run away. Everyone was chasing after him. But still she felt nothing. Where was her anger? She had screamed the truth, seen him defeated by a word. Was it enough?

'Calm down, laddies. I've found it. It was on the—'

'Give it here, Owen.'

'No, give it to me!'

Mikhail was gone away.

'Hush the pair of you. I think Gavin should have the flashlight and lead the way. Do you have a problem with that, Peter?'

'No! Just get your fingers out!'

Brussels without Mikhail would be unbearable. She had answered Henry truly—she would go to live in Spain.

'A cagoule. You must wear a cagoule, Peter.'

'Okay. All right. Okay.'

She barely knew Spain. She had run from it so young. Such a big country. Beautiful, people said.

'Are you coming too, Owen? William?'

'What for? Chasing the old boy up his mountain again? You're all barking mad.'

She would not return to Andalucia. Not yet. And she would keep away from mountains. A city. She preferred cities. Madrid perhaps, though Madrid had mountains. Barcelona? Henry had mentioned Barcelona. People said it was a marvellous city.

'Okay. We're off.'

'Thank fuck for that!'

Yes, Barcelona. Catalonia. A different kind of Spain. She would get a job there, make new friends, write letters to Henry if he would allow it. And perhaps, in time, she would forget Mikhail.

The front door banged below. Another, inside the house, was slammed also, by William, she supposed.

There was the murmur of American voices. 'What was all that about?' 'What's the big deal?' 'Some language that guy was using.'

'I do apologise.' Owen guided them towards the stone archway. 'There's no excuse for it, the belligerence of youth, storm in a teacup, nothing to worry about, another drink for anyone?'

For a short while, the hall was empty. Then James Urquhart, wearing leather slippers and a red silk dressing-gown and whistling softly, slipped down the stairs below and across the flagstones towards the kitchen.

Elena sighed, feeling her aloneness in this house of strangers. Those she knew best were gone, pursuing Urquhart. Again she wondered at the change in herself. She tried to imagine Urquhart, outgunned, defeated, running up his mountain, tried to find pleasure in it. Why did it mean nothing to her? Where was her anger, her obsession with *el malo*?

I didnae ken that they would kill the bairns.

His words were singing in her head.

Thou art so like, ma heart breaks even now.

She could see his blue eyes pleading, full of tears, telling her—*maldita sea!*—how Carlos killed her grandmother.

He threw ma sweet Teresa down. She was his wife.

Peter was right. Urquhart was a poet.

He would have killed me too.

Elena shook her head. Poetry was nothing—it did not buy lives, it did not earn forgiveness. She had carried her life's shame to Inverness to give to Urquhart. She had told him, he had understood. And then his tears had spilled. She had watched them follow his wrinkles into his beard, all his arrogance gone.

It was over. She gazed down into the empty hall and understood her dispassion.

The anger was over. And the shame also.

She had not passed it to Angus Urquhart. Her shame

had touched his romance, and both had disappeared.

Peter

They were going so slowly. 'Come on! Come on!'

Gavin, hogging torch and dragging feet. 'Like William says, what's the fuss?'

Searchlight finding it, the mountain path. Break into run.

Gavin alongside, light beam bouncing. 'You're mad. There's bugger-all point to this. I've only come out to keep you from breaking your neck.'

Teresa fell from a mountain path.

'The old boy pulls this trick all the time.'

They threw her off. She screamed his name. Which name?

'So here we go, chasing after him. Exactly what he wants.'

Angus, she would have cried. Angus.

'Pesky old bugger.'

Or Calum? Was Calum the name she screamed? His private *nom de guerre*? BARD'S IDENTITY DIES WITH HIS LOVER.

Gavin badgering. 'Are you going to speak to me, or what?'

'Yeah, yeah.' Stumble off track into squelching bog. Where were those steps?

'So *speak* to me then, okay?'

'About what, for fuck's sake?'

'About why we're out here. Why you're here at all.'

Real nobody, this Gavin. 'I came to find Calum—'

'Your father—'

'No, *Calum*. And she's killed him.'

'What?'

'Didn't you hear her, dumbo? Didn't you see him? She said it was all romance.'

'Big deal. So what?'

Hit of liquid ice in left sock. 'Are we lost? Pathetic mountain guide, you are.'

'Hold your water, it's this way.'

The steps at last. Tombstone ladder, weeping black rain. Gavin blocking his path. 'For fuck's sake, get a move on.' Push past and climb, with legs like pistons, eclipsing light beam, outrunning it. Fall forward onto hands, find next step, and next. 'Come on, you great lump of haggis, keep up with that torch.'

Light beam gaining. Race it, heart pounding, brain emptying, legs complaining, hands reaching, sweat breaking again. Cagoule hot, rip it off, knot sleeves round waist, up and up, head over heels, feet over light, mind over mountain, up, up, up.

'Slow down! It's dangerous ahead.'

Steps gone, hands groping in void, shuffling forward.

'Stop! Wait for me!'

Skyful of lightning, illuminating sheer drop to valley and black mass of sentinel rock. CRASH! BOOM! Push on through air pulsating with thunder.

'For Pete's sake, Peter, *stop!*' Relief of Gavin's hand on arm. 'Take this bit slowly. One slip and you're a goner.'

Blind on high wire, edging forward, feet in oval pool of light, mind dizzy with fear of tumbling arse over tip.

'That's it. We've made it. Here's the rock. Find it with your hands. The path is to the right of it.'

Palms flat on granite, feet following, up and round, up

and round, into smell, sound, taste of rushing water.

FIZZ!! CRACK!! Sky tearing, light pouring in. Strobe-lit view of croft and river. Fiona, Henry, dog, halfway there, turning, startled.

Gavin yelling. 'Stop, you two! Wait for us!'

WHAM!!! Heavens split again, welded to sentinel rock.

BANG!!! Brain seared, hands clutching at ears, mouth opening to scream. '*Calum! No!!*'

Vision of old man up to his kilt in tugging water, eyes black and blank.

Screaming his name through the darkness. Screaming like Teresa. '*Calum! Calum!*' Screaming to the others. '*He's here! Not there!*'

No poetry left. Screaming the clichés. '*Calum, don't do it! Don't jump!*'

Chapter Thirty-six

Peter

Blind and dumb. Screams going nowhere. Gavin waving flashlight aimlessly. Seize it. Henry did Morse in the scouts. Flash it at Henry. Short short short. Long. Long. Long. Short short short.

Too late? Swing beam out across river. No! God no! Nothing but water, water—No! vomit rising in throat. But yes, choke it back down, there he was. Calum, shaking head, dismissing world with hand, but still alive thank God, knees braced against the current, holding to a rock. Beside the rock nothing, a steady, sucking, black abyss.

Plunge into river, bellowing through din, 'CALUM! COME BACK!'

Throttled by sweater-neck, arms pinioned, wrestled to shore by Gavin. 'Don't even think about it, idiot. The current's lethal. If he's going, he's gone—there's nothing we can do.'

Jeans like freezing clingwrap in the wind. Impact of wet dog, barking, thrashing tail.

ZIP!!! SMASH!!! Firmament splitting again. Fiona arriving, face in torment, holding Henry's hand. 'What's wrong, Peter?'

'Look! There! Calum! You have to stop him!'

Pointing with head, arms still in Gavin's grip, flashlight on ground, but more lightning to see Calum by. 'Let go of me, you bastard!'

Thunder rolling down hanging valley like a giant bowling ball.

'Not until you promise to stay put. Most likely, he's just winding us up.'

'Fuck you, you Gavin creature, are you terminally thick! He's lost everything! His poetry! She said it didn't count!'

'*Father!*' Fiona shrieking through tumult. '*Father, come back!*'

'It *does* count! It has to count!' Struggling to escape armlock. 'Let *go* of me!'

'*Father! Come back! WE LOVE YOU!*'

'Of course!' Henry scooping up flashlight, then dropping it again. 'Of course, it's so *obvious!*' Henry yelling as though in exclusive possession of the truth. Henry unzipping and dropping his trousers.

Henry

He had suddenly understood two things.

The first was why Scotsmen wore kilts. He thrust his socks into a trouser pocket and dumped the lot into Fiona's startled hands. He pushed his feet back into his shoes, snatched up the flashlight again and began to edge out into the icy current. Jesus, it burned!

Hannah was barking, Gavin was shouting and swearing, but he ignored them. He swung the flashlight to his own face. 'W—ai—t.' He gave the word a big, silent mouth, hoping the old man could see, could lip-read. 'Wait. Please. I've something to say.'

For he must tell Urquhart the second thing he had so suddenly understood. He didn't yet have words for it, but he knew words would come and would show the old man he need not jump. He shone the light across the rushing stream, low so as not to dazzle him.

The current was deadly, ice-cold and strong, and deeper with each step. He struggled to stay upright on the shifting, slippery stones. His shinbones were throbbing in a way that dragged at his stomach, and he couldn't feel his knees. He ploughed upstream, away from the sucking mouth of the falls, steering a curving path towards Urquhart.

He found a rock that cleared the surface, and clung to it. He mustn't die. He refused to die.

'Stop!' The old man was yelling at him across the last few feet of water. 'Stop there, or I'm away.'

'All right. I've stopped.' He hurled his voice into the uproar of the falls. 'Can you hear me?'

'Aye. What have ye to say?'

'Just this, sir.' It seemed like nonsense. There was no power in it. But there was nothing else to say. He bellowed across the racing water. 'No one can live without romance, sir.'

Was it so banal? He didn't think so. He gathered courage. 'If they can...' He was gasping, pulling in gulps of freezing rain. He shouldn't have drunk all that brandy. '... they must be very dull... they might just as well... jump off mountains.'

The water rushed between them. He dared to touch the old man's face with torchlight. There was no smile or frown.

'The thing is, sir,' his lungs were seizing up, he pushed the words out, 'to find the right amount... of romance... illusion... of *hope*, damn it...'

It was useless. Urquhart was turning his head away,

towards the sucking edge. Henry found his second wind, enough to shout hoarsely, 'No, sir. Come back, sir, please. We *need* your romance. Peter needs it. Fiona needs it. Fiona loves you.'

He collapsed onto his rock, exhausted by the effort, fearful of the numbness creeping up his body. With shaking hands he managed to aim the flashlight again. The old man's mouth was moving.

'What, sir?' Henry forced more words past his rigid jaw. 'Please, what did you say?'

Urquhart let go of his rock and raised his face to heaven. 'I said I'm finished with it. There's nothing left to do.' He swayed in the current, his arms outstretched.

Henry had no more strength to speak or arguments to offer.

But yes! He did!

'*Elena!*' A strangled shriek, powered by fury, half-lifted him from the water. 'Listen to me, you selfish old bugger! You cannot do this to *Elena!* Is that what you want, you miserable, self-pitying bastard, to give her new reason to hate herself?'

Urquhart stood swaying on the edge of nowhere. It was all said. It was all done. Henry was spent and shuddering.

BANG! Simultaneously, lightning and thunder exploded. The flashlight was gone, out of his hands. He lurched after it as it swept away, still shining through the water. For a moment it paused, held by a stone against the drag. Then it was lost.

The darkness was terrible. The racket of the falls was all around, and the heavy pull of the current. He groaned in panic, pushing against the flow, desperate not to lose his footing, until, with a gasp of relief, he collided with his anchor rock.

He felt it shift on the riverbed, threatening to capsize. He was sobbing with cold and terror, trying not to lean on the unsteady rock, staring about him into blackness and nothing.

There was no sign of Urquhart.

Elena

The lights of the hotel dimmed, then were bright again. Elena yawned—sleep was what she most desired. She turned from the stairs towards the room of roses.

In the corridor were Georgie and Mabel. The child held the old dog by the collar and was trying to mount her, like a peasant with a donkey. 'Hello, Lena.'

'*Hola*.'

Mabel ceased pulling and lay flat with her head between her paws. She blinked with much sadness. Georgie hugged her tightly. Then he sat up and said with pride, 'I should be in bed.'

Elena yawned again, so that it was difficult to speak. 'Yes. I also.'

'But I'm not.'

'No.' She bent to pat the dog, who gazed at her with intensity.

'I have a new uncle. His name is Uncle Peter. He will give me lots of presents.'

She laughed. 'It is possible. Perhaps.' It was agreeable to laugh.

'I have lots of uncles. And one aunt. And two daddies. And cousins. And two dogs.'

'*Caramba!* You are fortunate.'

'You can be my aunt, if you like. You can give me presents.'

'Thank you. But tomorrow I leave here. I not return.'

Georgie looked at her. He had the Urquhart eyes. 'Why do you hate my grandpa?'

The question startled her. How terrible! What had this child seen and heard today? How could he understand?

I didnae ken that they would kill the bairns.

'I not hate your grandfather.' She stopped. As with Henry, it was important to speak truth. 'Georgie, I hate him before. Before I come here. But now he explain...'

What *was* her feeling for Urquhart? She struggled to know it. The child was waiting. The dog was watching. 'Still I do not much like your grandfather,' she decided.

Georgie turned away from her. He hugged the dog again. She must say more. What was the English expression? 'But I desire him no harm.'

Chapter Thirty-seven

Henry

He could scarcely breathe—his chest had clamped itself against the unbearable cold. His strength was vanishing. He must leave this rock, he told himself. He must find the way.

With the first step, he nearly fell. His legs were dead. The current seemed to double its force. He blundered against it, unsteady on the loose stones.

The water was deeper here! He froze in terror, unable to move or think. This was it. This was the end. He would slide under and be swept away.

A leaf above a storm drain. The image came back. Safe in *Palaeontology*, he'd had the nerve to think he had problems.

'I'm sorry,' he apologised to whomever might be listening.

And then he saw it. A tiny twinkling light, no brighter than a star. The toy torch! Fiona still had it! One numb foot at a time, he began to edge forward, powered by the craving to be somewhere warm. Hell would do.

'Henry Jennings.'

The voice came first, then the hand on his shoulder. They did not startle him, he was beyond surprise.

Urquhart linked an arm through his. They pushed side by side in silence towards Fiona's light.

'Henry Jennings,' Urquhart said again.

'What?' he managed.

'Thy mother was right, Henry. Thou'rt a guid mun.'

Peter

Please God, please God, no.

Brother and father lost. It mustn't be.

Chewing blood from finger, straining to see through the pitch dark, to hear through the murderous racket of the falls. Fiona weeping and pleading, waving her useless needle of light. Hannah whining, Gavin saying fuck all. And where in hell was the lightning when they needed it?

Then it was over. Fi's light found their faces. Henry and Calum, alive, arm in arm together, wading to shore.

Gavin, 'Thank heaven!' Hannah beside herself with ecstasy. Fiona blubbing as though a baby had been born.

No one lost. Nothing lost. Everything still possible.

Stretch hands to help them. One for each. Father and brother. Calum and Henry. Neptune and good old Hippocampus.

Neptune's frozen hand in his, stepping from the tide. 'Dinnae be making such a fuss, lass. Allow a mun to change his mind.'

Henry's cold paw. Squeeze it hard. Resist the urge to hug the bastard. Henry hissing through clamped teeth. 'My trousers, quickly, please.'

'Just how cold are you?' Gavin taking charge. 'Is it to be down the hill, or do you need to warm up in the croft?'

'Down, please. Most definitely, down.' Henry wild-eyed. Zipping up fly, pulling on socks.

'Aye, doon it is. I've been colder far than this.'

'I lost the flashlight.'

'No problem, Henry. You come with Fiona and me. Father, you guide Peter. Hey, look!' Pointing skywards. Storm clouds parting, exposing last night's moon. 'That's better. OK, don't rush it. The path is treacherous, right? So off we go.'

Gavin leading Henry, bent and shaking, then Fiona with the dog. All visible by moonlight. He and Calum bringing up the rear. Rounding the sentinel rock. Negotiating cliff-edge path.

He and Calum! Calum saved! His father! Burst of joy. Wanting to yell with it. 'You didn't jump!'

'Nae, lad. There's more to do, I see. Some other day perhaps.'

'She's wrong, you know. What she said is wrong. Your life, your poetry, it's *not* romance. It's worth much more.'

'Maybe thou'rt right. In any case, there's more to do. Thy brother made me see it.'

'More poetry?'

'Nae, lad. More life.'

Elena

It was too soon to sleep. She would sleep later. First, she must know they were safe. She stood at the window of the room of roses and saw them emerge from the darkness. They looked tired but content, cold yet easy with each other. Except Henry, her dear friend Henry, limping and stumbling as though alone. Tears sprang in her eyes for him—he had offered his heart to her with such humility.

The faces of the others were lifted towards the hotel. Fiona, Peter, and Urquhart himself, striding towards her with his kilt swinging. A man who had looked despair in the face many times and survived it. A man who could be defeated, yet rise again.

They did not see her in the dark window—their eyes were on the bright salon below. She had no part in their world—this she had told herself, defeated and in despair, preparing to run from this place, as she ran from every place. From her village, from Spain, from Mikhail, and now again, from Scotland and from Brussels. Always she believed she ran to find a better place, but always—now she understood the truth—she ran from herself.

Yes, Elena. Why do you need to remember this pain? How far must she run to forget Mikhail's voice?

Retreating from the window, she saw herself reflected. She saw a Spanish woman in a black suit, standing in a room of pink roses.

The black suit did not please her. She unbuttoned the jacket and threw it on the bed. She unzipped the skirt and stepped from it. She discarded shoes and stockings. She went to stand before the mirror.

In white shirt and slip, with bare feet, the woman seemed younger, though still Spanish.

Vale. It was fine to be Spanish. She *was* Spanish.

The black suit was all she had. But no, in the bathroom, she remembered, there was a pink robe. She fetched it, slid her arms into the sleeves and consulted the mirror again.

She looked more soft. More pretty.

The tears stung in her eyes. She wished Mikhail was not gone away. But it was too late for such a wish.

Yes.

She picked up the key to the room of roses and stepped with bare feet into the empty hotel corridor. Turning the key in the lock, dropping it into the pocket of the bathrobe, feeling shy but also clear and calm, slowly she made her way along to the stairs and down, towards the smell of shuttered Spain, towards the voices in the hall below.

Chapter Thirty-eight

Peter

Teresa! Venus! Helen of Troy!
Oh, thou art fairer than the evening air
Clad in the beauty of a thousand stars.
Through the blessed hotel warmth, a woman was gliding towards him out of heaven, swathed in pink towelling and with an angel's feet. His teeth were clattering like castanets, his flesh was chilled beyond reach of arousal, but his imagination was in full flight.

She was smiling at Henry, smiling at Fiona. She was stepping from the last stair to take Calum's hand. 'Angus. It is good you are safe.'

At last her smile came round to him, soft with the remembered taste of rain.

Sweet Helen, make me immortal with a kiss!
Her lips suck forth my soul: see, where it flies!
Then back to Calum. 'But you are like ice.'

Calum's frost-white hands in hers. 'Nae, lass. Thou'rt warming me.'

Fiona speaking. 'Henry is colder. Henry saved my father's life.'

'No. Please.' Faint protest through blue lips. Brother Henry, wracked with shivers, hobbling towards the carved oak chair.

Fiona tugging at him. 'No, not there. Let's get you to the fire. Someone fetch Owen, quickly, please.'

'I'll do it.' Calum striding off, unquenchable old man, with Gavin and Hannah at his side.

Fiona, arm round Henry, steering him through arch of stone into solicitous Yankee chorus.

Leaving only glorious woman, radiating warmth. 'I cannot follow. I am not dressed.'

Too right. Glowing inside her pink towelling robe. 'I'm freezing too, Elena. Feel how cold.' Take her hand, her warm, pink, willing hand. 'And wet. My jeans are wet.' Step close. Breathe in her smile. Yes, something was stirring down below. 'Let's try the back room.' Lead woman fast through passage and door, into the deserted bliss of many sofas.

Woman running forward. Kneeling. 'There is wood here, and hot ash. Will I start the fire?'

'There's no time. I'm dying. I need mouth-to-mouth.'

Woman laughing, turning from fireplace.

Sink to his knees, and steal the greater poet's words of love. *'Come, Helen, come, give me my soul again. Here will I dwell, for heaven be in these lips.'*

Henry

Fiona was chafing one of his hands. Gordon the waiter had put a balloon of brandy in the other. The Americans were hauling the sofa nearer to the fire. Hannah charged joyfully around.

But Elena had disappeared.

'I'm all right. I'm okay. Really I am.'

Big Owen was here. 'No you're not, you're hypothermic. Don't drink that brandy. Take it away, Gordon, please. Bring sweet tea instead. Three sugars, milky, double quick. And one for Father too.'

How lovely she had looked, how warm and kind. Yet she had barely glanced at him. Her smile had blessed him briefly, then moved on. He had done everything, risked everything, but it was nothing, nothing at all. Elena did not love him.

Wrapped in a tartan blanket on the vast sofa, Urquhart looked small and meek. Fiona was in tears. She hugged her father, who lowered his white head. 'Thank heavens you're safe,' she scolded him. 'And Henry. They were both in the river, Owen, out in the middle in the thunderstorm, right on the edge of the falls. Henry was so brave. He saved Father's life.'

'No. Really. Please stop saying that. Your father made his own decision what to do.'

'Nae, lad, it's true. Thy words recovered me.'

Henry's feet were tingling with pins and needles. The American voices were receding. 'Hey, let's give these folks some privacy. It's time we turned in.'

Gordon slipped a mug of tea into his hands. The first sip scalded, the first swallow burned his throat. His blood surged as the sugar hit. Elena did not love him, but he was alive, which was something.

The second mug was on the hearth. Fiona's arms were wrapped too tightly around Urquhart for him to pick it up. 'You really scared me, Father. Today was my fault. I could never have forgiven myself.' She began to cry. 'Tell me you won't try this again tomorrow, or next week.'

'Nay, lass. I willnae.'

She wasn't satisfied. She gripped his shoulders. 'Promise me, not ever, ever.'

The old man lifted his face. He spoke softly. 'Ma poor

wee bairn. Thou'st had misfortune enough.' His voice deepened and softened and lost its Scots. 'I promise thee, Fiona. Thou must not fear it. I'll think of it no more.'

Elena

She was on a sofa beneath Peter Urquhart, laughing and kissing him, hardly thinking. But then his knee, cold in the wet jeans, pushed between hers, and suddenly she was shivering. The pink bathrobe was loose. He was unbuttoning her shirt and burrowing his refrigerated nose between her breasts.

Her mind had been clear when she came downstairs, but now it was not. She could not organise her thoughts. 'Wait, Peter. One moment, please.'

He did not wait. He did not answer her. He lifted his face and kissed her again.

Her body desired this...

Yes, it desired embraces...

Yes, though shivering, also it was arching with desire...

Yes, and she was free...

Mikhail was gone away. She was free to do this. Yes... Yes...

But these kisses, these hands, they were making her less free...

Yes, but this Peter had so much fire in him...

His mouth, his body...

Yes, but she did not know him...

He was a stranger...

So much was changed in her...

So much was changing still...

What did it mean to kiss this man? She could not

remember what had seemed so clear...

His hand was lifting her slip. His breath rasped in her ear, her head. He was stopping. No, he was not stopping—he was unzipping his wet jeans.

'Peter! Please! Wait!'

He took no notice, pulled her hand to touch him. 'Hold me. I'm cold. Warm me, Elena.' Swelling and lifting in her fingers.

Yes, she wanted this, yes, her body told her, yes, but, 'No!' She struggled to escape his weight. She fell from the sofa to the floor. She stood up, tying the bathrobe tightly, retreating, smiling. Still wanting him.

His mirror eyes were full of laughter. 'Come back. I should've said. I'm fully equipped.' He fished in the pocket of his jeans, extracted a soggy condom packet. 'Though not often this lucky.'

No, she decided. 'No,' she said. She shook her head. She could not explain. She could not understand the reason.

He did not believe her. She tried to stop smiling at him.

He frowned. 'You know you want to. Don't pretend you don't.'

He reached for her hand again. She took another step away.

'Don't tell me you buy into all that holy bollocks: thou-shalt-not? Come on, Elena, I know you better than that.'

How could he know her? She did not know herself.

'Come on,' he repeated. 'Where's the problem? At least *we're* not related.' He laughed. 'Or have I missed something?'

Henry.

Henry was the reason.

'Peter, of course. I cannot pretend... of course I want. But I must not. I cannot explain. Not today. Not tomorrow. I mean this. I am sorry. I am sorry I... that I...'

He stood to re-zip his jeans. He returned the condom to his pocket. 'That you teased me?'

He frowned. He would be angry. He bit his lip and looked at her. She held herself ready for his curses.

'No,' he said at last. 'You've had a lousy day. But more to the point, Henry would be pissed off, wouldn't he? I didn't think of that.'

Her mind was clear again, and grateful. 'Thank you. You understand exactly.'

He grinned. 'Great tits, though. Pity.' He took her hand.

And she took one more kiss.

Chapter Thirty-nine

Elena

The time had come to sleep. She parted from Peter with more kisses and laughter. She climbed the stairs and returned alone to the room of roses. She washed her face and teeth, dropped her clothes to the floor and lay on the bed with a sigh of peace. Her guilt and confusion were gone.

'You've had a lousy day,' Peter had said.

'What will you do?' She could hear Henry's kind voice, feel his shoulder touching hers.

She was not mad. She was not alone. The shame was behind her. Ahead was any life she chose.

What did she choose? To go to Barcelona? Yes, but not to run away.

She yawned and rolled onto her side. On the table by the telephone lay the photograph of Angus Urquhart. So well she knew this face. Eighty years old, upright and proud, a man whose eyes mixed bad and good together. Pride with fear, wisdom with foolishness.

She no longer hated this man. She did not venerate him as Peter did, and yet...

And yet he had shown her...

What had he shown her?

She yawned again and closed her eyes, letting herself remember. She saw him stride from the dark mountain with his arms and kilt swinging. And below, in the hall that smelled of Spain, she felt the fire from his blue eyes and the chill in his old hands.

How to face pain with courage: this he had shown her. How to refuse despair and leave the past behind.

Was this romance?

No. It was not. It was the way to live.

The day was finished. Slowly her mind was relaxing, her eyelids falling. How tired she was, and heavy with approaching sleep. As she reached to turn off the light, Angus Urquhart's picture slid past her hand onto the carpet of roses. She lay in the darkness, thinking of Urquhart, Henry, Mikhail, Peter.

She would refuse despair and leave the past behind.

She would begin to live.

Henry

He was warm again, but sad. He had undressed and cleaned his teeth, but he wasn't yet calm enough to sleep. Instead, he sat straight-backed on the edge of the bed in his small, bare room, staring out at the black mountainside, forcing himself to think things through without the help of ghosts.

Was it only yesterday he set off from Guildford, with his mother at his side and Marjorie Macpherson's invitation folded warm against his heart? It seemed an age ago, but more, it was a different man who'd followed the call to Inverness, a man he no longer wished to be.

Which left the question, who was he now? How would he go on from here?

He was alone, that was the main thing. His mother was gone: dead, cold, cremated, scattered, no ghost left, nothing. This afternoon, right here, he had scolded and cursed her. He yearned to say, I'm sorry, I understand, I know you never meant to break my heart, I hope you had some happiness.

How useless even to think these words. She was not here, he could not have her back, he must content himself with memories.

He smiled, remembering again those last three years when she had grown so close and shared so much. Marjorie's books, for example.

Try this, Henry dear. It's so sad and Scottish.

How she had loved those books. And now he understood completely why. Maggie McConn and her Fergus, Maggie Jennings and her Angus—how closely they echoed the romance in her own life. And she had chosen to share them with *him*. Yes, after all, it was he, not Peter, who came closest to knowing her heart.

'Thank you, Mother,' he whispered, not expecting a reply. 'And thank you, Marjorie.'

Marjorie. How odd it felt to speak the name. Her ghost had vanished too, erased by Michael McCoy's smile. He no longer needed her voice. Her books no longer tempted him. They had the aura of stories consumed in childhood. He might still revere their magic, but it was inaccessible to him—he would never again experience it with a naïve mind.

He gazed forlornly into the unromantic Scottish darkness. A form took shape there. A new image shimmered faintly against the mountain. He blinked, but it persisted. Elena.

He blinked back tears.

Elena's ghost stepped in through the window. Her

dark-golden voice soothed him. 'Don't be unhappy, Henry. I shall be with you always. You need never be alone.'

Her smile, warm and welcoming, hung in the air before him, swelling the tears in his eyes. He felt so very, very sad.

'It's no use, Elena,' he whispered. 'I'd love to. And it's horribly, excruciatingly tempting. But it's bad for me. Fatal in fact.'

He made himself comprehend the truth. However he'd dressed it up, his feeling for Elena was romance. Mistaking her for Marjorie, fancying himself her cavalier, he had painted a stranger in the colours of his dreams. What had he imagined? Elena pushing a hoover in Guildford? Himself peddling financial advice in Brussels?

Her image faded. The room was empty. The mountainside was bare.

This was reality. The tears spilled down his cheeks.

He let them fall. There was no shame in them. There was no one here to see.

He was altogether alone. He had no choice but to be, and to make something of, this middle-aged financial adviser, somewhat overweight, wearing blue-striped pyjamas and weeping as he murdered one more ghost.

Peter

Coming awake on sofa, shivering with cold. Stiff neck, damp jeans. Limp libido.

Groan and stagger upright. Grope his way back to the hall.

Aquarium lights still on. The insufferable Gordon, plumping cushions, dishing out malevolent stare. 'The family have retired for the night, sir.'

Mouth rusty with sleep. 'Uh. Right. So, any chance of a bed, then? Or shall I kip here?'

Faintly perceptible smile. 'Please be so good as to follow me.'

Trail after the bugger, scooping up rucksack from hall. Through door under stairs, along chilly passageway festooned with clanking plumbing and sacks of root veg. Delivered with supercilious bow into a musty cupboard. Peeling, brown wallpaper. Divan-bed with mud-coloured duvet. Moonlit view of dustbins. A cobwebbed, ensuite bog.

Unshoulder rucksack and mobilise tongue. 'Well thanks a bundle, Gordjus. Jus' what I need. Sorry though, never give tips. Against my religion. Night-night, sleep tight, you snot-ridden shite.'

Alone. Quick, strip, and dive beneath duvet. Shiver, fidget, rotate, pushing out heat into heavy, damp feathers. Nothing 'twixt him and sleep but haze of frustration.

Hand on prick, call up hot Señorita, great tits and giggles in pink towelling robe. Yes, nest getting warmer, mind losing grip, wank-fantasy morphing to Teresa in high Sierra, Calum at it like Ernest Heming—

Wham! Shock action replay of CALUM... HIS... FATHER.

Prick collapsing. Roll onto back, and stare into darkness afloat with images of eyes like his own. Mind-blowing. Wonderful. Calum his father, plus a job-lot of brothers thrown in. Count the names off like sheep. James. Owen. William. Gavin.

And Fiona.

Fiona, his sister. And all because Calum... because

294

Calum and Ma...

Sleep out of the question. Mind full of Calum and what it would mean—Angus and Peter, father and son, muse and disciple, bards of the past and the fu—

Oh no, start up in horror. Blood turning to ice in his veins. His poems no good. His poems no fucking good. Could it be, son of genius, he just didn't have it? Panic like a shower of stones. Switch on the light.

Holy shite! Jump like a scalded cat! Woman in pink towelling robe! A ghost? Don't be daft.

'I am sorry. I startled you.'

'Blimey, you didn't half!' Still spooked and shaking. Woman advancing, untying bathrobe. Smiling. 'I asked Gordon. He said in here. I thought, shall I knock? But then I thought no, I'll surprise you.'

'You terrified me.'

Bathrobe on floor. Woman coy. Terror receding fast.

'Shall I go then? Or would you like a cuddle. To keep the ghosts away?'

Tasty vision. Lady Godiva minus horse. Venus de Milo with arms.

'Yes. Please.'

'Which please?'

'Cuddle, please.'

Woman sliding into hot, damp nest of feathers, switching off light.

Brain dizzy but, what d'you know, prick back in working order.

Fucking *amazing* day.

Chapter Forty

Henry

The next morning, Henry washed, shaved and dressed without benefit of ghosts, then stepped resolutely into the corridor. He must go home—he had Trevor's leg to see to tomorrow. But first he would have some breakfast, be sociable to this new family his brother had acquired, and part finally from Elena. He followed the spiral of steps down and emerged through the fireplace door into the back parlour.

Owen and James were there, each resplendent in his way. The first, in massive brown cords and a quilted, sludge-coloured waistcoat, was warming his legs on a lively new log fire. The second sat alert and cross-legged in the same chair he'd occupied the last time Henry passed through this room. But the checked trousers were zipped, and if James remembered being caught *in flagrante*, it didn't seem to faze him.

'Good morning,' said Owen.

'Did you sleep well?' said James.

Their smiles were genuine, putting him at ease.

'Yes, thanks, I did. And you?'

'Like a Rabelaisian dream.' James's grin was shameless. How did one shave around those spikes, Henry wondered, or were they detachable? 'But Henry, you dear, dear man. I've been hearing about your heroics.' Henry found himself returning the grin. 'A reward of porridge and kippers awaits you in the dining-room. I'll be on active kitchen duty in two ticks.'

Following the brothers through passage, hall and passage, Henry's heart began to beat faster. The boarding-school sounds of children playing tag on the stairs didn't help. 'Your guests will be having their breakfasts too, I expect,' he said nervously.

'They're long up and gone,' said Owen. 'Hiking on Skye today. They made an early start.'

'And the writer?'

'Don't worry about him,' said James. 'He skedaddled early, to Inverness.'

Henry's burden lifted. And sure enough, only Fiona and Angus were eating toast and marmalade in the chandeliered tartan Underground station.

'We're lumbered with you a while longer, Father, I gather,' said the irrepressible James.

'Aye, lad. And good morning to thee, Henry Jennings.'

The old man proffered his hand. Henry took it. There was no sign of Elena or Peter.

'Pour yourself some orange juice, Henry. Get stuck into the fruit. I'll be there in a flash with the hot stuff.'

At the tartan door James collided with Owen's wife. 'Fiona, the phone. A man for you.'

Fiona looked startled. She set off half-running.

Henry poured juice and pulled out a chair.

'Would that be *the* mun, dost thou think?' said Angus.

'I'd be surprised,' said Owen. 'It's been a good while.'

Henry pretended to examine the décor.

'Forgive us,' said Owen. 'You're as good as family, Henry, so no more secrets, eh? My sister is in recovery from an unfortunate affair of the heart.'

They could hear raised voices. It was William and Gavin, of course, bitching before breakfast, red face and red hair appearing round the door. Henry exchanged a smile with Urquhart, surprised how at home he was beginning to feel.

'Good morning,' said Owen, but they took no notice. In a brood of extraordinary children, there had to be some duffers, Henry supposed. Perhaps William and Gavin were so tediously irascible *because* they were duff—it was hard to disentangle cause from effect in families.

'The rotten cow,' Gavin was complaining. 'No sympathy after all the *donner und blitzen*, just a load of bloody nagging. Then, blow me if she doesn't take off in the middle of the night. I wake up and there she is, gone. Not a word, not even a note.'

'Time you got rid,' frowned William. 'You can't let them treat you like that.'

James had emerged from the kitchen with porridge, brown sugar and cream.

'Thank you,' said Henry.

'It's a real pleasure.'

'I wouldn't give tuppence,' Gavin was whingeing on, 'only she'll have taken the car, the bitch. If Fiona's full up, I'll have to bloody well bike it into town.'

'Oh dearie me!' James exclaimed. 'Whatever next?'

They turned to look at him. He was laughing aloud. Good God, was that a spike through his *tongue*?

'Her car's still outside,' he said, 'so the delightful Kim must surely still be here somewhere.'

Peter

Nose prickled by feathers. Clatter of dustbin lids startling him awake.

Spoon-curled naked around curvaceous woman. Eyes opening in chaos of red-gold hair.

Inrush of where and who. Loch Craggan, Kim—

And Calum!

Peter is ma son.

Would the thrill never cease?

Calum his father. Fiona his sister. Elena turned temptress, turned 'No, think of Henry'. Good old Henry, turned hero, talking Calum from the brink.

And now, luck of the devil, Kim, stirring and rolling to face him with mischievous eyes.

GUTSY GUY GETS THE GIRL!

Though, oh fuck, the bellicose brothers would skin him alive.

'Hi there, Peter.'

'Well, howdy, Kim.'

Woman stretching and yawning and grabbing his—

'Hey! So this is our secret, right?'

Grabbing and nuzzling and murmuring, 'Fine. If you say so.'

'No, really, hang on. What will you tell him?'

Woman rising, hair cascading, yards of it, grinning and climbing on top. 'Tell who?'

Guiding him in. Squeezing with knees. Starting to rock. Lady Godiva at home in the saddle, lifting and twisting her hair. Laughing. Repeating, 'Tell who?'

Metamorphosing man into stallion. 'Gavin, tell Gavin—'

Woman rocking and smiling, hair sweeping and drifting, murmuring, 'No problem. No problem at all. Gavin's history.'

Voltage rising, brain melting, from trot to a canter, woman dipping to whisper, hair like a golden mane. 'I've told him, it's over. It's over and done.'

Elena

The sun fell across her face. She wandered alone among wild flowers and olive trees. But someone was knocking. Opening her eyes, she saw the mountain beyond the window. 'Come in,' she called.

Janet Urquhart closed the door with her shoulder. She carried breakfast on a tray. 'Good morning. Did I wake you? I hope you like kippers.'

'Very much, thank you.'

'Did you sleep well? Yes indeed, I can see you're rested. Quite rosy in this rosy room.' She set the tray on Elena's lap. 'Take your time. On Sundays, we go slowly.'

'You are kind, Janet. And Owen also. While I have been discourteous, disagreeable—'

Janet touched her hand. 'With good cause, my dear. That was a terrible story. My father-in-law's an old devil. You quite put him to shame.'

Elena shook her head. 'No, I also.'

Janet was looking at her suitcase, tipped out on the floor. 'Dear me, you've brought so little. Do you have clothes for today?'

'My suit and one clean shirt. Tomorrow I will be home.' She looked at the suit. 'Black no longer pleases me,' she confided. 'I will buy colours.'

'Black is smart,' said Janet. 'I know what you mean though. Some days, smart doesn't feel right, does it? Okay, I'll leave you in peace to enjoy your breakfast.'

As the door closed, Elena remembered her resolution. Today she would begin to live. 'Home,' she had said. It was time to go home. Eating the kipper, mouthful by mouthful, she planned what she would do. It seemed much, it seemed difficult, but it was not. In reality it was small and simple. A few steps, one by one.

She would return to Brussels.

She would give notice to the Commission. A month's notice.

She would pack or sell her possessions, or give them to charity. She would give her smart black suits—she would buy soft shapes and colours. A pink bathrobe.

She would find a job in Barcelona. Anything to get started: teaching, or welcoming tourists perhaps. She would find a small place to rent, one room, like Mikhail's room in Brussels.

Before she left Brussels, she would return to Mikhail's room one time more. And to his office. She must be certain he was gone away. She must be certain he had left no message.

She would leave messages. With the Commission, at his office, on his mobile. To help him to find her. If ever he should want to find her.

And then she would go. She would not run from Brussels and Mikhail. She would leave her messages, and then she would go, calmly, home to Spain.

She had eaten enough. She set the tray aside. She took a breath.

Vale. She was ready. It was time to shower. To pack. To

put on the black suit. To leave.

Before she went, she would find Henry. She wanted his address, his number, his email address. Perhaps a kiss of friendship.

And she would find Peter, for a kiss of laughter.

Finally she would find Angus Urquhart. She would take his frail hands and tell him *adios*. She would kiss him also, on his cheek between the white beard and the blue eyes, to prove her forgiveness.

None of this would take much time.

She crossed the room to stand at the window. The sun shone brightly. Loch Craggan was brilliant with many reflections. The Land-Rovers had vanished, the gravel was marked by their tyres. Only Fiona's car, red and yellow, and two others remained, belonging to the family perhaps.

At the edge of her vision, something was moving. She shaded her eyes to look along the road towards Inverness. A car was speeding towards the hotel. Already it was near. On the roof a sign read 'TAXI'.

She grabbed the pink bathrobe and ran from the room, tying it as she went. Along the corridor, down the stairs through a tangle of playing children and across the hall. Fiona was there, pulling open the heavy door.

'The taxi,' Elena said. 'Will it wait for me, please? I need to leave soon.'

She stepped through the open door into a freezing wind. Pulling the robe tight around her and hopping from one bare foot to the other, she waved to the driver across the gravel.

The driver came towards her. 'Yes, ma'am?'

Behind him, his passenger was standing and

stretching.

But no, he was not stretching, he was waving. He was returning her wave.

The passenger was Mikhail.

Chapter Forty-one

Peter

Count of ten after woman skedaddled in dressing-gown. Then, following holy aroma of kippers, heft rucksack and saunter along basement corridor, up stairs—

And straight into snarl up.

Inrush of iced air through the open front door. Elena, pink-robed and ecstatic at some new arrival. Fiona all smiles, children staring. Other doors opening. Quick, melt into crowd.

Not a hope, no escape, for here came dear brother Gavin, looming gang-handed from direction of dining-room, eyes locking and switching from suspicion to certainty. 'Where is she, you bastard?'

Seized from behind by Will. Trowel on the innocence. 'What? Who?'

'You know bloody who!' Gavin's fist slamming shoulder. 'My woman, that's who.'

Big Owen arriving. 'Cool it, the lot of you. There'll be no more scrapping.'

Calum Calum arriving, surveying him proudly. But William's grip tightening, Gavin's fist bunching.

'Hey... guys...'

Brother Henry arriving, his eyes passing beyond them and filling with tears. For yes, here was the main event: Elena and stranger, tight in a body-hug.

Frantically gesture. Yell, 'Gavin. Look, Gavin. Now

isn't the time.'

Reprieve. All heads turning to gawp at the lovebirds. Shoot stranger a grin.

Stranger unsmiling, eyes widening, fixing on him—what in hell's name?—and pointing the finger. 'It was you!'

What was he on ab—Oh shit! This was Mick! 'Who? Me, mate?'

'Elena, this man yesterday answers your phone.'

'Peter?'

Her face full of happiness. Quick, think on his feet. 'Yes, it's *such* a long story. And a Hollywood ending, right?'

'But Peter, where is my phone?'

Leap out of Will's armlock to frisk hanging cagoules. Here it was, in a pocket. Smashed in three pieces. Turn and present them. 'Don't know how, but I dropped it. I was bringing it to you. And your message of course, Mick. But then, I don't know. Something must have distracted me. On the mountain was it, Elena, climbing up in the rain?'

Home and dry. Her eyes understanding. 'Yes, Peter, of course. I will explain to Mikhail.'

'Last call for breakfast! Who fancies a wee nibble?' Excellent timing for James to arrive with his *double entendres*.

'Me, please.' And oops! for here down the stairs came Kim, poured into jeans and a spangly sweater, smirking and brazenly swinging her bag.

Gavin growling at her. 'Don't think you can fool me. I know where you've been.'

'But I thought we'd agreed, Gavin.' Portrait of innocence. Essence of cool. 'I thought we'd agreed we were through.'

Elena

There were so many people, but she could see only Mikhail. And feel him, his arms strong around her, his rough cheek against hers, his familiar smell wrapping her in safety and peace. There was so much noise and argument. She wanted only to be alone with Mikhail.

'Tell me, how did you find me? My messages, why do you not answer?'

'When you leave, so angry, I too leave Brussels. I have interview for job, which I not tell you. I not take mobile. I return yesterday, Saturday. I listen your messages, read your note, ring your mobile. I speak this man, Peter. But then your phone is dead. I very afraid.'

'But, Mikhail, yesterday evening, still you do not answer.'

'I am in aeroplane. Your note say Scotland. The computer, it show Inverness. Angus Urquhart, Inverness. I ring many people name Urquhart. They explain me how to say "Er-cut."'

He was laughing and kissing her. She tightened her arms and pressed her face into his neck, hearing his wonderful voice in her ear. 'So I am arriving Inverness. I am afraid for you, not knowing what to do, but I switch on my mobile. And yes, you are phoning. No message, but I have number. I ask for you. You are sleeping. I speak Janet Urquhart. I speak Fiona Urquhart.' He turned her to see Fiona's smile.

One more question. 'But, Mikhail, on Thursday someone is in your room.'

'Ah, I give key to Boris. For if I take job. For if Boris want my room when I take job.'

Of course. A new job. He was saying goodbye. 'It is true then? You leave Brussels?'

'Yes, Elena, already. I start work Thursday.' He held her apart from him and spoke with sadness. 'I try to explain, many times. But you are too angry. You say, "No, Mikhail, no." His fingers gripped her shoulders. 'Elena, now I take job. Is for you I take it. And I want for you to come with me, but I think you will not.'

She understood. The fear lifted. 'I will, Mikhail. Wherever it is, I will come.'

He began to smile. 'Madrid? You will come to Madrid?'

Madrid, not Barcelona. She nodded. His smile grew. 'This is true? You will come to Spain?'

'Yes. Truly, yes.' His smile dissolving all problems. *There was no problem, there is no problem, there will be no problem.* She hugged him tightly and whispered in his ear. 'I was wrong, Mikhail. Completely wrong. About Spain, you always were right.'

Henry

Hannah nudged his hand with a wet nose, asking to be petted. He bent to give her ears a good rumpling. 'Poor old girl. Is no one making a fuss of you?'

He was trying hard not to feel sorry for himself. He was trying to feel pleased for Elena. She smiled so humbly at him as she went by in her pink bathrobe on the arm of her lover. He could see she knew how lucky she was, how the cards could so easily have fallen differently. Like no one else he'd met, she understood what this damned loneliness was like.

They were trooping off to the dining-room in quest of kippers and another good story, but he'd had enough to eat and, truth be told, a bellyful of stories too. 'Come on, Hannah,' he said. 'Let's have a look in here.' He wandered through the stone archway into the deserted guest-lounge.

He should be heading back to Guildford, but the prospect depressed him. He would be sad there without his ghosts. Trevor's new leg tomorrow would seem tame after this adventure.

What would he normally be doing on a Sunday morning in February? Some chores. Ironing his shirts perhaps with the radio for company, before toddling to the pub for a bit of oblivion.

There was a radio here on the table by the great glass wall. He switched it on and heard Sue Lawley's voice. Desert Island Discs—good lord, it was late, he must get going. He stared glumly through the glass at the road to Inverness.

The castaway was no one he knew. Some old lady who had once been famous, relating how she'd met her husband, with whom she then spent 'so many happy years'. Did Henry believe this? He didn't know. But at least the old lady seemed to believe it.

'And record number two?' prompted Sue.

'Ah yes,' she said. She had to have this one, to remind her of their meeting.

The violins faded in. Henry recognised the tune. It was one of the songs his mother used to sing, in the days before Urquhart stole her away, in the days before Gaelic lullabies.

I wonder who's kissing her now

Damn it, the music was bringing tears to his eyes. In his mind he was dancing again, down the soft-carpeted stairs of the Royal Highland Hotel towards his destiny, or in the sun-splashed arcade with Elena on his arm.

Someone touched his elbow. He turned, blinking, ready once more with the brave smile, and with the thought that he really must leave.

It was Fiona.

I wonder who's kissing her now

The desire to dance overwhelmed him. And it seemed that Fiona wanted to dance too, because his arms were around her and they were gliding over the polished floor. It felt enormously good. She had her head against his chest, and he allowed himself, just for a moment, to imagine that this was his woman.

All too soon the song faded out and Sue Lawley resumed the interview.

'That was magical, thank you,' said Henry. 'But sadly, I must...' He stopped, disconcerted, because Fiona was wiping her eyes. 'Oh dear, have I upset you?'

She was embarrassed. 'It's nothing. Only the music. How stupid of me.'

But no. There was something *he* was being stupid about. Half-remembered words nagged in his head. Something she said yesterday.

I was in a state myself. Needing to talk.

Something Urquhart said too.

Thou'st had misfortune enough.

Yes, and at breakfast, Owen's words. *An unfortunate affair of the heart?*

He had paid no attention. He'd been too busy mourning his ghosts. Dear God, had he learned nothing? Record number three was playing, some bit of Elgar. He took hold of Fiona's hand. Hannah was pushing between them, but he took no notice.

Fiona's eyes were large, and grey, and serious. Her face was completely still. His head was full of words he might speak.

Say no, I can take it. But I have to ask. You are lovely, Fiona. How could I have missed it? I haven't been paying attention. And if, amazingly, it's true... true that you're not... that there isn't someone. Then, what would you say? What I mean is...

He looked at her mouth. It was quite, quite still. Yes, he had learned this much. He knew for a fact that words were not wanted, that the only right and possible course of action was simply to kiss this mouth.

As he gathered his courage, it moved. It broadened into a smile, an absolutely beautiful smile.

It was the smile he'd seen on Friday as he blundered into the library out of the blizzard.

It wasn't Marjorie Macpherson's smile, or his mother's, or Elena's.

It was Fiona's own smile, and it couldn't be bettered.

He bent his head and kissed Fiona's smile.

Chapter Forty-two

Elena

The plane rose, and banked, and steadied, and began to head south. Elena surveyed great stretches of green and grey hills, searching among them for Loch Craggan, or the way to Loch Craggan, but recognising nothing.

Mikhail's grip on her hand relaxed. She turned to find him deeply asleep. He was so full of relief, he had said— that they would be together, that she had agreed to come with him to Madrid.

'What is the job?' she had asked him.

'It is only computers until I have Spanish. *Que ya aprendo bien.*'

It was true what he had said. *I take this job for you.*

She could scarcely comprehend how she was blessed. Already the clouds had swallowed the Scottish Highlands, where the miracle had happened. Glancing down at herself, she saw the black suit and black-stockinged knees. She wriggled her feet, eager to be in Brussels and then Spain, impatient to begin the future with Mikhail. She smiled as her toes found the sheepskin boots that Henry helped her to buy.

The steward was here with a trolley of drinks. She put a finger to her lips. 'Let him sleep.' She leant back, directing her smile to the luggage compartment above her head. Inside it, too big for her suitcase, was her new sheepskin coat for the winter cold of Madrid, and also, in a carrier-bag, a pink towelling bathrobe.

'Janet, you are truly an angel,' she had cried. 'This carries all my good memory of what has happened here.'

All had gathered on the gravel to say their goodbyes. Beyond them the taxi waited and Mikhail held out his hand. She climbed into the taxi, repeating, 'Thank you, thank you, everyone.'

It was then that Urquhart had reached through the taxi window. He did not speak or smile, just dropped a piece of folded paper into her lap. It was in her handbag, with the broken mobile phone. She must read it again.

Gently she moved Mikhail's hand to his own knee. Such big, solid hands he had, keeping her warm and safe. She opened her bag, unfolded the paper and read once more.

To Elena Martínez
with shame and deep-felt gratitude.
You released me from romance.
A.U.

Peter

'So?'

'So?'

'So what next?'

Elena was gone, big send-off on gravel. Henry and Fi, surprisingly chummy, had also vamoosed, rattling back to Inverness in her two CV. Bye, Fiona. Bye, Hannah.

Kim was leaving. Lingering at the open front door, letting the cold in, nonchalantly swinging her bag. 'I mean, do you expect you'll be staying in the Highlands awhile?'

Vision of mouldering houseboat, weighed down by rent arrears, plus office bristling with unstuffed envelopes and suits demanding tea—

No contest. 'Definitely. Why would I leave? Loch Craggan: home to the Urquharts. Doctor, chef, builder, mountain guide, rediscovered poet, undiscovered poet—'

'While me, you know, I'm kinda *persona non grata*, dumping Gavin an' all.' She was sighing and pulling a face.

Push hands into pockets and shrug. 'Guess that's right. Guess that's so.'

She was pulling out car keys and turning away, her golden mane floating and shining. 'Plus I gotta go to work tomorrow.'

Step between her and the door. 'Oh yeah. Doing what?'

Her eyes deadly serious. 'Trainee solicitor.'

'You're kidding. You don't look the type.'

'Do I not, you contemptible sexist!'

'No offence. I suppose you wear different kit, different hair.'

She was frowning and taming the mane with her hands, tugging it from her face. 'You should see me in my suit.'

Touch her, pull her towards him. 'I should like to, a lot.'

'Would you indeed?' She was smiling again.

'With black stockings? I can hardly wait.'

'Is that so?'

'Yes, that's so.'

'Pity you'll be stuck out here then, isn't it?'

'So what can we do about that, Kim?'

'What do you suggest?'

'How about your place?'

'If you're sure you can tear yourself away from the

Urquharts.'

'Course I can. Give me the address, I'll be there.'

Woman fishing out business card, laughing and pleased. Card safe in condom pocket. Wave her goodbye. Lady Godiva in jeans and a silver VW.

But Calum—his father—came first. Turn, and there he was, waiting. Calum Calum, a wonder of white-hair and old bones in the empty stone archway. 'There's more thou'lt be wanting to know from me, lad.'

Too right. Follow him in, fair exploding with questions, of which first and most vital—

'First thou'lt be wanting to know what truly I make of thy poetry.'

Oh God, face to face in aquarium, dwarfed by the mountain and by Calum's whole life—the climax, the moment. Watching his mouth move, and guessing the answer.

PETER'S POETRY NO FUCKING GOOD.

'Tis truly nae bad. There's much promise. There are moments of glory. I feel sure it will come.'

Take the words from his mouth. 'But I haven't lived long enough? Haven't gone deep enough?'

Old man smiling, relieved. 'Thou'rt young. It will come.'

Henry

'Goodbye. Safe journey.'

They were at the barrier. The train was about to leave. Fiona lifted her face, and he kissed her. Her lips were so friendly. She didn't mean goodbye.

He kissed her again, hard like a romantic hero would.

Then held her at arm's length. 'I'll ring when I get there.'

She flashed her amazing smile. 'Please do. It doesn't matter how late it is.'

'Are you coming, mister,' said the guard.

He snatched one more kiss, patted Hannah, then ran for the train. He made it into the rear carriage, and the door immediately shut itself behind him. He wrestled unsuccessfully with the window. Slowly the train was pulling out, leaving Fiona, Inverness and all these crazy happenings behind.

The whole thing seemed suddenly absurd. Unreal. He made his way to a first-class compartment, sat down and tried to steady himself.

He was going home. Home to Guildford. Trevor's leg, the pub, the garden. Home, where soon Fiona would visit him. Home, from where soon he would visit Fiona.

His heart was dancing in his chest. He was grinning like a ventriloquist's dummy. Did he never learn? His mother had broken his heart, then Ingrid, then Marjorie, and then, so nearly, if he'd allowed it to happen, Elena. The ghost of experience whispered urgently in his ear. 'Watch out, it will be exactly the same. Romance will turn its cold hose on you.'

There were no ghosts. He would listen to no more ghosts. He concentrated hard on the farms flashing by.

He wanted so little. To meet a woman's eyes in a smile. To smile at the thought of her. Such small human comforts.

The train was picking up speed. Highland wilderness rolled past the window, giving him no clue. His ghosts were dead. He had to find the answer by himself.

How dangerous it felt to believe in Fiona. He had

vowed to stick fast to reality, and he was swimming in romance again. Solitude waited for him in Guildford, if he wanted it. Pottering to the pub, chatting with Trevor, watching the flowers grow—a good life that many might envy.

Plus he knew how to do it. It was safe.

Fiona.

Her smile. Her face uplifted for his kiss. Too wonderful, that was the problem. He couldn't let himself believe it. He got up and paced the compartment.

What had he told the old man? That the trick was to have the right *amount* of romance? Yes, it was true. But how much was right?

Fiona.

She *wasn't* a ghost, he felt sure of it. He hadn't invented her. If she would have him, he knew he would love her for the rest of his life. Not a doubt.

But supposing she wouldn't? His innards contracted with fear. Because *that* was the romance: to imagine Fiona would love him, when, in reality, tonight, or tomorrow, or next week, or in a year's time, she might say, 'I'm sorry, Henry. I made a mistake.'

Like Ingrid did.

But she might not.

Fiona.

Her smile could not be doubted. Nor her serious grey eyes.

Be brave, Henry told himself. Be romantic. Have a little faith in yourself.

What were her last words?

It doesn't matter how late it is.

He grinned with joy.

316

Postscript

Hello. Yes. It's me again. Michael.

Sorry.

I wish I could stop there. Pour a brandy, toast Henry's grin, and type 'The end'. I wish it were that simple.

I hoped to atone by recording my folly, but if anything I feel even worse.

His photograph is beside my keyboard. Foxgloves and mock-orange. His trusting smile. His candid eyes. I thought I was over him, but—oh dear.

We met face to face for only a few seconds, yet the memories haunt me. His bafflement in the reference room, his shock in the hotel back-parlour. Impossible to explain or to help him: the harm had been done. I'd posted the flier. I'd hosted the workshop. He'd opened the door.

I'd take it back if I could.

It did the trick, more fool me: no more letters, not one. And I haven't dared write to him. What could I say? I hope he's been able to forgive.

So, besides remorse, what's left to tell? The ladies? I still have their names on a bar-snack menu from the Royal Highland Hotel. Margaret Fraser, Annie Duncan, Veronica Mackenzie, Alice Anderson—

They drew cards: the king and jack of hearts, the queen of spades. Two brothers, one older, one younger. A woman of mystery. But soon they were finding real people more interesting. The young man wearing black who barged past them as they arrived and dodged in later to consult a phone book. The Latin-looking woman that Annie spied as she came in and who was there as we left, hovering at the librarian's elbow. Dear Henry, who appeared in the doorway so briefly. The old guy who reminisced about Malaga at their December meeting. And the stern little librarian—wonderful, they said she was, and sorrowful lately. And me, of course, me. They were so chuffed I'd picked them to come out to.

Meanwhile, my concern was all for Henry. My god, what had I done? What would he think of me? I needed to share the problem. I didn't tell them I'd actually invited him. I just said, 'Let's suppose...'

And so it took hold of them. The library and the workshop, the blizzard, the lights failing, our booted trek to the Royal Highland Hotel, the charming young man in reception, the clink of glasses under the tulip chandeliers. It was fun to make themselves part of the picture, like the Escher design of two hands each drawing the other. I took comfort from hearing my predicament explored.

Next day, I pottered around town, taking a few snaps, making notes on locations. Then, come afternoon, I hired a car and went off in search of the hotel the librarian had mentioned. I'd said I fancied something a touch out-of-this-world, and she'd assured me her brothers' hotel wouldn't disappoint.

It didn't—it was ludicrously gothic. And on the landing going to dinner, I met my first ghost. The Latin-looking woman I'd glimpsed in the library, her clothes dishevelled, eyes puffed from weeping. The hairs rose on my neck. I almost said it—*Elena*?—before running away.

The reassuring substance of the other guests awaited me below—the amiable dog, the pompous waiter, a fine range of malt whiskies and an excellent Scottish dinner. And later, the very excellent Scottish chef. But then—oh agony!—there was Henry. Walking in exactly as I've told you, shocking me out of my skin, drawing crazily polite words from me, then vanishing through the fireplace door.

How was he there? And why? Now I felt truly haunted, with a queasy sensation of being awake in a dream. I signed off from the chef and left early the next morning, terrified of seeing Henry again. Bolted back to Inverness and the Royal Highland Hotel, pursued by the shame that has never since left me.

Early afternoon, I thought a Sunday paper might calm my nerves. There were none in the hotel lobby, so I headed out to the station to look for a newsagent.

It was then that I saw them.

They were at the barrier. He was carrying his Gladstone bag. She was wrapped in her tartan shawl and had the dog on a lead. The dog from the hotel.

I blinked and rubbed my eyes, but they were still there, solidly and absolutely themselves. Henry and the librarian. Solemnly kissing each other.

I wanted to run away. Or to shout—make them change into two, quite different people. But I couldn't move a muscle. It was as though I didn't exist, as though I were merely the ghost of an artist with a pencil in his hand, hovering above that Escher drawing.

Henry caught his train. The librarian waved, then turned and walked her dog towards me. I couldn't bear to look any longer. I ducked my head, and fled, across the road, into the sun-splashed Victorian arcade, shaking and trying not to cry.

That's it. Ye have it all. The end.

Acknowledgements

My thanks go to my mother Beryl and sister Pip; to *West Hampstead Writers*; to the reading groups at Clapham Library, Northcote Road Library and Lavender Hill Library; to Alan Bevan, Charlotte Mendelson, Cynthia Shepherd, Davinia Andrew-Lynch, Ian Jewesbury, Janet Mitchell, Joanna Devereux, Jonathan Masters, Kate Ibbotson, Kim Busen-Smith, Margaret Clare, Paul Lyons, Roger Hurrey, Sarah Naughton and Stephanie Busen-Smith; to ever-wonderful Jan Fortune and Adam Craig at Cinnamon Press; and to Alison Joseph for her workshop *Shaping the Story*.

I consulted numerous sources while writing this novel and found particular inspiration in *The SAS at War* by Anthony Kemp.

Praise for Bobbie Darbyshire's books:

Truth Games
'Shows the deft touch of a psychologically astute social satirist.'
Nina Finburgh, actor

'Examines the pain and egoism that sexual freedom brought in the 1970s. Characters drawn *con brio*.' Bob Boyton, author of *Bomber Jackson Does Some*

OZ
'The storytelling never falters. A constantly evolving plot keeps you hooked until the last page.' Sarah Rayner, author of *One Moment, One Morning* and *Searching for Mr Yesterday*

'Touches on a tough and important subject—the burden children can be for those who have them at the wrong times in their lives.' Chris Boyd, screenwriter

The Posthumous Adventures of Harry Whittaker
'A mad handful of compelling characters, a generous helping of humanity, and a perfect ending. Fizzes with life.' Ali Bacon, author of *In the Blink of an Eye* and *A Kettle of Fish*

'Hugely enjoyable. So funny and original. Bobbie Darbyshire writes with wit, wisdom and warmth.' Sarah Rayner, author of *One Moment, One Morning* and *Searching for Mr Yesterday*

The Third Bus
'For fans of Clare Chambers' *Small Pleasures*, an astute, late-coming-of-age novel that shows the difference an ordinary person can make to so many people's lives just by being himself. And what a moving ending—I couldn't stop thinking about Felix's journey for a long time after I read the last page.'
Emma Bamford, author of *Deep Water* and *Casting Off*